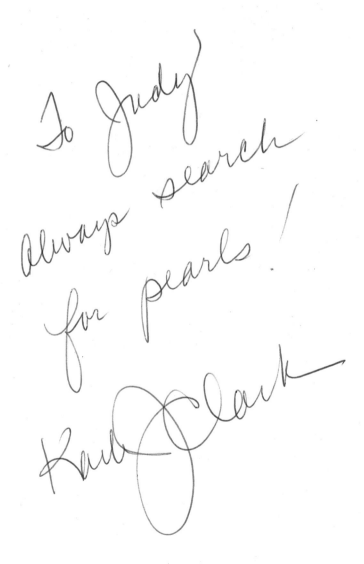

To Judy

Always search

for pearls!

Karl Clark

Knotted Pearls

And Other Stories

By

Karla Clark

authorHOUSE™

1663 LIBERTY DRIVE, SUITE 200
BLOOMINGTON, INDIANA 47403
(800) 839-8640
WWW.AUTHORHOUSE.COM

First published by AuthorHouse 12/08/04

ISBN: 1-4184-9296-5 (e)
ISBN: 1-4184-9297-3 (sc)

Library of Congress Control Number: 2004098862

Printed in the United States of America
Bloomington, Indiana

This book is printed on acid-free paper.

Also by Karla Clark

Between Courses: A Culinary Love Story

To my mother and father,
the string on which the pearls were strung

Acknowledgments

I have been abundantly blessed in life and owe thanks to God and the many people—family, friends, and colleagues—who are responsible for these blessings.

To my husband Scott, for the unique burden he bears being married to a woman who loves to write, and for insisting we spend our wedding money on an IBM personal computer instead of new living room furniture all those years ago.

To my sons Jordan and Jonathan, for the unfathomable joy they have brought me on their journeys from childhood to manhood.

To my father Frank Manarchy, for loving me doubly— enough for a father and a mother.

To my mother Marge Manarchy, who must be pulling strings in Heaven.

To my siblings and their families: Linda, Sean, Ryan, and Mike Cleary; Dana Manarchy; Paula, John, Nicholas, Margaret, Thomas, and Sarah Marie Sentovich; and Frank and Karen Manarchy, for unconditional love and support.

To my husband's family, who have embraced me as one of their own: Scotty and Christine Clark, Bob and Pam Schuckmell; Steven, Jeff, Paul, and John Zawlocki and their families; Steve and Sue Ives; Jim, Cheryl, Jason and Justin Gourley.

To my editor Linda Cleary, for her unfailing instincts, and to my proofreaders, Suzanne Untersee, Kay Sentovich, and Carol Hanson for their attention to detail.

To my book club girls—The Book Babes—Jane Sudderberg, Nonie Broski, Lisa Greco, Maureen Morrisey, Dawn Pratt, Karin Kellogg, Julie Anderson, Annelise Ives, Lisa Lillie and Jean Cooper, for treating me like a real author.

And to the great people at Author House who have made thousands of new writers' dreams come true!

Contents

Errors, like straws, upon the surface flow;
He who would search for pearls must dive below.
—John Dryden

A gem cannot be polished without friction,
Nor a man perfected without trials.
—Lucius Annaeus Seneca

Stones of small worth may lie unseen by day,
But night itself does the rich gem betray.
—Abraham Cowley

Roses Just Roses

"In eastern lands they talk in flowers,
and tell in a garland their loves and cares."
—James Gates Percival (1795-1856)

I KNEW THAT if I accepted the summer job at *Roses Just Roses*, an established flower shop in midtown Manhattan, I'd be a living, walking, breathing cliché. But I'd already been living my life as a walking, breathing pun (my name is Rose Peddles) so I was willing to take the leap from pun to cliché. Besides, I needed the money for school and I was sick of waiting tables. Furthermore, I loved flowers and I'd been told more than once I was a natural-born salesman.

But if honesty is what you're looking for then the real reason I took the job was this: the owner—a little, bald Greek man—looked exactly like my sweet old Uncle Murray. And seeing that my dad had just died three months earlier (struck down as a pedestrian while on his way to court to divorce my mother) you might say I was hungry for a father figure.

Mr. Zenovia fit the bill. It took a total of three seconds to see that he was a complete and utter sweetheart of a man. Short and sixtyish, he had Paul Newman blue eyes and a Kirk Douglas dimpled chin. Mr. Z told me he hired me because he immediately picked up on my natural sales abilities but also because I looked exactly like his cousin Gladys Zenovia when she was twenty-one—same short brown hair, same dark brown eyes. We spent the first couple of days acquainting ourselves with each other and with Uncle Murray and Cousin Gladys: "Oh, Mr. Z, I see you take cream in your tea. So did Uncle Murray!" and "Well, I'll be darned, Rose, Gladys was also partial to polka-dotted dresses."

I came with some experience with roses, but in growing them, not in selling them. My grandmother was quite the rosarian and I'd spent every summer since I was four with her in New Jersey. My parents were jet-setters and unfortunately, I, their only and adopted daughter, didn't travel well. I was a sickly kid—allergies, asthma, migraines (I could just imagine my mother, sole heir to her father's medical plastics company, looking down at me in my crib, saying, "I should think we could get a refund.")—so I was shipped to Nan's each June and shipped back each August.

To my good fortune, my long list of allergies does not include flowers. Cats, dogs, and dust mites send my histamines into turmoil, but blooms and blossoms cause not a sniffle, so when I happened to walk past *Roses Just Roses* and saw the "Help Wanted" sign, I did an about face and walked right in. And when I saw Mr. Z wearing my Uncle Murray's face, complete with gap-toothed smile, I knew destiny was knocking. The pay wasn't great, but the owners and employees were warm and folksy, and the place itself seemed to match what I'd had in mind for myself that summer—something comfortable and uncomplicated.

It had been a knotty year. Actually the last three years had been complex and confusing. I'd spent the last thirty-six months dividing my time between attending Columbia University studying Fine Arts and attempting to find my birth parents. I was a pretty good college student but a rotten detective. The records were sealed shut. I resigned myself that I was stuck forever with a mother who matched her slippers to her nightgown to her robe to her toothbrush to her nail polish, and no father whatsoever, not really even a memory. My adoptive father, though kind to me always, was nearly an elective mute. I guess he felt my mother talked enough for both of them. How ironic that just at the point in his life when he'd finally summoned the courage to free himself of her, he was run over by a crazy cabby.

Two weeks after we buried my dad, my boyfriend dumped me, and I mean dumped me. I'd like to say I gave him the two best years of my life, but, to be honest, he was just one of those get-you-along boyfriends that just kind of lasted too long. Still, it's easier to be the dump truck than the dirt. The good news was that I was a free agent. And that part felt good.

Roses Just Roses was one of those family-owned shops that had been around for just about forever. In the early twenties it was a barbershop and for a short time in the forties it was a tattoo parlor. But for the last fifty-three years it had been a flower shop. Mr. Z's father opened Zenovia Floral in nineteen forty-three—even during the Depression you had to have flowers for funerals. When Mr. Z took it over in nineteen sixty-seven, competition had become fierce among midtown Manhattan floral shops. To differentiate, Mr. Z decided to specialize. His wife Iona wanted to carry roses, orchards, and carnations. Mr. Z wanted to carry only roses. They bickered and bickered about it until finally Mr.

Z banged his hand on the table and shouted, "It'll be roses, just roses." And that's how the place got its name.

Before customer contact was permitted I was required to spend one day in the back room with Iona, learning about the different varieties of roses they carried. Who would have known there were so many! Iona said there were as many as seven hundred and fifty catalogued varieties and their shop featured one hundred of them. Ruth Ann and Shirley were the floral artists that put together all the orders. Ruth Ann was in charge of the walk-in business and Shirley managed the corporate accounts.

I was sent home with three different catalogues and four photo albums filled with page after page of roses—a hundred varieties in thirty different colors. Iona told me that I would be quizzed the following day on the names and characteristics of the different roses. Iona kept her word, too, although it was an oral exam that she administered, and she gladly helped me when I got stuck. When she was comfortable that I could tell the difference between a fragrant, Olde English, and a Ecuadarian, she gave me a chart that showed what the different colors of roses signified (red is for love, orange is for fascination, etc.), and asked that I commit it to memory. Then there was the price list with which to become familiar. I began to have second thoughts about the job being uncomplicated. Still I thought floral shop patrons had to be easier to please than diners.

On the second day of my employ I was handed over to Mr. Z. "First thing you got to learn, Miss Pet-als," he said, emphasizing the 't', "is the *nice-to-know* and the *need-to-know*. Example for you: nice-to-know that Dr. Trevor Freeman likes to send coral-colored roses to his pretty, young nurse on the first Monday of every month. *Need-to-know* that the bill is always sent to his office, *not* to his home. And it's nice-to-know that Mr. Thomas Nucci likes to put three fresh roses on his first wife's grave every week—a white one for reverence, a red one for true love, and a peach one for gratitude. *Need-to-know* that we don't send an invoice at all—Mr. Nucci comes in to pay so his second wife doesn't give him the business about so much attention to the deceased wife."

"I never realized flowers could be so...so political," I told Mr. Z.

"It's a racket all right."

"I'll be discreet, I promise."

"You'll do fine. You got a good face. Like Gladys. Your eyes are darker though. And you have higher cheekbones, too."

"And you're a might bit shrewder than my Uncle Murray. He ran a produce market on Fifty-Second. Nothing much political about fruits and vegetables."

"I don't know about that, Missy. Wasn't there something way back when about President George Bush, Senior, not liking broccoli. I think he took some slack for that. Possibly cost him re-election. I guess there's a little bit of politics in just about everything," he said as he went to unlock the front door.

My first customer was a young guy, my age probably, somewhere between a driver's license and a college degree, with longish blond hair, and shapely tan legs that stuck out of his khaki shorts like the legs of a solid oak table. He gave the impression that he was too cool to buy flowers for anyone, but I poised myself for a sale. "How may I help you?" I asked. (See how I used an open-ended question, rather than a closed-ended question that would elicit only a yes or no answer?)

"I work here?" he said. (I was certain he purposely phrased this as a question to punctuate the sarcasm in his voice.)

Right then and there I wanted to take a tweezers to his almost-one-continuous eyebrow. I was about to say something like "Doesn't your eyebrow get in the way of things?" when an inner voice reminded me that that was the kind of talk that got me fired from my last three waitressing jobs.

Thankfully, "Oh," was all I said as he headed for the back room. Iona had mentioned to me the day before that her nephew Byron worked here in the summer, making deliveries, but this guy looked as much like a "Byron" as I looked like a "Victoria." Honest, you'd have guessed his name to be something milkshake smooth like Pierre or Paul. Somehow, with just those three words— "I work here?"—I knew my perfect, sweet rose of a summer job was going to have one thorn in it, and he had better legs than I.

Soon Iona emerged from the back room with Byron trailing her. If he were younger, she may have pulled him by the ear. She didn't, but the effect was the same.

"Rose, this is Byron, my sister Nell's boy."

"Nice to meet you," I said.

"Mmmm. Hmmm. You too," he said. "Okay, now, which funeral home is it?"

While Iona gave her nephew directions, my first real customer walked through the door, announced by the clanking cowbell that hung from the doorknob.

"Hello, Miss," my first real customer said, in a spiffy British accent. "Have you any daffodils?"

"Daffodils? Oh, no, I'm sorry sir. We only carry roses."

"Only roses you say?"

"Yes, sir," I said, gesturing to the *Roses Just Roses* sign above me. "We specialize in old fashioned roses. May I ask, what is the occasion for the flowers?"

"Yes, well," he said, clearing his throat. "They would be for a certain young lady who has expressed a partiality to daffodils."

I could feel the eyes of Iona and Byron upon me. My first test.

"Well, maybe your friend is actually partial to flowers that are yellow in color. May I show you some gorgeous yellow roses? Do you know about the floral code, sir?"

"Floral code?" the man said as he followed me over to the refrigerated case.

"Yes," I explained. "In the nineteenth century each flower and color was designated a specific meaning so that messages could be sent between people through bouquets. Conversations between courting couples could be carried out over extended periods of time without a single word being used!"

"Imagine that! Well, what does the color yellow mean?"

"Yellow signifies gladness and joy, friendship and freedom. It can also mean 'welcome back' and 'remember me.'"

"Oh, well. Maybe not yellow then." He cleared his throat again. "Would you have something that means, say, 'Let's get together sometime, shall we?'"

"Ahhh. Actually, we do. The color peach says 'Let's get together.' Would you like a dozen boxed or wrapped with filler and fern?"

"She's goooooood!" I heard Iona coo to Byron. I saw Byron roll his eyes.

Unfortunately, the British gentleman was just beginner's luck. The rest of the day's customers proved more challenging, especially the bride-to-be that came in with her mother. The two of them couldn't have agreed that the earth was round much less on bouquets and boutonnieres. And several more people came in requesting gladiolas and carnations and irises until I wanted to point to the sign above the cash register and scream, "*Roses, DUH!, Roses.*"

I had problems with the ancient cash register and charged one lady fifty-one ninety-five for a dozen thirty-two-inch long stem roses, when I should have charged her fifty-five ninety-five. I told Iona she could take the four dollars out of my paycheck but she just laughed and said not to worry about it and by the way, what was I doing for dinner?

Since I was doing nothing for dinner, I joined Mr. Z and Iona at a diner down the street where they had the best Reuben sandwiches ever. We sat in a booth, Iona and Mr. Z on one side and me on the other.

"Miss Petals, you did good today," Mr. Z said between a bite of his steak sandwich.

"I did?"

"Oh, sure," said Iona. "Our own daughters never did as well." Iona told me their two daughters had both left New York City to attend college in California and then neither one came back to live. Their daughters and their families (six grandchildren) visit for Christmas and for a week in the summer.

"What about you, honey?" Iona asked.

"Yes, where's your family?" Mr. Z wanted to know.

Ah, the dreaded family question. I explained that I was an only child, adopted, that I had just lost my father in February, and that my mother was spending the summer on Martha's Vineyard with her sister.

"You poor thing!" Iona said. "Where are you staying?"

"At my mother's apartment. It's not far from here. Walking distance even."

"But you aren't walking, are you?" Mr. Z asked.

"No, my mother gave me my father's car after he died, a big blue Caddy. I can barely see over the steering wheel but I'm not complaining. It's better than biking it everywhere."

"Well, that's a relief!" Mr. Z said. "A pretty little dumpling like you shouldn't be riding around this city on a bicycle. And should your car ever break down, you just call me and I'll pick you up."

I smiled but I really didn't know what to say. I'd never in my life had anyone except Nan so concerned about my welfare, and even Nan had fostered my autonomy early on. Iona and Mr. Z's kind words gave rise to a couple of tears and I quickly had to feign a coughing attack to account for them. Mr. Z patted me on the back a couple of times as Iona took my right arm and raised it in the air.

"I'm okay, thank you," I said, but still the tears came. "Maybe I swallowed something wrong." I took a sip of water from the glass Iona handed me. "There," I announced, "I think I'll be just fine." And honestly for the first time in months I really was.

When I went home to my mother's apartment I ate half of a half-gallon of Neapolitan ice cream, but only the strawberry and the vanilla flavors. The chocolate I gave to my cat, Captain Mustache, because chocolate is his favorite. That was what I'd been doing since Simon dumped me—eating insane amounts of ice cream. Captain Mustache was really starting to put on weight.

I watched Letterman and couldn't help but wish Dave would be nicer to Richard Simmons. After the "Just Pants" blurb at the end of the show I flicked off the TV and hopped into bed. I thought with pleasurable anticipation about my job at the floral shop. What a wonderful little place, I thought. What wonderfully sweet people. Except, I had to wonder what was up with that Byron kid.

The next morning I took my place behind the counter, put on my *Roses Just Roses* apron, and said good morning to Stuck-Up So Stuck-Up Byron who had just come through the front door.

"What's so good about it?" he snapped. He was dressed exactly the same as the day before: white tee, khaki shorts, sandals. I thought about the florist my mother always used—their delivery boys dressed in tuxedos. Byron looked like a beach boy.

"What's so *not* good about it?" I returned, as I tied and retied my apron so as to keep my hands busy.

"Oh, man, I can just tell by looking at you that you're one of those cheerful Pollyanna types, aren't you."

"I am not."

"You are so."

"I am not. Mostly I'm brooding and deep. I use a lot of black and purple in my paintings. I even have a dark side. But at least I'm not hostile."

"I'm hostile? Me?"

"Yes, you. I only just met you and you're treating me as if I offended you in some way."

"DUH, you did."

"How did I offend you?"

"You took this job."

"And how did that offend you?"

"My girlfriend, Misty, wanted the job, but Aunt Iona wouldn't hire her on account of her nose earring. Or maybe it was the tongue ring. One or the other. Anyway I almost had Aunt Iona talked into reconsidering but then you showed up."

"Well, how in the heck was I supposed to know about Misty? And what kind of name is that, anyway? (The nerve of me, Rose Peddles, asking this question!) Please don't tell me she's Goth."

"Misty is not Goth. You are so pathetic."

"You're the one who's pathetic. And it's not called a nose *earring* and a tongue *ring*; it's a nose *ring* and a tongue *stud*. Anyway, both are childish and gross." (How dare I say this so superiorly when my own white blouse and black polka-dotted short skirt camouflaged a belly-button ring.)

"What's going on out here?" It was Iona. "Byron, you rascal, are you giving our Miss Rose Peddles a hard time already?"

"Rose Petals? Rose *Petals*? That's your name? You gotta be kidding!"

"Now, Byron, be nice or I'll tell her your last name."

"What is it?" I asked.

"Lord," Iona told me.

"Byron Lord!" I screamed. "You're Lord Byron backwards?" I couldn't help but laugh.

"I am not," Byron spat. "My last name is Lorden. She just likes to rev me up so that I'll make the deliveries faster."

"Now, really, you two," Iona said. "You do have something in common, you know. Byron's an art student, too, Rose."

"You are? I would have guessed a musician. Or surfer."

Finally, Byron cracked a smile. "See that? Who's giving who a hard time, Aunt Iona?"

"Come on you," Iona said to her nephew. "Let's go over today's deliveries."

Before I could even imagine what kind of artist Byron could be (I myself was a watercolorist and we watercolor artists believe ourselves to be the elitists of the entire painting world) the cowbell clanged on the front door and three customers walked in one right after the other. The first guy was easy. All he wanted was one perfect red rose. For twenty-five ninety-five, you can get an absolutely perfect imported red rose. Ruth removes the guard petals—the outer most petals that help protect the rest of the petals from damage—right before she wraps it. And honestly, it is perfect.

The second customer, a woman, wanted a vase of roses sent to the Fours Seasons Hotel where her son and daughter-in-law were celebrating their first anniversary. "What a sweet gesture," I said as I wrote out the order.

"Sweet my foot," she said. "I have an ulterior motive. Every time that spoiled little brat looks at those roses she'll be forced to think of me!"

I held back a smart remark, but I'm sure my eyebrows, which had levitated in disbelief, adequately expressed my thoughts. I couldn't help but wonder if this woman happened to be a friend of my mother's.

The third customer, an elegant-looking man in a dark suit, approached and introduced himself as Jonathan Redmond, Attorney at Law. He was pleasant but to the point. "I wish to send my client's wife some roses. Her husband has just been sentenced to ten years in the state penitentiary. What would you suggest?"

I stammered at first. Mr. Z had warned me about floral customers who think they must give you all of the details surrounding their purchases. I took a quick glance at my cheat-sheet of rose color meanings. "If I may ask, sir, is your client's wife *happy* about her husband's conviction?"

"I beg your pardon."

"Well, if she's happy that the louse is out of her hair, I think a dozen yellow roses, signifying gladness and joy, would be appropriate. If you want to thank her for her part in indicting him, then nothing says thank you like deep pink roses. If your client is innocent and you're going to appeal, a bouquet of red and white roses symbolizes unity. If you're glad he's out of the picture and you'd like to move into the picture, coral roses convey desire. If you're beyond desire, then red roses. Red is for passion."

"Well, I have never—" he said, but then broke a smile. "Wrap up two dozen long stemmed red roses and put them on my account. And make sure that my office is billed, not my home. Jonathan Redmond, 529 Lexington Avenue."

"She *is* good," I heard Byron say to Iona.

One afternoon in June, a tiny wisp of a girl, waif-like and blond, entered the shop. The way she matched from head to toe—black tube top, black Capri pants, black sandals, and black nail polish—made me pause to wonder if she, too, could be a friend of my mother's. I greeted her with my usual, "How may I help you?"

"My boyfriend works here?" she said/asked. But I interpreted this as "You stole my job, you ignorant slut."

"Just a minute," I said. I went to fetch Byron thinking, "Why are they always blondes?"

I hung out in the back room while Byron visited with Misty. I sat on a stool and watched Ruth Ann put together a stunning arrangement and listened as she told me about all the famous people and characters that had roses named after them. "Ingrid Bergman, Michelangelo, Minnie Pearl, Elizabeth Taylor, Dolly Parton, Christopher Columbus, Mr. Lincoln. Tinker Bell, Snow White, Goldilocks and Pinocchio, too," she said. Then Shirley told me about all the famous people who had come into the shop over the years: James Cagney, Dean Martin, Mary Tyler Moore, Harrison Ford. All this talk prompted Mr. Z into sharing what he called "rose lore," little tidbits about roses, like how Cleopatra tried to seduce Marc Anthony by welcoming him to her chamber with her floor covered in two feet of rose petals. Or how she soaked the sails of her ship in rose water to perfume the breezes. I could have listened all day but I heard the cowbell on the front door ring, which meant either Misty had left or a customer had entered, or both.

It was both. When I headed out front I came face to face with the most wastefully handsome man I have ever seen in my life. I kid you not. The man had good looks to spare.

He was casually dressed in a soft blue shirt and tan Dockers but he wore them as elegantly as if they were silk and cashmere. I don't often swoon over men (my old boyfriend, Simon, was average looking and that's being kind) but this guy had my skin darn-right goose bumpy. Byron was on the phone and ignored the man completely, so when he saw me he smiled and proceeded to power-walk over to me. He leaned over the counter and said in a breathless voice, "Quick! I just spotted the girl of my dreams having lunch in a café down the street. Flowers! I need flowers!"

"We have roses," I said, injecting urgency into my voice.

"Roses! I need roses!"

I grabbed an order pad and pistol-fired these questions: "How many? What color? Boxed, wrapped, or in a vase?"

"I don't know! What would you suggest a man in my position give to the most gorgeous total stranger he has ever laid eyes upon?"

"Hmmmmm. You seem to be fascinated with her."

"Yes!"

"Orange roses convey fascination."

"Fine!"

"But you also seem to be utterly enchanted with her."

"Yes!"

"Lavender roses signify enchantment."

"Great. Give me some of those."

"May I ask you one thing?"

"Sure."

"Is she blond?"

"Yes, but what does that have to do with it?"

"Nothing, I just had a feeling."

Byron, now off the phone, shot me a look.

"Please, I'm running out of time!" the wastefully handsome man cried.

"Okay, okay, I know just the thing. It'll be twenty-nine ninety-five and I'll be right back."

He gave me an impatient look. When I returned with a single peach-colored Austrian rose, he changed the look to you-must-be-crazy. "Thirty bucks for ONE rose?"

"She's fascinating and enchanting, but the girl of your dreams isn't worth a measly twenty-nine ninety-five plus tax?"

"Well—"

"This, sir, is an imported rose from Austria. The Austrian rose says, 'Thou art all that is lovely.' The color peach says, 'Let's get together.' The rest is up to you." I held out my hand for his money, then I handed him the perfect peach rose. "Good luck," I said. He smiled a million dollar smile as he turned to leave. I so wanted to shout after him, "Please let me know what happens!" but I knew that would be way out of line, and besides Byron was staring at me funny. "What?" I asked.

He shook his head. "Did I say anything?"

Maybe he didn't right then, but later, when I had dinner at Iona and Mr. Z's house (Iona invited me to join them at least two or three times a week), Iona told me that Byron had seen me in action and said that I could sell ice-cubes to an Eskimo and matches to the devil.

"Are those compliments?" I asked.

"As close as you'll come with my nephew," Iona said. "Now finish your beef stroganoff, you. You've lost weight and we need to fatten you up."

She was right, I had lost some weight. So had Captain Mustache, due to the fact that dinner with Iona and Mr. Z filled me up both physically and emotionally. I no longer went home and consumed halves of half-gallons of ice cream. Working with these kind people had transformed me. For the first time in my life I was without a boyfriend, apart from my girlfriends, separated from my father, and estranged from my mother, yet I had never felt more alive. The aching need to locate my birth parents had subsided. Maybe because I was pretending that I'd found them. Iona and Mr. Z had all but adopted me. I found myself wishing I belonged to them. They were the kind of people who made a girl wish she had never pierced her bellybutton.

That night I fell asleep happy, but then I dreamed of Mr. Wastefully Handsome. We were slow dancing at some night club and he whispered into my ear that he didn't care that I was only five feet tall, and that my nose turned up just a wee bit, that my hair was too short, that I dressed like an art student, or that I was saddled with an incredibly silly name. He loved me. He loved me in spite of it all. I woke up wondering if there would ever be someone who would love me *because* of it all.

Almost a week to the day after Mr. Wastefully Handsome had come in for the peach Austrian rose, he returned. This time he was dressed in a lightweight tan summer suit and his hair was slicked back with gel. I don't know how he could look even better, but he did.

"You are amazing!" he said as he approached the counter.

"The rose did the trick?"

"Did the trick? She was like putty in my hands. I couldn't believe it was that easy. I never knew the power of roses. One stinking rose and I had her phone number and a date for the next night."

"I'm glad it worked out," I said.

"Actually, it didn't work out. She was gorgeous but dumber than dumbbells. I didn't ask her out again."

"Oh, I'm sorry."

"Don't be sorry. Your part was successful. And now, there's this new broker at work."

"Another blonde?" (I had to ask.)

"No, actually, a brunette this time."

"I see," I said and then noticed that Byron had appeared out of nowhere and was digging around in the drawer where we kept enclosure cards.

"By the way," Mr. Wastefully Handsome said to me, "my name is Perry Roget, like the thesaurus, and I think we'll be seeing quite a bit of each other. Now, what do you say? I'd like another one of those Australian roses that says you're hot and I want you."

"It's an *Austrian* rose, and it says '*Thou art all that is lovely,*' and '*Can we get together sometime?*'"

"Right, right. Hey, can you maybe write that first part down for me, the 'thou art in heaven' part."

I wanted to gag. Why oh why are the beautiful ones always shallower than the shallow end? But I kept my cool, especially because Byron was wearing a cat-ate-the-canary look.

When Mr. Wastefully-Handsome-But-Abundantly-Shallow left with his thirty-dollar rose, Byron said, "I could have told you."

"You could have told me what?"

"Not to waste your time drooling over the likes of a guy like that."

"Byron, please, he's a stock broker, he's straight, he's apparently got some money, he dresses impeccably, and he must have been the mold God Himself used to create the most gorgeous man on earth. I'll waste every morsel of my time drooling over the likes of Perry Roget."

"Like the thesaurus."

"Do you even know what a thesaurus is?"

"Vain. Conceited. Stuck-up. Egomaniac. Proud. Supercilious. Haughty. Self-important. Insolent. Grandiose . . . does that answer your question?"

"Yes, Byron, but honestly, you're being altogether too hard on yourself."

At the end of July I invited Iona and Mr. Z to my mother's apartment for dinner. I wasn't much of a cook since I never had much of a teacher (even Nan couldn't cook), but I was very accomplished at ordering out: "This is Rose Peddles. I'll have the usual but make it three."

At the conclusion of dinner I presented Iona and Mr. Z with a gift. I'd been working on a watercolor for weeks. Finally, I'd completed it and had it framed. It was my best work and part of me was sad that my instructors would never see it. I was mostly pleased with the color of the guard petals. And the water droplets almost looked wet.

The next morning when I came into work, Mr. Z was pounding on the wall behind the counter with a small hammer. "Just in time, Miss Petals," he said. Then, with great ceremony, that sweet man hung up my painting and then stepped back to admire it. "You can almost smell the fragrance of it," he said. That stirred up a few tears. My mother had never hung up a single piece of my work and I had presented her with many. I don't know if she filed them in a drawer or in the wastebasket, I only know that not one ever showed up on a wall.

Mr. Z came around the counter to give me a squeeze. "Rose," he said, "you are something special. You're just as sweet as my cousin Gladys. I hate to see the summer come to an end." And here's the part that made me spill more tears: Mr. Z had tears in his own eyes.

Summer wound down quickly with August being a notoriously slow time for the floral industry—no holidays, no holy days, just mothers scurrying to get kids ready for school. Captain Mustache and I began eating halves of half-gallons of ice cream again. I found myself wondering if I should give up my dream of teaching art to inner-city children and jump instead headfirst into roses.

Byron and I began playing double-solitaire at the front counter to pass the time. I'd beaten him shamelessly for something like twenty-three straight games. Finally, I found an ounce of mercy in my heart and I let him win. Afterward he complimented my watercolor.

"I like your painting. It's really good."

"What's your medium?" I asked. "You've never told me."

"Same as you."

"No, I would have thought you were an oil man, or acrylic."

"Well, I'm not nearly as good as you. If you want the truth, I took one look at that," he pointed to my painting, "and considered changing my major."

"Byron, thanks for the compliment, but what else could you possibly be qualified to do?"

He punched me in the arm and then dealt out a new game. "Haven't seen the Thesaurus in here lately. Has he been in?"

"Oh, him. He was in on Monday. Another thirty bucks on yet another gorgeous rose for yet another gorgeous woman. I think he's up to eleven women now. I so want to tell him to go to a craft store and buy a carton of artificial roses."

"You did it, you know. You created a monster."

"I know, I know. I lose sleep over it."

"Why are women always attracted to guys like that?"

I looked at him incredulously. I knew I shouldn't say it but I did anyway. "The same reason guys are attracted to women like Misty."

"Misty's history."

"She is?"

"Been history for two weeks now."

I didn't know what to say.

"She dumped me like dirt."

"Like dirt you say?"

"For some stock-broker. Some really 'dreamy and romantic' stock broker."

"Byron?"

"Yeah? You can't be out already, I just dealt this hand."

"No, it's not that. Just that, well, remember? Perry Roget is a stock broker."

His eyes popped out.

"And you can't argue that he'd probably score a perfect ten for dreamy and romantic."

"Wow," he said. "Wouldn't that be something?"

"But what are the chances, really. I don't know why I mentioned it. It wasn't very nice."

"Forget about it. I have."

"Two deliveries, Byron," Iona called from the back.

"Okay, coming," he called. "See ya'," he said to me and threw his cards down on the counter. His face looked so long, I must confess to feeling a pang of guilt for having planted the seed about Misty and the Thesaurus. It was intentional and mean. Possibly even hostile.

"Hey, Byron," I yelled before he disappeared into the back room, "I'd like to see some of your work sometime."

"No, you wouldn't."

"Yes, I would."

"No, you wouldn't."

"Yes, I would."

"No, you wouldn't."

"Yes, I would."

"Maybe. We'll see."

He came out of the back room nearly camouflaged by our most expensive item, a crystal vase filled with two dozen long-stemmed red roses with baby's breath and fern.

"You're not going to believe this," he said as he set the vase on the counter and pulled the delivery ticket out of his pocket. "Look who ordered these." I knew who it was before he even pointed to Perry Roget's name in the "sender" box.

"And the recipient?"

"A Miss Michelle Bun," he read and then wiped his brow in pretend relief.

"Michelle Bun? What kind of name is Bun?"

"A beautiful one. One that spared me the humiliation of losing Misty to a reference book."

"I'm sorry about Misty, Byron, I really am. I'm a recent dumpee myself. A few months ago. You get over it."

"I guess," he said and headed for the door.

It wasn't until after he left that I noticed some roses on the counter. There were three of them. I looked around. I had no idea where they'd come from; I only knew they weren't there a minute ago. It occurred to me that quite possibly they had fallen out of the arrangement Byron was just about to deliver, but then I remembered that those roses were red. These were each a different color: one orange, one lavender, and one coral-colored. I held them in my hands and took in their fragrance. I had not grown tired of roses just roses.

When Byron came back inside to retrieve his second order from the back, I said, in my most smart-alecky voice, "Okay, I know the lavender one is for enchantment, and the coral one is for desire, but orange can be for either fascination or enthusiasm. So which is it?"

"What are you talking about?" he said, not even slowing down to give me the time of day. "I got deliveries to make, you know."

"These aren't yours, these three roses?" I felt my face flush. To assume does make an ass out of 'u' and me.

"Rose!" he said, and I couldn't tell if he meant the flower or me. When he emerged again from the back room, again partially camouflaged by another arrangement, I said, "Are you sure these don't belong to you?"

Without stopping, he said, "Yes, I'm sure, Rose, because they belong to you." At the door, he turned and I think I saw a smile behind some light pink roses. "And the orange," he said, "is for fascination. Definitely fascination."

◘

Everything Delicious

"A happy family is but an earlier heaven."
—Sir John Bowring (1792-1872)

THEY SAY A mother can distinguish her newborn's cry from all others in the nursery. I will confess, the crying all sounded the same to me, the father—a symphony of screechy, throaty wails that produced gooseflesh on my arms and sent my heart into tachycardia. Even after the fifth time around.

It's not like Margie talked me into five children. They just arrived, one by one, every two or three years, beginning the second year of our marriage while I was still in residency at Rush Presbyterian St. Luke's Hospital in Chicago. My wife is Catholic and Italian and need I say more? Five children...all of them girls, four of them genetically architected like their mother, small-boned with heads of thick wavy hair in varying shades of brown, each with dark chocolate eyes, and one of them, the last and luckless one, constructed remarkably like me. And I assure you, a day does not go by that the red-headed freckled one doesn't remind me that *I'm* to blame for her coloring, as if her mother had nothing to do with running out of melanin by the time she came along.

You *hear* my girls before you see them. Indoors and outdoors their voices reach high decibels causing me to obsess about the risk of hearing loss to those in proximity. I don't mean to say that my daughters lack femininity, just that they are uproariously and resoundingly feminine. Together their voices produce tintinnabulation such that would send any of a number of my patients suffering from tinnitis or ear-ringing over the edge. It would seem that they only whisper when I walk into a room. Then it's: "Dad, this is girl talk," or "Dad, it's private." My daughters possess this attitude of empowerment that frightens me at some deep level, leaving me to wonder how—or if—I can father them into womanhood.

Often, but not until after the birth of my youngest, I have laughed at my own error in choosing to specialize in otolaryngology rather than in obstetrics and gynecology. Surely those branches of medicine that study the physiologic and pathologic function of the female reproductive tract and the healthcare of women would have better equipped me to be the father of daughters. As it is, my training as an ear, nose, and throat specialist has left me without a clue.

I think of these things as I lie here on the last day of August on a too-firm king-size bed in a freezing hotel room on Coronado Island in San Diego. I've been in this same position—head propped up with four pillows, knees bent, with the remote control balancing on my stomach—for a couple of hours. I'm awash in guilt. You see, I'm not supposed to be here.

Please now, don't jump to conclusions; it's not what you think. There's no other woman, nor have I succumbed to a drinking binge, as have some of my esteemed colleagues who are also here at this medical convention. It's nothing as dramatic as either of those scenarios. I guess I'm either hiding out or else I'm conducting an experiment. I have yet to decide which.

I'm here as a guest of the wonderful people at Glaxo Smith Kline who requested that I speak on the topic of acute maxillary sinusitis at the annual convention of otolaryngologists. Margie usually accompanies me on these trips but the girls just started school last week (three different schools) and she assured me that "everything would simply fall apart if I left right now," so I came alone. And now I've decided to stay an extra night. And just to show them (them being Margie and Sarah and Cassie and Jenny and Lisa and Kelly), I am not even going to notify them of my change in plans.

I attribute this breach in my otherwise sensible nature to the shock I invariably experience whenever I am away from my wife and girls for extended periods of time. It's as if I undergo a withdrawal syndrome—so accustomed am I to having my life designed and arranged by this group of females. In a sense, they have spoiled me rotten; in another, they have ruined me completely. Do they at all fathom that they are my earth and I am merely the little moon that revolves around them day and night? Here's what this is all about: they never miss me when I'm gone and I miss them more than I would miss a limb.

The idea of staying an extra night came as the result of my frustration after three days and three nights of phoning home without ever getting through to anyone other than Kelly's voice on the answering machine. Certainly I understand that the person who is away from home misses the persons who are back at home more than the persons back at home miss the person who is away from home…but still! I left my itinerary with the number of the hotel on the refrigerator so if anyone wanted to know if I'd arrived in one piece, she (or she or she or she or she or she, for that matter) could have placed a simple phone call. As it was, I had to tell the answering machine that I'd arrived safely but late after a minor scare with one of the plane's engines, that my sinusitis talk went well, and that I beat Jack Rider, the cocky head and neck surgeon, whom I can barely stomach, in a round of golf.

I attempted one last call at eleven this morning, right before check out time. Margie is usually home until noon on Fridays because she helps our seventy-four-year-old cleaning lady clean and then she takes her out for lunch and writes out her bills for her. This time I didn't bother with a message, just slammed down the phone and allowed myself what my oldest daughter Sarah calls a "Rodney Dangerfield moment." But it's true, I get no respect from the women in my life.

So, here I lie, watching CNN, and wondering when Margie will realize that I should have been home hours ago. Didn't I tell her I'd be home by nine p.m.? It's almost eleven here which would make it around one in the morning in Chicago. Certainly she couldn't have gone to sleep? One would think (one would hope) that one's spouse of almost twenty-one years would be calling the hotel and pacing the floor in a situation like this. All I can do is picture my wife sleeping soundly in our bed, her cheeks pink with warmth, and her shoulder-length brown hair spilling over her pillow. I like to watch her while she sleeps, smiling contentedly as she dreams about everything wonderful and everything delicious.

I think back to circa 1980 B.C. (before children) when we were *it* for each other. She would pull all-nighters right along with me and quiz me for my exams. I'd laugh at her pronunciations of some of the medical terminology like *peptostreptococcus* and *phyohemagglutinin* and *isopropylaminoacetic acid,* but the truth is I never would have made it through med school without her. We were so close. But with the addition of each child we were pulled further apart. And now when I come home at night, after a day of attempting to improve the hearing, smelling, tasting, breathing, and swallowing of my patients, it's as if I drown in a sea of circulating estrogen before I can even reach my wife.

Usually it's Kelly, six, the one who looks like me, that attacks first, waiting for me at the side door. "Daddy, I want to be a mermaid. I can be a mermaid, right? Lisa says I can't be a mermaid."

"Well, or course you can be a mermaid. And if you ask her nicely I'm sure Mom will sew you a mermaid costume for Halloween."

"No, Daddy. I want to be a mermaid *when I grow up!*"

And if I tell her that I'm sorry but mermaids don't exist so she can't really be a mermaid when she grows up, she'll find some way of blaming it on the fact that she has red hair and freckles and then that would lead to blaming it on me. "Well, of course you can be a mermaid when you grow up. If Daryl Hannah can do it, so can you."

But then I have to deal with Lisa, nine, who is next in the sea of obstacles that stands between my wife and me. Lisa doesn't talk, she roars. "I can't believe you'd lie to her, Dad! Children mustn't grow up thinking they can be whatever they want to be. Some things are not possible. Illusions are not healthy and should not be perpetrated (I'm sure she means perpetuated) by well-meaning but coddling fathers."

There, that's exactly what I mean by a "Dangerfield moment." But there was a time, early on, when my fourth

27

daughter, Lisa, respected me, even idolized me. Career day comes to mind. The day Lisa, then seven, dragged me into her second grade class for a Daddy Show & Tell where the fathers speak to the class about their occupations. I'll never forget how my daughter introduced me: "This is my Daddy, Dr. Daniel Stuart, and he's a doctor and he knows everything about your body and what it does and all the real names for the parts of your body and the real names for the gross stuff your body does. Ask him anything. He knows ab-so-lute-ly everything."

Standing at the front of a room full of seven- and eight-year-olds proved to be more challenging than addressing an audience of my peers. They shot questions at me with machine-gun speed. What's the real name for passing gas?" *"Flatulence."* "The real word for burping?" *"Eructation."* "For goose bumps?" *"Pilomotor reflex."* "Bellybutton?" *"Umbilicus."* "Snot?" *"Mucus."* "Puke?" *"Emesis."* "Blood blister?" *"Hematoma."* "Adam's apple?" *"Laryngeal prominence."* "Hiccup?" *"Singultus."* "Sneezing?" *"Sternutation."* "Chickenpox?" *"Varicella."* "Sleepwalking?" *"Somnambulism."* "Going to the bathroom?" *"Urination or defecation."* "Headache?" *"Cephalalgia."* "Bad breath?" *"Halitosis."* "Sweating?" *"Diaphoresis."* "Sore throat?" *"Pharyngitis."* "Ear infection?" *"Otitis media."* "Stomach ache?" *"Gastritis."* "Charley horse?" *"Cramp."*

All right, perhaps I was guilty of grandstanding, but the way my daughter looked up at me, you would have thought I was Hypocrites.

Tomorrow, I'll rise early, play nine holes, enjoy a big lunch at the hotel, and then head for the airport. Perhaps when I'm in flight, news bulletins will air on the major networks about the missing ENT from Chicago. Perhaps there will be a small span of time where they, my wife and daughters, resign themselves to the fact that they've lost me. Then what, I ask? Maybe they should think about whom it is that makes their life so wonderful and delicious, anyway.

So, I get by Kelly, I get by Lisa, now I'm stopped by Jenny, our middle and most studious daughter, who does her homework at the dining room table so as not to be distracted by the others who usually sit at the kitchen table while their mother makes dinner. Jenny's the brightest of the five but also the hardest on herself. "Dad! Look! Can you believe?" she asks as she holds out a poster covered with a collage of magazine photos.

"What? This is nice. Nice job."

"I got a B+! A lousy B+!"

"No way! That's an A if I ever saw one. Still, honey, it's a B with a plus."

"Dad! It's still in the B family! It's not fair."

We almost lost Jenny once. I was in Miami speaking at a sleep apnea clinic when Margie paged me in a panic. She'd brought Jenny—three or four then—to the immediate care as she suspected she had an ear infection. The attending physician diagnosed acute otitis in both ears and prescribed amoxicillin. Twenty-four hours later, Jenny was worse instead of better—vomiting and complaining that her head and neck hurt. I told Margie to get her to the ER. They admitted her for bacterial meningitis and started her immediately on intravenous antibiotics but it was touch and go for a while.

At one o'clock San Diego time (three a.m. Chicago time) I hit the power off button on the remote and then turn out the light. First I get situated on my back, then on my right side, then on my stomach. I know I'm only kidding myself if I think I'll actually sleep, but my eyes are tired and I want to be fresh for my golf game. I re-position myself on my stomach, turn on my side, my back, and then do a complete three-sixty.

In my daydream Cassie almost crashes into me as I step out of the dining room and into the small butler's pantry that leads to our kitchen. This is the daughter that roams the house with the cordless phone glued to her ear talking always to "a guy." She ignores "call-waiting" until I get so frustrated I call it "Dad-waiting." The most I'll get in the way of a greeting is a perfunctory wave of her fingers. She's sixteen but looks twenty and loves to flaunt her curvaceous body all over the place. I worry that she's become a *femme fatale* (I've seen her working a crowd of sophomore boys) but she wasn't always such a temptress. When she was four, she was more charming than mysterious. When she was four, the only man she loved was me. And that might have been the last time she loved me…when she was four and I brought her home a gift from one of my trips, a sterling silver necklace and matching ring. I don't think she took them off for two years, not even for baths. "Daddy, it's the best gift ever. I just love jewelry. Next time, get me a diamond and then we can get married."

"But I'm all ready married to Mommy, sweetheart."

"Oh, silly, she won't mind. Besides, Mommy says we have to share."

A couple of weeks ago I found Cassie on our family room sofa buried underneath a boy I had never seen before. I'd just come in for the TV Guide. I didn't know what to do. I got so flustered I ran to get Margie who escorted the boy out of the house and escorted Cassie to the laundry room. In our house you don't get grounded, you get laundry—everybody's laundry—washed, dried, folded, and put away, for an entire week. Afterward, I was the one who got a talking-to: "Dad, you act as if I committed a sex crime or something. I'm sixteen and you may as well know now that although I am not an advocate of promiscuity, I am not an advocate of virginity either. A woman who marries a man without checking out the merchandise first is a full-blooded fool."

On sleepless nights when Cassie has a monopoly on the part of my brain that processes worry, I catch myself wondering if she still has that little necklace and ring set.

I'm almost to the kitchen. I can smell tomatoes and garlic. I see my wife but then I see Sarah, our oldest, too. They're fighting. It seems Sarah spent a hundred and seventy-five dollars on a pair of shoes. Sarah, who, when she was little, wouldn't keep shoes on her feet. My firstborn, colicky child. She sounded like a goat when she cried. I wasn't prepared for how wiry she was. I thought babies were soft as mush. But this child was strong, exerting her own power and will from the moment she drew in air. Such hardihood! Such tenacity! And could she scream! And she's still screaming. Margie's holding the shoes up in the air and Sarah's stomping her feet. It doesn't take me two seconds to assess this as one of those "no win" situations so I hold up my hand in stop sign fashion and say, "Hey! Don't involve me in this. I know nothing."

Wrong thing to say! Margie forgets that she hasn't seen me all day, she forgets that today was the day I had a deposition, she forgets that tomorrow is our anniversary and I just bought her a new washer and drier (her idea, not mine), she forgets that I come home famished, but mostly she forgets that I need to be assured on a regular basis that I am not invisible when I walk into my own home. And so now before I even get to kiss her on the cheek, she's mad at me. "You were supposed to say that a hundred and seventy-five dollars is too much even if it is her own money," she says, her Italian hands speaking louder than her mouth.

I look at Sarah. I point to her mother and say, "I agree with her. Sorry."

"WIMP!" Sarah spits. A Dangerfield dagger right to the heart.

I've been known to go off the deep end late at night in hotel rooms. Once I ordered a seven-course meal at midnight, which I consumed with a half-bottle of half-decent wine, giving no thought to the severe bout of acid reflux that would accompany me the following day on the plane ride home. There was a time in Phoenix, in a hotel in the desert, when it was so quiet I couldn't sleep at all so I went for a run at three a.m. Another time, I called housekeeping ranting and raving that I could find no Gideon Bible in the chest of drawers. The poor lady from housekeeping didn't know how to respond to my question as to what the world was coming to when you couldn't find a Gideon Bible in a hotel room chest of drawers. And speaking of chests of drawers, there was another sleepless night where I remember sliding onto a barstool in the hotel lounge next to a drunk who kept up a running commentary on the size of the bartender's breasts. "How about those headlights?" "A guy wouldn't even need a pillow." "Now that's what I call a chest of drawers."

The phone startles me out of semi-sleep. It's four-fifteen in the morning here, which makes it six-fifteen in Chicago. They're just getting up. I let it ring a few times. It's a little late now but I realize that I never really choreographed how I'd tap-dance my way through this. With a sinking feeling I remember that I stink at impromptu. I say hello.

"Daniel?"

"Yes? Who's calling please?"

"Excuse me, this is your wife! Where are you?"

"I'm here at the hotel. You just called me, remember?"

"What's going on? I thought you were supposed to be home last night."

"I was."

"Daniel, I don't understand."

"Hi, Daddy!" It's Kelly, on another phone.

"Hi, honey."

"Dad, are you coming home?"

"Who's that, Cassie?"

"Yes, Dad, it's me."

"Daniel," says Margie, "I had a migraine last night so I went to bed at seven. I thought when I woke up you'd be here."

"I'm—"

"Dad, please come home," Cassie says. "Mom is so weird when you're gone."

"She is?"

"Yes, she is."

"Weird, how?" I want to know.

"I'm not weird when your father's gone, Cassie."

"Yes, mother, you are. It's like you mope around. And you're bitchi— okay, crabbier. And you get mad because no one compliments your cooking. '*Everything's delicious, hon*,'" she says, imitating me. "And—"

"That's enough, Cassie. May I please talk to your father? Do you mind?"

"Bye Dad, I miss you."

"Who said that?" I want to know.

"Dad! It's me, Cassie. Geez!"

"Mommy, can I ask my Daddy one thing."

"One thing, Kelly, then you hop in the shower."

"Daddy?"

"Yes, honey?"

"Can I be a mermaid when I grow up?"

"You know, Kelly, I've been giving this mermaid thing some thought. Mermaids don't make all that much money and if you want to own horses you'll need a better income...and legs."

"Oh, yeah. I'm glad you told me. Come home soon."

"Daniel Paul Stuart, you better tell me what's going on right this darn minute."

"Well, I missed my flight and—"

"Are you feeling left out again? Is this like last year when I chaired that committee and I had no time for you? Is that what this is about? Oh, Daniel—"

"Honey, I missed my flight and I tried to call but nobody was home and then I had a headache myself and I fell asleep too and—"

"Oh, all right, whatever. Just come home. I do miss you and I have been moping and rather bitchy and you are the only one that appreciates my cooking."

"I've got a seven o'clock flight. I'll be home for lunch."

"Hey! Why don't we go out for lunch, just you and me? I'll make Sarah baby-sit. Let's go to Luna Blu. Everything is so delicious there."

As I hang up the phone I catch my reflection in the dresser mirror. I'm smiling.

I pack up and with just a sliver of guilt in my heart I begin my journey home—where my five daughters think I'm nothing but a clueless nerd with a good vocabulary; where my main value lies in the God-given talent of roaming the house and flicking off the lights thereby conserving energy for the planet; where I will never win by taking sides in any argument between any two of the inhabiting females; where every word is screamed and shouted and bawled and bellowed and yelled and whooped and roared; and where everything—*ab-so-lute-ly* everything—is delicious.

◖◗

On Ellen Avenue

*"Let me live in a house by the side of the road
and be a friend to man."*
—*Sam Walter Foss (1858-1911)*

A BIRD'S EYE view of two used-up, dirty-white bungalows on the southwest end of the ever-evolving Ellen Avenue: two clay-colored shingled roofs in ill repair, two crumbling brick chimneys, two sun-scorched brown lawns, two rusty chain link fences that might as well be stone barricades, two flourishing rectangular gardens, one flower, the other herb and vegetable, splashing shocks of color and drenching the otherwise drab monotony with a spray of beauty.

The house on the corner of Ellen and Raleigh is the bigger and nicer of the two bungalows, hemmed in by bulky oaks whose acorns at summer's end are like gifts, tiny trinkets dropped upon passersby, souvenirs of the season. Once this house was home to seven, but now only

Della remains, her husband dead six years, her five sons married or otherwise occupied, her ninety-two-year-old aunt, whom she'd cared for up until last month, hanging on by a shoe string in that urine-scented nursing home on Cleaver Street.

Della, with a tall glass of lemonade in her thin hand, a hand that suddenly has too much skin on it (she can pinch more than an inch at the knuckles), has stepped out into her backyard on this ninety-eight degree August day with hopes of catching any degree of breeze. There is none, but even standing in the shade of the big oak is preferable to melting in the stifling wall of heat in her kitchen. She's been baking again. "Well, you got to eat, don't you?" is her explanation to anyone who asks why in God's name she would choose to turn on her oven in this heat. Or, she'll say, "The bananas were perfectly over-ripe." Or, "I like to have chocolate chip cookies handy when the grandchildren come by." Truth is, the grandchildren don't come by anymore, all seventeen of them awash in the magnitude of their own lives. More truth: her sons rarely come by either. Maybe to cart her off to a doctor's appointment. A couple times to borrow money. For Mother's Day. Easter and Christmas. Her birthday. (Three out of five usually remember her birthday—but never the one she lost sleep over, the one who grayed her hair, thinned her down with worry to a hundred and ten pounds that one terrible year. A tall woman like her, five feet nine inches, down to a hundred and ten pounds!)

But look! Della does have company—that dingy, once-white terrier mix mutt, the one her middle son, the one she lost sleep over, asked her to look after while he went off camping in the mountains ten years ago with that bosomy Latin-American redhead. David ended up marrying the redhead, who swiftly proclaimed a severe allergy to "good-for-nothing-stinking-mongrels." In the end, Goliath (the name was a farce, David's doing, of course) had proved not to be a miserable excuse for a dog but an amiable companion, all the more appreciated when Aunt Emily was moved to the nursing home on Cleaver Street. Surely without Goliath, Della would be wandering around her house and yard talking out loud to herself. Someone—a nosey neighbor maybe—would witness this and before she knew it she'd have an address on Cleaver Street and a roommate named Aunt Emily. (She now understood the real reason that dog is man's best friend.)

"Go get the hose, Goliath!" she says in that high-pitched, excited voice that one uses with dogs and babies. "Go ahead, get the hose. Come on now!" She claps her hands together. Sometimes she is surprised by the sound of her voice. It sounds staticky, like a well-worn record album. "Good boy. There's a good boy," she says when the dog returns with the hose hanging loosely in its mouth. She pats his head like she used to pat the blond heads of her five sons. Goliath sniffs around the marigolds that form a golden hedge around the perimeter of the garden while Della waters everything for the third time today. She sprays Goliath who immediately shakes off the water and tilts his head to give her a puzzling look, one that seems to say *why on earth would you think I would enjoy that?* She sprays her own legs and feet, lifting her housedress to indecent heights in the process. It feels wonderful. She slaps some water on her cheeks, on the back of her neck, the sensation bringing her back in time thirty or thirty-five years when in this very backyard she, a respectable housewife and mother, ran around in her bare feet, housedress raised to indecent heights, chasing her five sons with the garden hose. Milton was away on business and the boys were so hot and crabby they were nipping at each other like garter snakes. Ray, her oldest, started it, spraying his brother Lucas right through the kitchen window. Lord that was fun! And afterward, it was as if her boys had a new respect for her. Mom was human after all, capable of some spontaneous fun. Later, when the boys told their father about the water fight, Milton looked up from his paper, adjusted his glasses and raised his eyebrows, nothing short of shocked. Della just smiled. She knew when she married him he was a fuddy-dud.

Della's garden is glorious with rich swaths of color and texture, magazine perfect, a study in pluralism and democracy—the Shasta daisies co-habitating with the pink and magenta zinnias, the deep blue delphinium living harmoniously with the bleeding heart and the candytuft, the Lady's mantle with chartreuse-colored star blooms and moss-green leaves sharing the sun with Virginia Bluebells. Della has a knack for composition, planting in such combinations as daylilies with purple perilla, heliotrope with dusty miller, love-in-a-mist with iris and cosmos, cleome with liatris, Chinese basil with Japanese anemone. John Bowman, an African American man from church, assists her with the garden. Last year he helped her expand it, permitting the addition of new varieties of perennials and flowering shrubs. Now it bursts with color from the first pink blossom of spring to the last auburn sedum of fall. She lives for it, the garden. And for Goliath, of course.

"You could have thrown a tomato plant in there somewhere, or some chili peppers," the redhead had said to Della, when she and David returned from the camping trip and announced the good news that Goliath was now hers.

"I make a mean-ass salsa," the redhead had told her. Della, not knowing that the redhead and David were already married had treated the girl briskly, saying, "I'm a baker, not a canner." Had she known she was speaking to her middle son's new wife, she would have carefully curbed her terse reply. "Sure, maybe next year I'll add tomatoes." Or, "I love a good salsa." The point being: she didn't know.

Still watering, Della sees a rainbow in the arc of the spray and for some crazy reason this makes her cry. As she wipes away the tears, she catches movement in her peripheral vision. Goliath barks twice and Della turns slightly to the right, straining eye and ear. Sure enough, it's her neighbor and ex-best friend Jeena (why would anyone spell Gina, Jeena?) Bell. Bell was the woman's last name but forever people called her JeenaBell, as if it were one word. It's JeenaBell all right, making a racket with a mallet, hammering a wooden stake at least five feet tall into the ground to accommodate her prize-winning Big Boy tomatoes that keep climbing like Jack-in-the-beanstalks to the sky. Tomatoes—Schlamadoes. Della was a baker, not a canner. A flower gardener, not a vegetable gardener. Pretending to water the bed that lined the fence separating their two yards, Della snatches a peek at JeenaBell's garden of plenty. Fat, red tomatoes hang like forbidden fruit from the tallest plants she's ever seen (big deal, Miracle Grow). JeenaBell's long green zucchini border on the pornographic. Those large bell peppers will be perfect stuffed with JeenaBell's delicious meat dressing. There's lettuce and radishes, onions and carrots, cucumbers and green beans. JeenaBell even grew sweet corn. Sweet corn! She cans tomatoes, tomato sauce, tomato juice. She cans dill pickles, bread-and-butter pickles, pickle relish. She cans anything and everything, the bottles lining wooden shelves in a cool corner of her basement. "That woman can can!" Anne Maloney from across the street would say, laughing at the sound of the repeated words.

For all intents and purposes (you'll appreciate the irony of this later on) JeenaBell delivered David. In her Chevy Impala. With her own son in the car seat howling for his milk. Once, they were thicker than thieves, Della and JeenaBell, hosting neighborhood coffees and Christmas galas and summer block parties. Once, in their forties, they lay in the sun all day drinking Manhattans (neither had ever been drunk in her life) until they couldn't even get up off their chaise longues. Their husbands, laughing, left them there all night. In the morning they were sunburned and covered with mosquito bites.

When JeenaBell's mother died, and Fritz was out of work, Della cut every blooming flower out of her garden and filled baskets and vases and jars with the colorful blossoms, then carted them all over to St. Jude's for the funeral Mass. Likewise, when Della lost her father, JeenaBell cooked for days, putting out a spread fit for royalty. "No one can cook like you, JeenaBell," Della would tell her. "And no one's thumb is greener than yours, DellaBell (she called her that sometimes)," JeenaBell would reply.

Christmas bordered on the ridiculous, what with all the gifts the two friends gave each other. Milton and Fritz would tease, "Maybe these girls like each other *too* much." But all their gifts were inexpensive homemade items that were stitched, sewn, hot-glued, cooked, canned, or painted.

This Christmas, neighbors on Ellen Avenue will find baskets filled with JeenaBell's canned goodies upon their doorsteps. JeenaBell will slip in jars of raspberry jam or grape jelly or apple butter—depending on the tastes of her friends—or jars of dill pickles, pear halves, mint jelly, chutney, tomato sauce. But there won't be a basket for Della this year, hasn't been one on her front porch since Christmas of seventy-eight. That's when the trouble with David and Amelia had begun.

In March of his junior year, citing a certain unexplainable restlessness, David left college, promising his father he'd return in the fall. Once home he fell into an easy groove of helping Milton out at the hardware store during the day, practicing his guitar at night, and palling around with his musician buddies on the weekends. They even played at a couple of dances at the high school. Milton was soured. He hadn't doled out good money for college so his son could earn a degree in "billiards, loose women, and rock 'n' roll."

He was a good boy, Della maintained, he just possessed a spirit that was freer than his brothers. David was a musician after all, an artist. She fancied that quite possibly she was going through what Paul McCartney's mother had gone through (not knowing that Paul McCartney's mother had died young). Besides, David *was* learning responsibility—every other week he handed his mother twenty-five dollars.

Once, he didn't make it home. And then often he didn't make it home, telling his mother the next day that he'd "crashed" at so-and-so's, not to worry. But Della succumbed to the usual parental worries: drinking, drinking and driving, drugs, girls, trouble with the law. The usual. But it never occurred to Della that all of the above could come in the pretty little package that lived next door.

Ameila was by far the prettier of JeenaBell's two daughters but not in any spectacular way. Her shoulder-length mousy brown hair was worn long and straight, parted down the middle like all the teenage girls wore it. She had nice brown eyes that she highlighted with sky blue eye shadow. But what saved the girl from mediocrity was her body. Her pleasant if ordinary face was attached to—well, as her sons had put it more than once—a body that wouldn't quit. (Quit what? Della wanted to ask, but of course she already knew.)

That fall when David stayed back from school he was twenty-one; Ameila was not quite seventeen. Della saw how David looked at Ameila, but Peter and Steven looked at her that way too: the *little-girl-next-door's-all-grown-up* look. David actually gawked. But what could Della say to him? It wasn't the same with sons as it was with daughters. Sons needed their space. You couldn't go around interrogating sons the way you could daughters: *Who sat next to whom?*

What was she wearing? Where does she live? Who are her parents? Did you kiss her? No, boys needed space or you'd push them away forever.

So, of course she was the last to know: Ameila was pregnant. Three months along by the middle of June. David denied paternity. "I swear to God, Ma, it's not mine. Amelia's been around the block a few times, believe me."

It was the beginning of the end. Milton worried that if David didn't marry Amelia she might press charges—even if it was consensual, it was still statutory rape if the girl was under age. "You'll just have to do the right thing, son," Milton told David. And so they married.

At first Della and JeenaBell rallied, putting aside shock and shame to help their children make a life for themselves and the baby. Together they painted the complete interior of a tiny upper apartment they'd found up on Cleaver Street. Each woman donated pieces of furniture—odds and ends really—and other sundries needed to set up house. JeenaBell sewed cheery kitchen curtains and a comforter and matching bed ruffle for the crib. She filled her daughter's pantry with canned provisions while Della filled the flower boxes with impatiens and variegated ivy.

But David and Amelia couldn't come together. They did nothing but fight. Once Ameila lost control and hit David over the head with his guitar. It wasn't unusual for Della to find David home in his old bed some mornings when she went up to wake Steven.

"She can't cook," David told Della one morning when she found him sipping coffee at her kitchen table.

"You can cook. You're a great cook," Della told him.

"She's so dumb. She's never even heard of Helen Keller. Hell, she's not even interested in getting her G.E.D."

"Oh, so now the college drop-out is turning up his nose at the high-school drop out?"

"Maaaaaa! I don't love her."

"But there's the baby, David."

"Yeah, the baby. Somebody the hell else's baby."

"David!!"

There was the baby. And that baby surprised them all, coming out three weeks early, coming out the color of chocolate milk. David moved out that night before Ameila and the baby even came home from the hospital. Della never told anyone, not even Milton (she was so ashamed), but David had left a note, a good-bye note on his dresser. It said: *Mom and Dad, Imagine! This may be the first time in history that a black baby has set a white man free. I'm free. Tell her I'll send money. Love, David*

The next time Della heard from her middle son was three months later. On a postcard from Los Angeles he scrawled: *I'm okay. Really, I'm okay. Love, Dave*

He never did send money. Della and Milt gave Amelia cash to help cover the cost of diapers and formula and sleepers and such. Ameila and the baby, a lovely plump girl named Bianca, moved in with JeenaBell, staying until Bianca was seven. Maybe it was providence that JeenaBell's husband Fritz had died of a heart attack the year before. He'd been spared the grief.

Della watched the girl grow. From the kitchen window, from her bedroom window, from the back porch, from the garage, from her pew three rows behind them at church. Della watched Bianca flourish like one of the lovely flowers in her garden. The sound of her laughter and cry became as familiar to Della as those of her own boys had once been. But she never spoke to the little girl. Not once.

There was a time, a hell-hot day not unlike today, that Della, kneeling in her flower garden, looked up from the dirt to see a small brown hand holding out a huge, oddly formed tomato, the sight of it alone making Della's mouth water. Through the leaves of her hydrangea bush Della saw Bianca's sparkling eyes. She must have just turned

four. She smiled at Della, then brought her free hand up
to her mouth to stifle a naughty giggle. Della found herself
extending her hand to accept the offering, when…

"Bianca!" JeenaBell called out sharply.

Startled, Bianca dropped the tomato to the ground.
Splattt! It cracked down the middle, oozing juice and seeds,
scenting the air with that pungent, summery smell.

"Come on back here, sweetie," JeenaBell called. "We
don't talk to that woman, remember?"

"Why not, Grandma?"

"We just don't. That woman is invisible to me. She
simply doesn't exit."

"Is she a ghost?"

Della strained her ears but never did hear the answer.

That's when Della decided it was time to go talk to
Father Will. Milton was against it. Our business is nobody
else's business, he told her. But everyone on Ellen Avenue
and beyond knew about "the little situation." Some sided
with Ameila: W*hat kind of low-down, good-for-nothing
man would abandon his wife and baby like that! That poor,
sweet child! There are laws against that.* Others sided
with David: *Why should he raise someone else's kid? One
that's not even his color? That little hussy trapped him into
marrying her. Who wouldn't run?*

Of course Father Will knew all about it, didn't even
pretend not to know, which made Della feel that maybe
she was right to come talk to him. Father Will didn't take
sides either, another good sign. He simply praised Della for
providing money for the child's needs and praised JeenaBell
for taking her daughter into her home with open arms and
helping to raise Bianca.

"So where do we go from here?" Della wanted to know.
Tears now.

"Where do you want it to go, Della?"

"I want things to be back the way they were. Before David and Amelia wrecked our lives. JeenaBell was my best friend for twenty-two years and now she treats me as if I were invisible."

"She's hurting too, Della."

"Hmmpf."

He took her hand and gently sandwiched it between his. "Dear Della, you know how stubborn JeenaBell is. It'll have to be you that makes the first move. You'll have to be the brave one. It will be one of the hardest things you will ever do, I promise you that. But I also promise you this, the healing and the peace that will wash over you afterward will be like a little taste of heaven. More beautiful than all the flowers in your garden."

More tears. Then, "Father," as she rose to leave, "sometimes I wish she *was* my granddaughter. She's prettier than a purple pansy."

Della rose the next day with a sense of courage and peacefulness (was she already tasting heaven?). Milt was away on a three-day business trip and the younger boys were off early to their summer jobs. This was the day, Della decided, setting aside the morning paper, not wanting to taint this wonderful feeling with the sad news of a house fire or a traffic fatality or a drug bust.

Everyday for the next three years, Della woke up thinking this is the day. She even sang it: *This is the day that the Lord has made, let us be glad and rejoice.* But never was she able to make that first move. An opportunity would arise and her legs would stiffen or her voice would choke off, her vision would blur, her hearing would falter, or her feet would become cement blocks. Pride had a way of paralyzing a person.

Each day she promised herself and each night she chastised herself. It became even more painful for Della when she started finding presents hidden under her hydrangea bush—the very bush where Bianca had held out that fabulous tomato. At first it was the glint of a shiny silver dollar that caught Della's eye. She was sure it was Bianca's because she had seen the child's uncle present it to her earlier that day. She threw it over the fence into JeenaBell's yard, aiming so that it would land on the cement patio and be easily discovered, and went back to her garden. But then more things appeared. Then daily things appeared: bits of pretty ribbon, a marble, a stick of Juicy Fruit gum, a walnut, a broken red balloon, a heart-shaped rock, the lid to one of her grandmother's Ball canning jars. The gifts kept coming: a barrette, a broken shoe string, a Barbie doll head, one of those plastic baby bottles that when inverted looked like the milk was gone (surely she didn't want to give that away!). And kept coming: an unopened Cracker Jacks prize, a mood ring, a Hot Wheels car, a wallet-sized photograph of Bianca in a frilly pink dress. Della began to look forward to her morning "peek" under the hydrangea bush.

One day there was nothing. Out in her backyard, Della heard the slam of JeenaBell's back screen door and she watched JeenaBell kiss Ameila and Bianca and load their suitcases in the trunk (oddly, in the front) of Ameila's Volkswagen Beetle. JeenaBell waved and cried and admonished them to call when they arrived. They were gone in an instant—leaving nothing but exhaust—before Della could even say good-bye. Or hello.

Della sank into a funk. What if that baby really was her granddaughter? What if David and Ameila's genes for blond hair and fair skin had somehow mutated? They both had been guilty of abusing drugs and alcohol, and Ameila never stopped smoking cigarettes during her pregnancy. Maybe Bianca had been smoked, like a ham or a salmon to her particular dusky shade. Could something have happened in the womb that flicked on a gene for dark skin and curly hair?

"Don't kid yourself, Mom," Steven told her years ago when she asked him about it. "It's a scientific impossibility. That little girl's father is a black man. That's all there is to it. Might have even been the drummer in David's band."

Della never saw Bianca again. Anne Maloney, from across the street, heard that Ameila and Bianca had moved to Minneapolis, that Ameila had married again, had three more children, all girls, and was now teaching blind children. JeenaBell visited often, driving two hundred miles all by herself, until her eyes went bad and then she rode along with her younger daughter for visits. Bianca would be about nineteen now. Ameila never returned home with her daughters, not once.

But David returned home many times. He would breeze in and out, with a different girlfriend, a different rock band, a different dog. It surprised his mother that he never once bothered to ask, even as an afterthought, "Hey, what ever happened to Ameila and the baby?" One time when he'd visited with the bosomy redhead, he opened up the fridge to grab a pop and his eye caught hold of the wallet-sized photo of the little girl in the frilly pink dress stuck with a smiley-face magnet to the refrigerator.

"Who's the cute kid with the tan?" he asked.

"Your daughter."

"Oh," he said, popping the pop-top.

Later that night when she hugged him good-bye, David leaned in close and said, "Ma, you know that wasn't my b—"

"I know that, David, but wasn't it really? In some way?"

He only looked at her funny. "Gotta fly, Ma. I'll send a postcard from the Big Apple. We open for the Doobie Brothers! The Doobies, Ma!"

JeenaBell's confounded hammering is starting to give Della a headache. She throws down the hose and presses her bony fingers to her temples. The afternoon heat is debilitating—she needs another lemonade, or maybe something stronger. A Manhattan, maybe. Yes, a Manhattan.

She pulls open the screen door and steps into the kitchen, still hot but wonderful-smelling from the banana bread she baked earlier. The few bottles of liquor she keeps in the house are stored in the cupboard above the microwave. She has to drag a chair over to reach. What was in a Manhattan, anyway, was it sweet Vermouth or dry Vermouth? She couldn't remember the last time she had one much less mixed one. She takes out a bottle of Bourbon and decides it was *sweet* Vermouth. She mixes it up the way Milton used to: two fingers of bourbon and one finger of sweet Vermouth in a short glass over ice, garnished with a cherry.

She looks at the kitchen clock above the sink as she takes a tentative sip and wonders what the neighbors would think of a seventy-two year old widow taking a nip at two o'clock in the afternoon. *They just might join you*, a small voice in her head says. So she stirs up another, and then backs out the screen door using her elbow to depress the handle.

As she makes her way to the fence Della's not surprised to find the first few steps so painful. Her legs go weak and her heart tries to jump out of her chest. What surprises her is that it doesn't get any easier. By the time she reaches the fence, both glasses are dripping with condensation and almost slip out of her hands.

She clears her throat once. "Care—" It comes out a squeak. She clears her throat again. "Care to join me for a Manhattan?" she calls out over the fence.

JeenaBell emerges from behind one of her giant tomato plants. She squints at Della, then uses her hand to shade her eyes. "What was that?" she asks, using the other hand to cup her ear. (Leave it to JeenaBell to make Della ask twice.)

"I said: Would you care to join me for a nice cold Manhattan?"

JeenaBell arches her eyebrows. She throws down her mallet and wipes her dirt-caked hands on the back of her gardening slacks. She scowls at Della, producing all sorts of wrinkles in her face—on her forehead, nose, at the corners of her eyes—as she slowly makes her way over. When she reaches Della she stares at the Manhattans in her hand and it's a full ten seconds (Della counted) before she stretches out her hand to Della and says, "Don't mind if I do."

◼

A Chunk of Change

*"It is a poor and disgraceful thing
not to be able to reply,
with some degree of certainty, to the simple questions,
'What will you be? What will you do?'"*
—John Foster (1836-1917)

FROM MY BED I watch the Monday morning sky. The color of trash cans, it opens and regurgitates rain in straight sharp needles down on my neighbor's gray-shingled roof. The lines of water ricochet, then stream down the slanted sides of the roof and collect in the eaves. If the downpour continues, my neighbor, a guy with muscle shirts and whiskers, will risk saturation and electrocution by climbing his aluminum ladder in order to clean out the gutters. "Now that's using your head," I'll say under my breath from the safe distance of my second floor bedroom. The last time he was up on the ladder during a storm I felt like marching on over there and showing him the label (in these times of hyper-litigation there's got to be a label) on the side of the ladder that says: "Warning! Do not use in electrical storms." The thing is, under the muscle shirt, there are muscles.

Soon I'll need an ark. This rain is unwelcome and unnecessary. For days now, the ground has been sodden and springy, drunk with moisture. My mom's basement flooded yesterday, my landlord's front yard has sprouted freaky-looking mushrooms, and my sheets are damp at night. Enough is enough. I lie in bed and whistle George Harrison's "*Here Comes the Sun*" in hopes that it will.

I listen to the rumble of thunder in the distance. The lightning isn't close, still, it startles me each time the flashes of light stab my bedroom walls. The hell with it. I reach for the phone and call work. Eddie is pissed, tells me it's the fourth time this month. Says I better invest in some multi-vitamins or better yet, have those tonsils yanked out. I swallow hard and tell him I had better get off the line, that all I can hear is static.

So. It's not like people are depending on me or anything. Like you do a doctor, or a teacher, a short-order cook, or even a lawyer. Hell, anybody can collect garbage. There's nothing to it. All you need are two strong arms, a pair of thick gloves, a good back and a weak sense of smell. Maybe my calling in sick will force Eddie to bring Theo back. Theo got suspended last week for idling his truck in somebody's alley while he enjoyed a smoke on a former girlfriend's back porch. Yeah, this would be a good time to get Theo back. With any luck, he'll get struck by lightning. I'm only a quarter joking.

I know I'm in trouble when my stomach starts grumbling in unison with the thunder. I take this as some sort of sign (I'm big on signs) and I get myself up and drag myself to the kitchen. I open the fridge—evidently old habits are hard to break—even though I know its contents by heart: a half-empty bottle of ketchup, one can of Old Style, and some messed-up applesauce. I settle for a nutritious breakfast of Cheerios and water. If the water is ice cold, it's not all that bad. I carry the bowl to the living room and flick on the black and white (it's actually a big-ass color set, but I'm going for a little sympathy here) so as to enjoy breakfast with the ever-chipper Katie Couric and Matt. I never liked Katie Couric until her husband died. Tragedy changed her somehow. Tragedy has a way of doing that. I plop—as much as one can plop while holding a bowl of cereal in his hands—into a webbed lawn chair, just one of a matching set of four, which together constitute my living room ensemble. This is what I got when Julie and I broke up. This fancy living room furniture, the TV, the CD player, the microwave, and the waterbed. In my book, I made out.

When my cell phone rings I jump. It could be Eddie firing my ass. It could be my mom begging for a pack of cigarettes in her booze-bruised voice, or it could be my kid brother Benny in need of a ride. It's actually some woman saying, "Good morning, Tweety. This is your seven o'clock wake-up call." When I tell her that I'm not Tweety, she says, "Ooooops!" and hangs up.

I push down the reset button and then dial up home. Home being my mom's house where I lived until two years ago when I moved in with Julie. I pray Benny will answer. It rings and rings. I count eleven rings. I'm just about to hang up when I hear a gravely hello.

I say, "Benny?"

"No, it's your mother. What time is it?"

"Give me Benny, Mom. He's got a math test today, he can't be late."

"Your car running?"

"Yeah."

"I'm almost out of cigs."

"Sorry to hear it, Mom, give me Benny."

"You've turned mean, Petey."
"People change, don't they."
"Is that thunder I hear?"
"Get me Benny, please!"
"I'll get Benny when I get some cigs." BANG.

The thing is my throat really is sore. I'm not faking it, I can barely swallow. Eddy's right, I should have my tonsils yanked. I might as well confess, I had the surgery date all set, then at the last minute I chickened out. I can't help it. I have this aversion to blood and needles. So now you know what the rest of the world knows about me: I'm a medical wuss.

And a glutton for punishment. In ten minutes, I'll call home again and my mom will answer again and I'll ask for Benny again and she'll leverage cigarettes again. One of us will hang up but I'll keep calling back in hopes that at least the ring of the phone will be enough to wake up my little brother. Benny's a junior at my old high school, and I swear, if I don't keep pushing, the kid's not going to make it through. And here's the real shame—he's sharp as a tack and, unlike me, he's good at school. School and I just didn't get along. I had the smarts but I wasted myself. Evidently, in addition to blood and needles, I have an aversion to authority. Even now, when I go to sign the back of my paycheck and it says, "Do not write/sign/stamp below this line," I'll do it, just to do it. For me, a "Keep off the Grass" sign is an open invitation. I know this is warped and immature behavior, especially for a guy pushing thirty. I know it is. But it gets my blood pumping.

Benny's my half brother, my only brother. For thirteen years I was an only child and then my mom remarried and *poof!* I got this cool little brother. Sometimes I have to remind myself that he's not my own kid. In a lot of ways I raised him. Just taught him how to drive last summer. I'm on him all the time about being smart, staying in school, staying away from drugs and thugs. I don't want him to drop out like I did. He'll regret it, like I do. He could go to college. He should go to college. He's a real hacker—he's been programming since he was twelve. He can't miss this math test.

I can tell when she answers the phone that my mother is still in bed. Her voice is different when she's flat on her back.

"Mom, get Benny up. He's got a math test."

"He's up all ready. Now what about my smokes?"

"No can do. I'm home sick today."

"Is that right?"

"Yeah, that's right."

I prepare for a day in front of the television. I situate my lawn chair, enhancing the built-in comfort with a pillow from my bed. Nothing but soaps and game shows. At least Julie let me take the TV. But without cable the choices are limited. Without Julie just about everything seems limited. She didn't kick me out...more like shoved. Three weeks have gone by and I'm still not altogether sure of the reason. She couldn't quite articulate her reasoning, but I know it was about "enoughs." I wasn't romantic enough. I wasn't ambitious enough. I wasn't decisive enough. Oh, and here's the best one of all—I wasn't macho enough. But I was stupid enough to stay for two years.

That's just the way I am. Put me somewhere and I stay put. Like now, I can probably sit here for hours, hardly changing positions at all. I eat my cereal and enjoy my grandmother's favorite soap, the one she used to call "The Young and the Rest of Us," until a sudden bolt of lightning blows out the reception. I am left with static. I try some other channels. Nothing. I watch the static for a while. It holds my interest for about twenty-two seconds. A part of me thinks that this is just deserts for calling in sick. This could be a sign.

I wander for a while. The bare wood floors are cold. I say "test, testing" out loud just to hear my voice. The words echo. For the last three weeks I've been kicking myself for not moving back home. I could be there for Benny. I could get him up, make sure he gets breakfast, get him off to school, help him with his homework, set a curfew. But, see, there's my mother.

Now look at this, this is depressing—my CD player, sitting on the floor over here, with no remote control and no CDs. They turned up missing when I moved out. I think Julie hid them just to spite me. I had this awesome collection of CDs, very eclectic. A little of this, a little of that. Julie said she'd call me if they "turned up." But she won't. She's hard that way.

Not macho enough because I wouldn't punch out the guy at the auto body shop who couldn't fit her in until a week from Thursday. Not decisive enough because I always answered, "Whatever you want to do," when she asked, "What do you want to do?" Not ambitious enough because I'm perfectly happy being a sanitation engineer. (Maybe not happy...more like staying-put-comfortable.) Not romantic enough because I didn't remember things like the fourth anniversary of our first date and the second anniversary of when we moved in together. The thing is, I never wanted to move in together in the first place. It was her apartment. She shared it with a friend and when the friend moved out she took her television, CD player, microwave, and coffee maker with her. Well, my TV and CD player were just sitting in my bedroom at home so I brought them over. And before I knew it I was buying Julie a microwave and a coffee maker and a kitchen table and chairs and a sofa and a love seat and a waterbed and a something called a curio cabinet. But she was never satisfied. She would stuff a decorating magazine in my face and say, "Wouldn't you just *love* to sit in this room?" Maybe it's a guy thing, but even now, I'm happy with what I got. I got my TV, my CD player, my waterbed, my microwave and my coffee maker. That's really all you need. Oh, and my car. The rest is just fluff.

I wander back to the living room and flick on the TV to see if it's back but it's not, so I head to my bedroom for a pair of sweat pants to throw on over my boxers. I plop down on my unmade bed and listen to the rain. Maybe I moved in with her because that's where all my stuff was. After all, don't they say home is where your stuff is?

Anyway, Benny was a freshman at West. He seemed happy and settled and I needed to get away from my mother. So, one night I didn't come home and then two nights and then *home* was Julie's. My mom never said a word. After all I was twenty-six. I'd been hanging around for the kid but it was time to vamoose. Benny hated me for a few weeks, but then he got all caught up in high school and he mellowed. Julie and I took him out for dinner every Thursday night, and I gave him a lift to games and movies and to friends' houses, my way of dealing with the guilt for leaving him there.

Julie thinks, *thought*, I spoiled Benny. "His wish is your command." And she always thinks, *thought*, I was too hard on my mom. "If she said black you would say polka-dot, or plaid. Anything, just to oppose her." That was the problem with Julie—she never looked beyond what she saw.

I saw Julie a few days ago. She was having lunch with two friends from work, I can't remember their names. But she was laughing. Uproariously. And I thought, no fair. No laughing allowed. I haven't laughed. Not once in three weeks. Okay, maybe a chuckle or a snort, but it was canned laughter, not the real thing. Not like she was laughing. That night in a weak moment of pathetic desperation, I almost called her. I had six digits of her phone number punched in. I had six beers in me, enough to make me think that maybe, just maybe, she'd consider moving in with me. Here. Starting over. I could change. I could rent Cary Grant movies and brush up on that romantic stuff. I could get a punching bag. Talk to my boss about a promotion to senior garbage collector. I could be decisive. If she asked what I would like to do I would tell her I'd like to go to the truck and tractor pull. I punched in the last number and got connected to the video store. At first I took it for a sign that I should rent the Cary Grant movies. But then again, dialing up the wrong number could mean it was wrong to call her. So I hung up.

I fall back to sleep for a while, an hour or so, and I dream that Benny not only missed his math exam but he dropped out of school. He not only dropped out of school, but he blew it up with a pipe bomb. I wake up in a sweat, thinking it's all my fault.

I mean he's sixteen, right? He's basically a man. Benny can take care of himself. I was an old man by the time I was sixteen. I was working after school, loading food onto trucks for a grocery wholesaler. It was my uncle who got me the job with Green Waste Management. "A garbage man?" I'd said at first. "You've got to be kidding!" But by then my mom wasn't working and we needed the money. The pay was surprisingly good and the benefits were excellent. Benny was in a private school for gifted kids. My mom's second husband, Henry, Benny's dad, was fifty-eight when Benny was born. The guy had three married kids and two grandkids. Benny was like this little miracle baby. Henry adored Benny. He was going to give him the whole world. But after only two years of marriage to my mom, Henry died from liver cancer and left my mom with a one-year-old. Henry had never gotten around to changing his will so his other kids got everything and my mom and

Benny got next to nothing. My mom was forty-seven and didn't get out of bed for two months. My grandma came and stayed for a while, but then I took over. I was fifteen going on fifty.

My cell phone rings and I jump like a frog. It's Mrs. Klem, the secretary at Benny's school. Benny never showed up this morning. My alarm clock says it's nine thirty-nine. I'll take care of it, I tell Mrs. Klem. Right away, Mrs. Klem.

I own a raincoat. Isn't that kind of scary? I throw it on and then wrap a clean tee shirt around my neck. My glands feel like they've doubled in size. I open the back door and swim to my car. Well, the good thing is you get to see my car. I love my car. In fact, right now I'm actually *in love* with my car. Look at this thing: a black Pontiac Grand Prix. Leather interior. All the bells and whistles. Surprised? Why does everybody think just because I'm a garbage man I'm going to drive some rusty piece-of-shit pick-up truck? A job only partially defines a person. Even Julie knew that. Or, she partially knew it anyway. When people asked her what I did for a living she insisted on telling them I was an engineer. Mine may not be the noblest profession, but as community services go I'd say it's one of the biggies. Which would you be quicker to give up—your weekly garbage pick-up or the neighborhood playground?

My mom's house is actually on my route. How's that for a sign? It's weird to pick up my own mother's waste. Each week I am forced to witness all the empty wine bottles. You'd be surprised what we see, we who haul away what you throw out. I see the envelopes from my mom's social security checks. I see her crossword puzzles. I see empty prescription drug bottles. And packs and packs of crumpled cigarette boxes. You would never know that the lady who lives here once won a prestigious teacher of the year award. That the lady who lives here once was on the board of directors at Benny's school. That the lady who lives here never use to touch a drop and thought smoking was unladylike. That the lady who lives here has a scrapbook of me for every year of my life up to the age of thirteen. That the lady who lives here used to cut the crust off my sandwiches and pick all the peas out of my vegetable soup.

I pull up in front of the house. I kill the engine and stare at my old house. I almost laugh. She used to have flowers in the window boxes and now there's not one thing about this place that reminds me that mom still lives here. Except for the fact that it too looks like it's on the verge of collapse.

Okay, maybe you won't believe this, it's up to you, but Julie's apartment was on my route, too. That's how I met her. She left for work at exactly the time we'd pull up to her garage every Thursday morning. About seven thirty-two. She'd get real ticked off if she had to wait for us to get out of her way. She'd turn up her nose at us, Theo and me, two greasy, grimy, smelly losers. Then this one Thursday, it was in the summer when the garbage was at its ripest and most malodorous, we pull up to her garage and there she is, bent at the waist, with her head half in her garbage can. I watch as she throws pieces of garbage over her shoulder. When she comes up for air I can see that she is crying. I mean here I am in a filthy gray jumpsuit, dirty work boots, with a red bandanna holding my greasy hair back and there she is looking like a stewardess in her crisp, navy blue bank teller uniform. Where I got the nerve I'll never know, but I walk over and say, "Are you all right? Can I help you with something?" Well, she looks up and this time she doesn't turn up her nose at me. Instead she tells me between sobs that she thinks she threw her pocketbook away. That she was paying bills last night and maybe threw it away along with the discarded envelopes and junk mail. Theo is calling, "Come on, man!" I just wave him off. She says she had something like eight hundred dollars cash in her wallet; she was going to pay her rent and make her car payment. And all the credit cards. And the pictures of her nieces. I think that's what got me—the pictures of the nieces. I grabbed a black garbage bag, one of four, and ripped it open. Of course, the wallet was in bag number four, but the take-home is that I found it. She was ecstatic. She almost hugged me, but then she probably smelled me. On a summer day such as that one I could have easily smelled like a combo skunk-puke-rotten egg platter. Don't think I'm exaggerating. She took a step back, ran her fingers through her straight blond hair and said, "How can I ever thank you?" She started to open her wallet and riffle through some bills. I said, "Please, don't insult me. I'm just glad I could help."

"No, really, I can't believe you found it. I have to do something to thank you. What do you like? Candy? Beer? Wine? Lottery tickets?"

"Nothing. No. Not necessary, really."

Theo started honking.

"Oh, come on, there's got to be something you like."

"I like lasagna."

"Lasagna?"

"Yeah, I really like lasagna."

"I'm sorry. I don't cook."

"I like the kind you just throw in your microwave. TV dinner style."

"You do? Well, I guess I could microwave you a lasagna. If that's what you really like."

"I go crazy over lasagna. I could bring garlic bread."

"Okay. Well…I guess I could have you tomorrow night. Does that work for you?"

"Tomorrow night's great."

The thing is I hate lasagna. I have no idea why it came out of my mouth. I kept thinking it was a sign, but I couldn't think of what. The next night, when I rang her doorbell, she opened the door, looked at me, and said, "Can I help you?" I wanted to crawl under the doormat. I said, stupidly, "I'm, I'm your, um, garbage man?"

I can't even begin to describe the smile that spread across her face. It was like a melting sunrise. It was surprise and relief and maybe even a little thrill all rolled into a pretty little mouth. I can't say what it was exactly, but I did mention that I clean up pretty well, didn't I?

It's still pouring. I sit in the car, using the excuse that I'll wait for it to let up before I get out and deal with whatever it is I have to deal with. You just never knew. Maybe Benny couldn't take her anymore. Once, my mom almost got better. A teacher friend brought her to a prayer group. She stopped drinking for a while. She smiled again. Took an interest in cooking. Told Benny and me that she found Jesus again. That Jesus was helping her to get better. That Jesus was her garbage man—that he was going to take all her pain and sadness and sin and failure and get rid of it for her. I really thought her faith could heal her, I really did. She even went back to work, substitute teaching at the high school. But that winter she slipped and fell on the ice and messed up her shoulder. Surgery and pins and physical therapy left her depressed. She got hooked on the pain pills and spiraled down from there.

Julie doesn't drink at all. Something that really attracted me to her, which is so totally unfair because I do. Quite a bit, in fact, but I can't stand to see a woman drink. Double standards? Yes, I know.

The rain doesn't let up for a second, so I open the door and make a mad dash for the front porch. You can tell the eaves and the gutters are all clogged up by the way the rain spills over in places. I should send my neighbor with the muscle shirts over.

The house is dead quiet. I leave my shoes on the rug in the front hall and hang my raincoat on the closet doorknob.

It drips rainwater onto the wood floor but honestly, there's no one who will give a rip. I climb the stairs and take a right to Benny's room. He's asleep, both arms slung over his head. Doesn't even stir when I come in and it's not like I'm trying to be quiet or anything. I sit on the edge of his bed and shake him a little. He sleeps soundly like Julie. Wakes up crabby like me.

"Benny. Hey, buddy. Wake up. You overslept. Come on you got that trigonometry test today. Come on."

After much shaking and begging he gets up and I guide him as if he were blind to the bathroom. I run the shower and right before he steps in he says, "Morning, Pete," as if I hadn't been gone for over two years.

When I open the door to my mother's room, a terrible smell almost overwhelms me. Something acrid and sour. I'm afraid she's died and decomposed. But she's alive and lying in her own vomit. I sigh, like I always do before I get a wash rag and a towel and clean her up and light her cigarette and make her coffee and listen to her cry about how much she misses Henry, Benny's father, the most wonderful man that ever lived. Never a word about my father, who died in a hunting accident when I was nine. Always about Henry. Henry made more money than your father, Henry brought me to nicer restaurants than your father, Henry was better educated than your father. Then there's the sling of lies: *I'm sorry* and *This is the last time* and *I'm turning over a new leaf* and *You can flush my cigarettes down the toilet* and *You can pour my bottles down the drain*. I listen to her voice in my head as I look at her pale, gaunt face. Once she held me, nursed me. Unfathomable.

I just stand here shaking my head. Then, suddenly, the rain stops. Just like that. After three days of merciless drenching, it stops. And then, a second after that, Benny shuts the shower off. The quiet is so complete it's startling. I can actually hear the thoughts in my head. They're clear as a bell without the confusing drone of the rain. For once, I know what I have to do. It's like I swallowed a decisive pill. I stumble over a wine bottle. I shut the door behind me.

While Benny dresses for school, I run downstairs to the kitchen and grab four heavy-duty garbage bags from the broom closet. I don't even knock on Benny's door when I return upstairs, just storm in, open his closet and start stuffing clothes into a bag. I toss a bag his way and nod for him to do the same. Without words, we cram as much as we can into the bags, then drag them behind us down the stairs, bump, bump, bump, and out the front door. We throw them in the trunk. Benny has to run back in for his backpack and when he gets back into the car he's crying. Then, I am. And just as we spring leaks, the sky does too, sending down sheets, mistaking us for parched desert earth.

"Damn rain," I say. Then I grab my cell phone and call school. I tell Mrs. Klem that Benny's sick today. That he'll be with me. She knows all about the situation at home. She asks me to send a written excuse tomorrow. Fine, I say.

On the way home I stop at the doughnut shop and run in. It's late in the morning and there're seven doughnuts to choose from. I take all seven plus four cartons of milk. I get back into my car just as a garbage truck pulls into the alley. I feel like I'm playing hooky. I drive away fast.

Once, when I picked up Benny and his friends from a football game, two boys in the back seat got tangled up in an argument about the difference between a nova and a supernova. I've always taken an interest in the cosmos so I knew the answer and piped in with my explanation, which simply put, was that a nova was a star that suddenly increased its light output tremendously and then faded away to its former obscurity in a few months or years, and a supernova was a rare nova outburst where the star shined as much as one hundred million times brighter than the sun.

The car went dead silent and then my little brother says, "Ahhh, what do you know, you're just a garbage man."

I said nothing. I dropped off Benny's friends and then pulled up in front of mom's house. I wanted to get into it with him about what he said. I wanted to tell the little shit that I got all A's and B's in school. And that a job didn't entirely define a person. I wanted to tell him how once, I saved a guy's life. It's true, I did. This old homeless man. It was a freezing February day last winter and I had just emptied the contents of an eight-cubic-yard bin from the medical center. I switched on the compactor and the heavy blades mashed the refuse together while Theo backed the truck up to the next garbage bin. I shouted *stop* to Theo when he was within reach of the bin, then I turned around just in time to see a scene from a horror movie: a hand in the hopper, reaching up to grab the side of the truck. For one second I froze but then I came to my senses and shut off the compactor. I heard the guy yell for help. I called to Theo and we had to dig to get him out. He was old and bloody from a cut above his eye. He'd lost a shoe. Had more hole to his sock than sock. He told me I saved his life. I told him I had actually almost killed him. Five more seconds and... He told me he'd been sleeping in the bin at night to keep warm. Then he hugged me for a long time, not caring how I smelled. I wanted to tell Benny about how it made me feel. Like I was somebody. I had saved someone's life. How many people can get up in the morning and say that?

But you can't tell a fifteen-year-old anything. So I said nothing and he thanked me for the lift and I went home.

But when Thursday came around, I skipped our house. I left Mom and Benny's garbage right where it was next to the garage. The next Thursday and the next and the next, I made Theo just drive on by. After a month, the neighbors complained to my mother and my mother threatened to call my boss and report me. I reminded her of what it would mean if her cigarette supplier became unemployed. Finally, Benny called me and said, "Okay, I get it. I'm sorry I said what I said. But if you want to know the truth, Pete, you're just too smart to haul garbage. It's a waste, it really is."

Needless to say garbage pickup resumed the next Thursday.

Now we pull into my driveway and I pop open the trunk. We haul in the wet garbage bags and throw them in my room. It's not until we sit down at the kitchen table and eat our doughnuts and drink our milks does Benny say, "I didn't know you moved. What about Julie?"

"It's over, three weeks ago."

"Oh. Sorry."

"It's okay, really. Actually, it's not, but things change. It rains sometimes, you know?"

"Yeah," he says, looking out the window. "Hey, look at that idiot!" he says. I don't even have to look. I know it's my crazy neighbor up on his ladder. I look instead at Benny. I almost laugh because he's got powdered sugar on his chin and a milk mustache that makes him look about six.

"Pete?" he says. "What about Mom?"

"I don't know, kid. Right now it's what about Benny. What about Mom and what about Julie come later. Okay?"

He nods but I can tell he's afraid. I tell him to go get comfortable on my living room furniture and that after a couple hours of TV we'll take a look at his math book. He goes but he trudges.

Since I'm on a roll, I figure, what the heck. I pick up the phone and dial up my ear, nose, and throat doctor. While I'm on eternal hold, I think about Julie. About the joke we used to share at the end of every working day. I'd come home and stand at the top of the basement stairs and strip off my filthy jumpsuit. She would ask what kind of day I had and I would answer with whatever I smelled most like that day. "It was a sour milk day today," I'd tell her. Or,

"Definitely a dirty diaper day." Rancid meat. Rotten fruit. Decomposing varmint. Julie always had a bad sense of smell but a good sense of humor. I thought that made us compatible.

I imagine her here in my kitchen, this kitchen that she has never even seen. "What kind of day was it, Petey?" she'd ask me and I'd say, "Julie, today was wine vomit. But it won't be ever again." And maybe she'd know what I meant and maybe she wouldn't. Probably she wouldn't.

Lingering with Annie

The passionate are like men standing on their heads;
they see all things the wrong way.
—Plato (427-347 B.C.)

I WILL TELL you the truth: I came to your country against my will. I had my own life back in Sicily: *mi amore*, Giorgio, and my girlfriends, too. And before I was imprisoned in my own home I had school and soccer. Yes, I was a rebellious teenager and complained often of my overprotective parents and schemed of ways to escape my father's monarchical reign, but, as is often the case, one does not realize what one has until it is taken away.

Before I tell you how I came to your Manhattan, you should know this about me: I am twenty years old and I am beautiful. I tell you this not because I spill over with conceit but because it is essential for you to know, for you to understand what transpired and why. You must know something of the passion that bubbles inside me like a fountain. Such a passion that once when I was sixteen my father caught me kissing Giorgio on the veranda in the morning and then Vincenzo Baldi on the veranda in the afternoon. My father said, "Tizianna, you possess the kind of beauty that is both a blessing and a curse." I laughed at him then because it wasn't until I came to your country that I found terrible truth in his words. I would love to blame America for taking my blessing and turning it into a curse, but as you will see, I can only blame my own family and myself.

I was in America for nearly a year. Still, more days than not I awoke and wondered where I was. Back at home I was awakened gently by Zia Ella, my great aunt who lived with us, and acted, in spite of my mother's protests, as our *domestica*. This is how Zia Ella awakened me at home: she knocked softly on my bedroom door, entered, and opened the drapes so that the yellow light of morning would splash into my room. She would then run my bath and sit at the edge of my bed caressing my face with her soft, doughy hands while singing an Easter folk song, replacing the *He* for Jesus with a *she* for me: *Arise! Arise! Come and see! She is risen! She is risen! Oh blessed be.* When I opened my eyes her perfectly round face was the first thing I saw. And when I emerged from my bath, she had my breakfast, which in Sicily is very light—espresso, a roll, and perhaps fruit juice—waiting for me on a tray.

In America, *I* did the waking up—three small children— and *I* did the breakfast, which usually consisted of colorful but tasteless cold cereal from a box.

You may think me arrogant when I say that I had never held in my heart the desire to see America, but it is true. Oh, my girlfriends talked and talked about the Empire State Building and the Statue of Liberty and the Grand Canyon as if they were the eighth, ninth, and tenth wonders of the world, but I was content to be where I was for I knew that few places on the planet could match Sicily's rustic beauty. Still, America started luring me through letters my Uncle Benito, my father's brother, sent us when I was a child. The letters arrived monthly and had two purposes: to inform my father of the "good life" in America and to persuade him to join Benito and his family in New York City.

My father, Count Lucio Bonagio (in Sicily, everyone is a count or a baroness), awaited the monthly letter with great anticipation. Zia Ella actually "served" it after dinner on a silver platter with *i dolci* (the sweet things).

Uncle Benito began his letters with trivia about the American legal system, a subject which greatly interested my father who was a judge, and concluded them with deliciously terrible gossip about the people who worked at his Manhattan *ristorante*. Uncle Benito never gave up on his dream that my father would one day join him in America and help him run the *ristorante*. But my father would never leave. He loved his homeland and was proud of his occupation. He had devoted his life in law to ridding Sicily of the strong arm of the Mafia. Still, Uncle Benito never stopped trying.

When Uncle Benito died ten years ago after a long illness, his youngest son, Tino, took over the *ristorante* for his father and the obligation of writing monthly letters to my father.

I must tell you, my father never did enjoy Tino's letters as much as he did his brother's, for although they were respectfully written, there was none of the legalese, and worse, none of the juicy *maldicenza* about the employees. My father wondered if he would ever know if the waitress's husband ever found out about her lover, the one with the code name Alfonso.

My father, always in possession of his judicial wisdom, would read Uncle Benito's letters to himself first and then share them—appropriately edited if necessary—with my mother, my brothers and me. But by the time he was reading Tino's letters, my brothers were all married and it was just my mother and me left at the table, and it was no longer necessary for my father to preview the letters as they usually contained only superficial information regarding the *ristorante*—new dishes they were serving, a review by an important dining critic, details of a remodeling project. Mostly, I chewed my food, uninterested. But when cousin Tino wrote that he was getting married and described his fiancé as an "angel from heaven," a pre-pubescent hunger for romance ignited inside of me, and I stopped chewing.

"An angel from heaven!" my mother exclaimed when my father read the words out loud. She scowled and once again I found myself wondering if my mother's attitude toward romance had been soured by the lack of it in her own life. Her marriage to my father had been arranged and their relationship had always been matter-of-fact: I am the wife, you are the husband; I do these things for you, you do these things for me. "An angel from heaven," my mother said again. "And I suppose you'll want us to attend the wedding of this celestial being."

"Why of course we will attend the wedding," my father replied. "Tino is my godson. And I promised Benito I would look after him. It was his dying wish, Camella. I promised him."

My mother dropped her shoulders in defeat. She hated travel of any kind and air travel most of all. But my father had spoken. And although my father didn't demand that we address him as *vossia* (meaning, roughly, your majesty) as his father before him had, his word reigned in the kingdom of our humble household.

We never made it to Tino and Annie's wedding. My father suffered a heart attack three days before we were to leave on our trip. He underwent by-pass surgery and recovered nicely, but we never even talked about another trip to America until five years later when Tino sent a letter inviting us out for a reunion of sorts so that we could finally meet his wife and now, their two small children.

It was planned that my parents, my brother Franco, his wife, and I would visit and spend two weeks in New York City. I was almost eighteen, just about to finish school and excited about attending university in the fall. My upcoming American *vacanza* made me the envy of all my girlfriends. Giorgio, however, my boyfriend of two years, was not thrilled about my leaving him for an entire two weeks, but I was able to appease him by pledging my undying love and promising to return with designer jeans.

Once again our plans were interrupted. All winter and spring my father, the judge, had been embroiled in Mafia trials that resulted in the history-making convictions of nearly four hundred Mafiosi. Needless to say, my father was pleased with the convictions, but undermining that pleasure was a deep fear of retaliatory killings. He was right to be fearful for just days after the convictions and two weeks before our trip to America, two lead judges in the case were assassinated and my father scooped up our entire family and hid us for the rest of the summer in the countryside of Regaleali, an hour southeast of Palermo. We hid in the vineyards on the estate of Vincenzo and Mirella Boni, brother and sister-in-law of Zia Ella.

At summer's end, when we returned to our home, my father returned a different man. He was sullen and gloomy. It was a sad thing that just as my father had begun to see the fruits of his life's work and things were finally changing in Sicily—the nearly four-hundred Mafiosi convictions, thousands of people marching in anti-Mafia demonstrations, businessmen forming associations to fight extortion, anti-Mafia newspapers being circulated—a strangulating fear took over. There had been a fundamental shift in the social acceptance of the Mafia's existence, yet my father could barely leave the house.

Suddenly plans were changed. I would not go on to university after all. It would be much too dangerous. I would take my studies at home with a tutor. My father stepped down from his position—his heart couldn't take it. Fear swallowed our home. You could feel it, you could smell it. With drawn curtains we lived in shadows and whispers. Zia Ella did the marketing and soon it seemed that we only left the house for Sunday Mass, and then after a while, my father requested that Padre Cono bring Mass to us. We entertained family only. Giorgio and my girlfriends, Tia and Melina, were allowed weekly half-hour chaperoned visits. If Giorgio had not found a way to climb up the trellis and sneak in my bedroom window every few days or so I would have gone quite mad.

As it was we went on half-living for nearly two years. My father had turned into—how do you say?—a recluse. My mother and Zia Ella were afraid of their own shadows, and I was the loneliest girl in all of Palermo, unable to enjoy even the simplest of pleasures: joining my friends at Mondello, a popular beach hangout outside of Palermo, or meeting them at the ice-cream parlor for *gelato*, or even for a simple *passeggiato*—a stroll down our main road early in the evening when everyone takes to the streets to socialize.

I was certain I would have to wait for my father to die before I was set free. Then in February another letter came from Tino. My father had written to him about what has since been called "the Palermo Spring" and about the retaliatory killings of his colleagues. Tino sympathized with my father, and even though he was preoccupied with problems of his own—his wife, Annie, thirty-two, mother of now three young children, had been diagnosed with ovarian cancer—he still corresponded regularly with my father, always attempting to persuade him to come and join him in America. But Count Lucio Bonagio would never leave Sicily. So instead he sent me.

This is how I came to your New York City to live with Tino Bonagio, my father's nephew. But I didn't come to help with the *ristorante;* my father offered my services as an Au Pair. I had disrespectfully laughed out loud when he told me this news. "An Au Pair? Me? What do I know about caring for children?"

"You will learn," was my father's answer.

I moped around the house, speaking only when spoken to. When my father asked me a question, I replied, "Yes, *vossia.*" I vowed I would go kicking and screaming, but in the end I resigned myself. After all, it was only for one year—per the rules of the Au Pair program.

I will never forget my mother's eyes (my father couldn't bring himself to come to the airport) when she left me off—they were dry and lifeless. She embraced me as she would a diplomat and told me that I would be fine, to please write when I was able. There were no words about missing me. Giorgio had come to the airport, too, and in spite of my mother's scowl, I allowed the poor boy to kiss me on the lips. I did not know how I would live without my beautiful Giorgio's kisses. Finally, Zia Ella held me tight and kissed my forehead and hair. Right before I boarded she wrapped my neck with a thick red scarf she had knitted for me. "*Fa cattivo tempo in Nuova York,* Tizianna!" she said, and I had to smile. Bad weather was the last thing on my mind.

On the plane I tried to pretend my circumstances were different: I was an exchange student going to study in New York City, I was a businesswoman on my way to negotiating a big contract for my company, I was a fashion designer bringing my latest creations from Rome. During the course of the long flight, my attitude gradually began to soften like melting *gelato.* Maybe this wouldn't be as bad as I thought. I began to consider with pleasure all the things I would do when I arrived in America: see a Broadway play, attend a rock concert, eat a cheeseburger at Hard Rock Cafe and a hot dog from a street vendor, ride the subway (at night), and maybe meet a movie star in a café or theater.

I found New York City at once beautiful and exciting in spite of the frigid February wind that slapped my face and burned my skin. I found it not unlike the hustle and bustle of my own Palermo, where you wake up to the sound of police sirens and endure crushing traffic congestion and chaos in the streets. The only thing missing were the soldiers who stand guard before the homes and apartment buildings of judges and politicians.

When I stepped off the tarmac, I was met by the Au Pair coordinator, who quickly whisked me away to the hotel where I was to take part in a four-day orientation and childcare training program. There I learned how the program worked: my cousin was to provide me with a private bedroom, a weekly stipend, one-and-one-half days off per week, including a full Saturday or Sunday, and one completely free weekend each month, plus a two week vacation with pocket money. I was to provide forty-five hours of childcare per week, shuttle the children to activities, run errands, and help with shopping and cooking. Upon completion of the intensive program, I was delivered to Tino and Annie's home in Manhattan.

When Tino opened the door to his apartment he smiled at me with my uncle Benito's face. My father had told me that I had met my cousin Tino once when I was five or six, but I decided then and there that my father was surely mistaken: even at a wee age I would have remembered his beautiful face. He had all the good features of my father's family—a regal, elongated nose, eyes that were like chocolate drops on snow, and a forehead that protruded slightly, all haloed by wavy dark hair.

He embraced me at once and I greeted him in the Italian way, kissing him on both cheeks. I looked around the room for Annie, but the angel from heaven was nowhere to be seen.

"You are wonderful to come," my cousin said to me, taking my bags. And when the coordinator left he said, "Please know that this wasn't my idea. I would never have asked such a thing of you. But your father was thinking of your safety…"

"Yes," I said, choking back the tears, as I thought of Giorgio and his soft kisses.

"You're an angel to come, honest. If you like children at all, you will love mine. They're sweet as strawberries, honest. And little trouble. You'll see. Honest."

Right then I knew he was lying. And not because he'd used the word "honest" three times, but because he said his children were "little trouble." I'll just bet, I thought. It was likely they were each a little bit of trouble adding up to big trouble. This is what I, the reluctant Au Pair, anticipated.

When Annie finally appeared she gasped when she saw me. I turned around to see what it was that had startled her so, but when there was nothing, I realized it was I. I have grown accustomed to my appearance, and in truth find nothing extraordinary about my face, but as I told you, I am said to be beautiful. At that moment, looking at Annie, I wished I could wipe off my fresh, young face and replace it with a face like hers, smooth and pale and plain as cotton.

"Welcome to our home," she greeted me, although there was not a spark of welcoming warmth in her voice. If I were a generous person I might have attributed her coolness to her illness, for I had not known her when she was well, but I suspected she'd carried this chilliness with her always.

I sat on a chair across from Tino and Annie and politely answered their questions about my trip. "Yes, thank you, the flight was fine." "Yes, the orientation went well." "Yes, it is colder than I ever imagined." But all along, I kept wondering: where are the children? I gave Tino full reports as to the welfare of my mother and father and brothers and their families. He used the friendly manner of a relative when speaking to me, but really we were strangers. I was distracted, expecting any moment for one of the children to pop up from nowhere and hurl a frog at me. I had seen movies about nannies and the kinds of things their charges did to them. Finally I just asked, "Where are the *bambini*?"

"Goodness, dear," said Annie, "the children are in bed. It's nearly ten."

So I had to wait until the following day to meet the little ones who were to be in my care forty-five hours a week for the next twelve months. Early the next morning, I was awakened by a series of soft taps on my bedroom door. In my sleepiness I thought it was Zia Ella, coming in to draw my drapes, run my bath, and serve my breakfast. But when I opened my eyes, it was not Zia Ella's face I saw, but that of Alicia, the four-year-old.

"She's pretty!" she said out loud. "But she doesn't look a *thing* like Mary Poppins." Then giggles and the blur of three little bodies scampering out of the room.

At breakfast, I had a formal introduction. Stair-steps they were—Ian, five; Alicia, four and *precoce* (I think you say "precocious"); and Isabella, two-and-a-half. Surprising even myself, I took to them immediately, loving especially Ian's baby-fine blond hair, Alicia's endearing lisp, and Isabella's eyes, the same sapphire blue as the Tyrrhenian Sea near my home. They found my name, Tizianna, to be very humorous and Alicia decided right away to shorten it to "Tizzy." Sitting at the kitchen table, I felt more a guest than a nanny, although this I should have expected as the coordinator told me that Au Pairs are meant to be treated as contributing members of the household, and to be welcomed into the home as family members, not as nannies or boarders.

For the first morning at least I wasn't allowed to lift a finger. Tino cooked bacon—different than our *pancetta*—and eggs. There was so much food! Pancakes and waffles, and something he called "hashed brownies." The children all talked at once about all the things they wished for me to do with them, the first order of business being to view their "Mary Poppins" video, so, in Alicia's words, "You will know what we are expecting." I almost choked on a forkful of eggs—I felt so much an impostor! I knew that I could never live up to their expectations for I had come to them a privileged and pampered young woman who had never so much as lifted a finger at home. Once in a burst of anger my mother told me that my only talent in life was a flawless face. When I cried to Giorgio about it he just laughed at me and said, "Actually, she's right." When I dug my fingers into one of his thighs to protest he added that I indeed did have one other talent—I gave the most incredible back rubs.

After Annie scooted the children off to be dressed for church (she refused my offer of assistance, saying, "No, no, please finish your breakfast") I sat sipping the rest of my coffee as Tino (who also refused my help) loaded the dishwasher.

"So what shall I do for you, Tino, sleep in your bed and drink your coffee? Only that?"

"Well, certainly, Tizianna, I won't make you sleep in my bed!" He grinned then at his own joke, and I am sure he was just trying to make me laugh, but I felt my face go crimson.

I fought back tears and stuttered, "I- I- I only want to know what is expected of me! I want to please you and Annie."

"Oh, Tiz, I'm sorry to embarrass you. I didn't mean anything," he said as he wiped his hands on a dishtowel and then placed one of them on my shoulder. "I'm bad that way. Ask the waitresses at my restaurant. I tease them terribly. It's just my way. Just give the children some cheerful attention and give Annie…well, give Annie whatever she wants, knowing that "whatever she wants" can change from minute to minute."

With this my tears came and I confessed outright that I had never run a dishwasher or a washing machine or a drying machine, and not because we didn't have these appliances at home but because all the domestic duties had been performed by my mother and Zia Ella. He laughed, wiping my tears away with two clean sweeps of his hand, then he showed me how to operate all three machines before we left for Mass.

When we returned from Mass and we again were alone in the kitchen I made my final confession: that I had never cooked. Not an egg. Not a slice of toast. Once again my cousin found me amusing. He said, "Well, Annie's never been much of a cook either. More often than not I bring dinner home from the restaurant." He showed me what he called their "quick" food—chili from a can, macaroni and cheese from a box, and red sauce from a bottle! But I need not have worried about the cooking because Tino brought home lots and lots of what he called "take out" even though I thought it made more sense to call it "take in."

But I shall say this, I was good with the children. Since the weather was so brutal that time of year we spent much of our time indoors, but they enjoyed my silly games. At the conclusion of my first viewing of the "Mary Poppins" film (there were many, many more viewings to follow) I explained to the children that I had songs, and I had stories, but I had no umbrella and no bag of magic. Ian's face fell with my news, but lightened when I began to sing a little song about a worm that fell in love with the other end of itself. I found that if I went back in time to the world when I was small I could retrieve all the little games and songs that Zia Ella had shared with me. In no time at all, I had won them over.

Annie, I am afraid, was a different story. At first, she was not so sick and at first we were not friends. She was polite to me, but distant in a way that made it clear that bringing me in as an Au Pair was not her idea. At first she would not let me so much as wash a child's hand. "I can do that, Tizianna," she would say (never "Tizzy" as the children called me, or "Tiz" as Tino called me) as if I thought her incapable. It seemed I couldn't please her and since she insisted on correcting my English whenever I misspoke (she was an award-winning journalist for the New York Times), I became increasingly self-conscious in her presence, thinking out my every word, until I spoke so slowly I am afraid I seemed a dullard.

Easter came late, in April. It was cold and gray and I felt I was in Siberia rather than America. Friends gathered at Tino and Annie's home for Easter dinner. How odd, I thought that their home was not filled with family as ours back home would surely be. Tino explained that his two brothers were in California and his cousins were at their parents' homes. I suspected their friends were really Annie's friends because it seemed that most of them were introduced to me as working for this magazine or that newspaper. I liked none of the ladies, especially the one in the hideous pink hat, who I overheard whispering to another one, "Has the cancer gone to Annie's brain? I wouldn't have an Au Pair who looked like *that* within inches of *my* husband!"

The children are what saved me. I never imagined that I would enjoy them so, but they were delightful and bright, uttering daily the most extraordinary things, reminding me

of the fantastic wonder the world was through a child's
eyes. We fell into a comfortable routine, the children and
I. I would wake them, caressing their small faces with my
hands just as Zia Ella once caressed my face, help them
to dress, and then serve a Sicilian-style breakfast—a roll,
fruit, some juice. On Mondays, Wednesdays, and Fridays, I
would drop off Ian and Alicia at school. Then Isabella and
I would run errands, do the marketing, or visit the library or
a museum until it was time to pick them up.

Annie seemed contented or maybe just resigned to being
at home alone for most of the morning. We would reunite
for lunch. Gradually, I took over the noon meal, simple
sandwiches and soup from a can (everything from a can in
America!). After nibbling just small bites of food, Annie
would look at her children longingly, then invite them to
join her on her bed for a story. She was very private about
her bedroom, where she both rested and worked, but she
would allow my presence for story time. I wished for ten
minutes alone in her room as I was certain her belongings
would tell me more about her than she herself had in the
two months since my arrival. Her room was like a library
with books and periodicals stacked on the floor in leaning
towers, like Pisa, at the side of her bed. I stole peeks at their
titles whenever I could. The subjects were odd and diverse:
one week they were all about Africa and the Congo, the next
week they could be about Iranian art and literature, the next
week they might be all on oceans or galaxies or flesh-eating
bacteria.

She was still fighting then, attempting to hold on to
her job at the newspaper, which I understood to be a very
important one. She insisted on writing her weekly column
at home but the fatigue showed in her face and in her gait
and I wondered why she bothered. I would sit in the rocker
while she read to the children. Then, although I couldn't
point to the exact moment or even the day it happened, I

was on the bed reading to the children and Annie was in the rocking chair staring off into naked space.

In July, I accompanied the family on a holiday to a place in the Adirondak Mountains, where all of Annie's family—mostly academic types—gathered each year. The week was relaxing and uneventful in terms of the negative, save for this one thing: Annie's youngest brother, a big lug of a university boy, pinched my rear end and tried to kiss my lips. I slugged the brute but thought it best not to mention the incident to Annie or Tino, as we would be leaving the next day and I would never see the boy again.

Back at home after the holiday, Isabella, the little one, took to calling me "Mama Tizzy." I gently corrected her, but she would just laugh and say it again and again. Since the beginning of the summer, Isabella had begun to prefer me to her mother. Tino noticed this and said it was only natural since she spent so much time with me but asked that I try to hide it from Annie. But this is something you can't hide from a mother. When Annie heard Isabella call me "Mama Tizzy" she said nothing but she sent daggers my way.

I called Giorgio that night, long-distance, without the permission that was requested of me if I were to make over-seas phone calls. I cried and cried and told him that it was all too much for me. I imagine my sobs were heard throughout the house because the next morning when I woke Ian the first thing he said was, "Tizzy, you won't leave us, will you?" I had explained to all the children many times that I was only allowed to stay for one year and that I would be returning home at the end of February. "But not before my birthday, February twenty-fifth," Ian always said. We marked the date of my departure on the calendar: February twenty-ninth, a leap year day. Alicia drew a big sad face next to the crude airplane I had drawn in the February twenty-ninth box. "But promise you won't leave before my birthday," Ian demanded.

"I promise, Ian, not before your birthday."

That night, Tino knocked on my door and asked if he could have a word. He sat, quietly, at the foot of my bed for some time, seeming to search for his words. Finally he said, "She's a different person now, you know. I wish you could have known her before she got sick. The cancer, it's robbed her of everything. She had such a passion for everything—her writing, the children, me. But she's getting better, Tiz. They think they got it all with the radiation. Yesterday she got a great report. Things will get better," he assured me, but it seemed to me it was himself he was trying to convince.

"I don't think she really wants me here," I said.

"Oh, but she does! She just doesn't say it. Annie's better with written words. She's never been able to express herself as well in speech. That's just how she is."

Your angel from heaven, a very mean part of me wanted to say. My mother, who I rarely admit is ever right, certainly was right when she scoffed at Tino's letter all those years ago describing Annie as "an angel from heaven."

"You are an angel from heaven," Tino said suddenly, just as I was thinking those words myself.

"I don't know what the children and I would have done without you. Please don't think of leaving us early." He scooted over to me and hugged me long and hard. And I was surprised to find that up close he smelled like my father. He kissed me on the forehead, then left closing the door softly behind him. How could I even think of leaving after that?

And then, Annie took a turn for the worse. The radiation treatments hadn't been successful after all, so next came chemotherapy. Tino's *ristorante* was closed on Mondays so he would bundle Annie up—it was August and hot as Sicily but she was always chilled—and drive her to the clinic for the treatments. When they returned, Tino would carry Annie into the house, like a new groom with his angel from heaven bride.

It was then, after her treatments, that Annie's illness took over the household. Her cancer grew to engulf us all. I don't understand how you can feel someone's sickness, how you can hear it and taste it, but you can, and we did.

I sometimes awakened to Ian's tears. He was starting to see the change in his mother and it was frightening for him. The only comforting words I had were in Italian: "*Stara bene poco un.*" (It will be all right, little one.) I knew my words were empty promises, but they seemed to have a calming effect on him. I rocked him back to sleep, noticing after I returned him to his bed, the dampness on my nightgown where I had absorbed his tears. Was that why I had come then? To soak up all their tears?

Soon there was hardly time to even reply to the letters my Giorgio sent weekly. I would toss the letters unopened upon my dresser remembering how back home the American mail was served to my father on a silver tray. The children occupied my every thought. It was my desire to keep them distracted from their mother's condition. I wanted the children to have at least a small part of their day that was filled with cheerfulness. And so as Annie gave up her newspaper column completely and endured the poisons they put into her, I put on happy face for her three children.

At the conclusion of the summer night class I had taken, I decided not to enroll in any classes for the fall semester. My Au Pair coordinator had some concerns about my schedule but I wanted to be with the children, not sitting in a classroom learning how to conjugate English verbs.

After her Monday treatments, Annie was not well for two days, spending most of her waking hours vomiting, until her face became pale and gaunt. One of her two sisters would come to help her on Tuesdays and Wednesdays. On those days she only saw the children a few minutes each day. By Thursday, she was a bit better, and by Friday, she was up and asking for the children.

There were some happy times. In September, Tino hosted a party for me at his *ristorante* where I was able to meet many of my father's *cugini*. Tino hired a band and there was this one boy—oh, well, it came to nothing so why even mention it, but just seeing him, talking with him, dancing with him made me miss Giorgio so much my chest ached. When I danced with my cousin Tino, I wished he was Giorgio. I closed my eyes for one moment to pretend, but Tino didn't feel a bit like Giorgio. Tino was rather a large man for a Sicilian. Giorgio was compact, no taller than I, but muscular, and what he lacked in height he made up for in his beautiful face and his complete sweetness.

By Thanksgiving, I was planning to leave.

And it had nothing to do with me missing Giorgio or my girlfriends or my mother or father or the Sicilian sun. It had everything to do with Annie. I could count on one hand the times the woman had been pleasant to me. For nine months I had provided wonderful care for her children, and still she treated me with the reserved coolness one might use with the man who repairs your kitchen sink. You allow him into your home and appreciate his assistance, but that's as far as it goes. Once—and I am not, how do you say? under-exaggerating (forgive me if that is not a word)—and only once did Annie ever thank me. This is the honest truth: once she sneezed and I said, "God bless you," as her own children had taught me. She thanked me for that. For a simple blessing.

That night the phone rang at about eleven-thirty. We were all in bed; I was finishing a long overdue letter to Giorgio and the sound of the ring as it pierced through my solitude made me jump. A few minutes later Tino came knocking on my door to tell me that the call had been from his night manager at the *ristorante*. There had been a grease fire in the kitchen and he had to attend to it. He asked if I would listen in on Annie—she'd been restless and was having difficulty falling asleep. I finished my letter to Giorgio ("only three more months, my love, and I will be home!") then I quietly tiptoed to the living room, bringing with me a book and a blanket, and lay on the sofa so that I could hear Annie if she needed me.

I had hardly read a page when she called, "Tizianna! Tizzy!"

I leapt from the sofa, dragging the blanket along with me, tripping over it but not falling, and raced to her room. Suddenly a horrible thought crossed my mind—what if she was dying? And then another—how would I know? And another—what would I do?

I found her in tears. When she could catch her breath she apologized for bothering me but said she just couldn't bear to be alone. And would I mind just sitting in the rocking chair, please. Of course, I said. I sat rocking in the dark, wishing for Tino to come home quickly as it was torturous to be alone with her, knowing the ill feelings she had toward me.

"I don't think I have much time left," said her voice in the dark.

"*Scusi?*" I said, my nerves causing me to revert to the Italian.

"I can feel it inside me, in the center of me."

"Maybe it is just sadness you feel," I offered, wondering why she was opening up to me now, after all these months.

"No, I just know." She sighed and said nothing else for the longest time. Just when I thought sleep had come to her, I heard her say, "I know I owe you an apology. You've been kind and I haven't."

I stopped rocking, wishing so that I could see her face.

"You couldn't possibly understand, Tizianna, but when they said the "C" word I simply disintegrated. Even before

I was symptomatic I had already died. Hell, I wrote a column for the goddamn New York Times. For ten years! You have no idea who I am, who I was."

"You are right. I do not."

"I hated how Tino reacted. Pampering me. Smothering me. Then this idea of an Au Pair and then your father offering to send you. And then you show up—looking like that!"

What was there to say, that I was sorry for my own face? Should the sun apologize for being bright? A star, for twinkling? It is just who I am. I said nothing.

"Alicia's a lot like me really," she said.

Maybe she was one of those persons who once she started to speak you could not stop her. Or maybe, she just thought that if she continued to speak she would not die.

"She's a good girl when things are going her way, but when they aren't, watch out. That's me. My life was like a beautiful symphony—everything was in perfect harmony. My career. My children. My husband. And I was the conductor. That's what I lost. Oh, all right, conductor is just another name for controller. So I was controlling, but it worked for us. Tino liked it that way. I always fixed everything. But this time I couldn't. But you could. You came and cared for the children, which meant Tino could get back to the restaurant and I could concentrate on my damned cancer cells. I'm supposed to visualize them exploding or imploding or something."

"Annie, what can I do for you?"

"Nothing."

I thought of things I did for her children. "I could pray with you, sing to you, read to you. I could—"

"Do you give back rubs?"

"Yes," I answered. "I do."

You would find it hard to believe that that was all it took—one back rub—and Annie and I were best of friends. And you would be right not to believe. Not best friends, no, but things were better. She never in words apologized, only said that she owed me an apology. And she never in words thanked me for my childcare, only acknowledged that the children were indeed well cared for. But Zia Ella always told me that blessings come by the inch. And if you keep giving an inch here and there, your blessings would increase. And so I lingered with Annie, hoping that she would wait to die until after I went home.

We tried so to make Christmas festive. Annie would get bursts of energy and she would help wrap gifts or sit at the kitchen table and blend some ingredients for chocolate chip cookies. She smiled a little more often, cuddled with Isabella more often, and even referred to me as "Mama Tizzy" a few times.

On Christmas morning, there were gifts for everyone, and I was very touched by the silk scarf and the lovely book of New York Times essays (which included one of Annie's) that were my gifts. The children were pleased with the Italian puppets I had my mother send for them. Tino went loco for the case of imported balsamic vinegar. I almost tore out my brains over what to buy for Annie, but then I came up with the perfect gift: an "IOU" for as many back rubs as she wanted from now until February twenty-ninth. She even smiled when she read the little voucher I had made up.

After tucking all the children into bed, I was invited back into the living room for a glass of wine with Tino and Annie. The three of us talked about our own childhood Christmases where the toys were more colorful and less electronic. After a while, Annie grew tired and Tino picked her up and carried her off to bed. It made me sad for my cousin. I wondered how he endured.

Later when I was in bed, dressed in the lavender satin nightgown that Giorgio had sent me for Christmas, someone knocked on my door. I was tempted to feign sleep for that is what I wanted—to sleep in the nightgown Giorgio had sent me and dream of him taking if off of me. I expected one of the children, who now came to *me* when they had upset tummies, frightening dreams, or ears that ached. But it was Tino.

Did I have a just a minute? Would I like another glass of wine maybe? I thanked him but told him that I was tired as I tucked the blanket up around my flimsy nightgown.

"But it's only ten o'clock Christmas evening. I'm wide awake!" my cousin said.

"And my neck is a little stiff," I lied, rubbing it. "I think I just need some rest."

"What you need, Miss Tiz, is a good back rub. Annie used to say *I* gave the best rubs, until you came along that is. Come on, turn around."

Innocently—honestly—I obeyed my cousin. I hadn't had a back rub in months and months. In fact, the only human touch of any kind I had received since coming here was from the children, if you don't count the pinch on my rear from Annie's overly friendly brother.

Tino was right, he was a good masseuse and soon I relaxed and felt the tension take leave of my muscles. I felt wonderfully slacken and loose. Then I felt something else. I wasn't sure—it couldn't be. Tino's lips on my back? On my shoulder? On my neck? But it was. I think I shuddered. Shivers raced up my spine and I froze, not knowing what to think or do. Then Tino turned me to face him, put his finger to my lips to shush me, and then leaned in to embrace me. I relaxed a bit, thinking the poor man just needed a hug.

But then he said the most awful thing, he said, "Did you know that you are the most gorgeous being I have ever laid eyes upon?" With his dying wife in the next room, he said this to me! I could have spat in his face. Instead I melted in his arms. And I let him unleash his frustrated passion on me. And if I were to tell you that I struggled and protested and painfully endured it, I would be lying.

I didn't know what self-loathing was until Ian and Alicia woke me the next morning, reprimanding me for sleeping in when games and toys were waiting for us. Like a—how do you say?—zombie, I played with the children, thankful at least that Tino and Annie were sleeping late themselves.

I had no idea what I was going to do. I just knew what I had to do.

Finally Annie and Tino rose for breakfast and Tino made a big show of pancakes and bacon and waffles and those hashie brownies. I couldn't look at him. I couldn't look at Annie. Annie! I held Isabella in my lap and realized that suddenly I felt more like a prisoner than I had ever felt in my father's home in Sicily. Shame makes for stronger bars than does fear.

When the phone rang I had no idea that it would be my way out, my way back home. When I answered it, the caller quickly informed me that he had the wrong number, but I heard my own voice continue the call even after he had hung up.

"How awful!" I gasped. Then in Italian, "*Tragico!*" I looked up to see concerned faces, then said, "It cannot be! How did it happen?" Then I forced some tears to come, which was the easiest part of all.

"What is it?" Annie asked, looking genuinely concerned.

"My father. His heart. Another heart attack. They're operating right now. I must go to him. You will understand, no?"

"Of course," she said. "I'm so sorry, Tizzy."

"Yes, Tizzy," Tino said.

"We'll call your coordinator," Annie said sensibly. "She'll make all the arrangements."

"But you promised!" Ian shouted when he realized what was happening. "Not until after my birthday! You promised!"

I scooted out my chair and transferred Isabella to her mother's lap, where she belonged. I knelt on the floor by Ian and pulled Alicia over so that I could address her as well. Then I fed them lies about how I loved my father and that they would want to be with their father if he were sick and that my father needed me and that I would come back for a visit sometime.

You could have drowned in the crocodile tears. Both of the children ran off to their rooms. I wanted to call after them that even Mary Poppins had to leave, but that would have been cruel. Annie looked at me as if I had betrayed them. If she only knew that it was she whom I had betrayed.

I called my coordinator and she arranged a flight for me the next morning. I rose early and cried as I packed my bags, leaving the silk scarf and the book of essays in the bottom dresser drawer. Tino came in, this time, without bothering to knock.

"You're really going?"

"My father—"

"Is fine, I'm sure."

"Well, he would have a heart attack if he knew."

He grabbed my arm. "You can't go. The children need you. I need you."

I pulled away. "I cannot stay and you know it. There's Annie, of course, but also we are cousins, for God's sake. I'm sorry, my heart is breaking, but there is not a thing that could make me stay."

I pretended to phone my mother, to check on my father's status and give her the time of my flight's arrival. I kissed the children even though they wouldn't look at me, wouldn't kiss me in return. Tino tried to make them kiss me but I told him to please stop.

Finally, I knocked on Annie's door. I owed her a good-bye at least. "I wanted to say *arrivederci*," I said, sticking my head in the door.

"Oh, Tizzy, do you have to?" she said.

I came in and stood next to her bed. She looked so small. I wanted to reach for her hand and touch her.

"I mean I know this sounds selfish," she said, "but could you possibly wait to see how your father's surgery goes? Oh God. I don't believe I just said that. I'm sorry."

"No, no, it's all right," I said, as I inched closer to the door.

"The children, Tizzy."

"I know, I know, but they knew I had to leave sooner or later. This is just two months sooner. I'm sorry. I'm so sorry."

She put her hands to her face. "I just don't know how we'll do it, that's all. Get along without you. I know I still owe you an apology and I owe you my gratitude as well."

"I enjoyed your children so much. I will never—" My throat closed up.

"Listen to me, Tizianna," Annie said in a voice I had not heard before. Maybe it was her conductor voice—it was strong and sure. "I know your father is fine. And I have a pretty good feeling what this is all about."

Surely my face was crimson. I covered my eyes in shame.

"And you know what? I can live with it. Maybe I couldn't if I had years to live, but we're talking months or weeks here, so I can live with it."

I looked up at her and realized that I was looking at the bravest woman that I would likely ever come to know. "I'm sorry, Annie, but I cannot." I leaned over and kissed her on the forehead then swiftly left the room. Tino, who was on the other side of the door, caught me by the arm, and said, "You'll have to live with it, Tiz, here or there. Why not here?"

"Please!" I cried, "Just let me go!"

On the plane, I tried to pretend my circumstances were different: I was an exchange student heading back to Sicily after studying in New York City, I was a businesswoman returning home with a signed contract for my company, I was a fashion designer returning from my American show. I looked out the window for the answers but the clouds turned into faces. Clearly I saw Alicia and Ian. Maybe Isabella's too. I knew that forever and ever those sweet faces would haunt me. What would become of them?

When I phoned Giorgio from the airport he was elated. He drove over immediately and we had a glass of wine in a crowded café at the airport. I told him everything. *Everything.* And he forgave me as I knew he would, loving me as he did and so elated to have me back home. And even now, I wonder if I'd waited a few days or weeks or months or years, would he have forgiven me? Or was he just caught up in the moment of being twenty and in love.

I never told my mother or father. They accepted my story that Annie wanted to die in the presence of just her immediate family. And she did just that. Two weeks after I'd returned home. Tino sent a letter saying she had died, blessedly, in her sleep. Her two sisters were helping with the children who were understandably distraught. "Please know that Annie forgave us, Tizzy. What's left is that we must forgive ourselves."

And I have forgiven myself for what transpired between Tino and me. I confessed to Padre Cono who walked me through the vulnerability and desperation that brought Tino and I together. "Humans are both the grandest and the weakest creatures God has made," he told me. Padre Cono granted me forgiveness and said that I was right to leave and turn away from sin.

But now, I'm not so sure. About my leaving. I always thought that I had done the right thing by leaving. The best thing. But I began to question it last year when Giorgio and I had a child of our own, our little Ana, and I put myself in Annie's shoes and wondered if I could have "lived with it" if it were me who was sick and Giorgio had done what Tino had done. And there's no doubt in my mind, I could have lived with it too. I could have lived with anything if it prevented heartbreak for my little Ana.

So I live with the guilt. I just live with it. And I touch my little daughter's cheek as I rock her and I pray an odd prayer—that she is blessed with a pleasant face, and not cursed with a beautiful one.

◼

Her Flesh, His Blood

"Present fears are less than horrible imaginings."
—William Shakespeare (1564-1616)

JAKE'S LITTLE GIRL pans in for a close-up of his hands. They're like something out of a horror movie. The blood has found its way into the creases of his knuckles and under the cuticles of his fingers.

Gia stands in the doorway, arms crossed, still as a tree, scrutinizing her father's every move. He slaps another slab of beef on the long wooden table and gives a hearty swing with the butcher cleaver. Gia jumps at the sound of bones splitting, but Jake pretends not to notice, keeping his eyes focused on the knife's point of landing. He mindlessly wipes his sticky, bloodstained hands on his white apron, then looks up to smile at his five-year-old. She doesn't return the smile; in fact, it looks to Jake as if she's fighting the urge to gag. He lifts the corners of his apron to get a look at it. It is pretty gory.

"You okay, G?" he asks as he sets down the cleaver and reaches for a large knife with a long blade and a slightly wide, bulbous tip. She nods her head but says nothing, just breathes heavily through her mouth. Jake ceremoniously trims a strip of fat away from a cutlet and tosses it into the big barrel situated at the end of the table. "He shoots! He scores!" he sings for Gia's benefit.

She doesn't smile. She just stands there, looking both odd and lovely. Gia is long-limbed like her mother, with Peri's fair skin and silky honey-colored hair. Only her eyes are her own. Where her mother's are a striking cool, lake-water blue, Gia's are more muted, the color of stonewashed denim. She doesn't look a bit like Jake, and this bothers him. Weren't the genes for dark hair and dark eyes supposed to be dominant? The only thing Italian about Gia was her name.

"You sure you're okay, lamb chop?"

"I'm fine, Daddy. I'm just watching you." She resumes breathing out of her mouth.

Jake laughs to himself. He used to do that when he was little—breathe out of his mouth—back when he stood where she's standing and watched *his* father cut meat. If you breathe through your mouth you avoid smelling the thick, raw, animal flesh stench that permeates the air. The stench that over the years has found its way into every crack and corner of the back room of his father's place, Mattino's Meat Market. A place that looks clean and is clean, but never smells clean.

The door to the walk-in freezer opens and Jake's father, Papa P, emerges shouldering a scarlet side of meat. Jake pauses—his knife hovering over the meat—to watch Gia's reaction. The bloody carcass affronts her and quickly one hand pops up to cover her eyes, the other to plug her nose.

Jake gives his head a shake. She's a puzzle, Gia is. She'd never been an easy child—colicky as a baby, timid as a toddler, fearful as a preschooler. And now, out of nowhere, her fears have evolved into full-blown phobias, which—take your pick—span the rational and the irrational: blood, all dead animals, certain live animals, spiders, strangers, boys with braces, men with beards, women with vivid red lips, ghosts, witches, darkness, planes, traffic signals ("how do you *know* green means go?"), stuffed animals with scratchy fur, all eleven of her "boy" cousins, any kind of raw meat, poultry or fish, ketchup, and her grandfather's meat market.

Papa P crosses the room and then drops the meat onto the table. The loud *THUNCK* makes Gia blink. Papa P throws her a smile. That thing he does with his mouth, the way he stretches it out for a millisecond—more like a tic than anything else—is supposed to be a smile. Jake's tried to explain this to Gia, that that's just how Papa P smiles, that he's "all business" when he's at the store. But she's still afraid of him. Afraid of his hands, whether they're bloodstained and sticky, or clean and dry and pork pink. Afraid of his soiled apron. Afraid of the sharp butcher knives that cling to the magnetic bar on the wall, especially the butcher saw, which looks just like a hack saw. Afraid of the walk-in freezer with the right-out-of-a-horror-movie meat hooks. Afraid of the knife sharpeners: the crisscross one, the ring type, the rolling sharpener, and even the sharpening steel—the *Zip-Zap*—which had been Jake's favorite as a kid (the next best thing to a real pirate sword). She's afraid of the heat-sealing equipment, the fluorescent ceiling lamps that buzz incessantly and cast a pinkish hue about the room, and the trap door where the stairs pull out to the basement. She's even afraid of Papa P's delivery truck because of the realistic rendering of a nicely marbled New York strip steak and silver butcher knife.

"She's afraid of just about everything," Jake finds himself saying to his wife at the end of just about every day.

Peri's response is always the same. She just waves Jake's words from the air with a sweep of a slender, pale hand, obliterating them from existence. "What do you expect?" she'll say as she blows on a freshly painted fingernail. "She's exactly like you."

It infuriates Jake when Peri does that—resolves all of life's problems simply by pointing a finger. After twelve years of marriage Peri has perfected her jump shot. She can toss blame in Jake's direction with alarming accuracy. (*She* shoots! *She* scores!) Those same lake blue eyes that had drawn him to her—he'd wanted to swim in those eyes— were now piercing, exacting, judicial.

Just this morning before Jake and Gia left for the market, he'd stopped in the bedroom to say good-bye (Peri has always had a passion for sleeping late on Saturdays) and she said, with her eyes still closed: "You're just kidding yourself. You can't cure her fear of blood by forcing her to watch you and your father butcher. You're wasting your time." She said this just as Jake was leaning in to kiss her forehead. He paused in mid-air, waiting for the next sentence which he expected to be a comment about genetics: "Isn't it funny how Gia got my genes for hair color, eye color, cheekbones, and stature, but she got your nervous genes and your worry-wart genes and your 'take-everything-too-damn-serious' genes." Or, she sometimes threw in plugs for pharmaceuticals— "The kid needs Prozac."

But this morning Peri added nothing else, just sighed and turned over. Jake unpuckered his lips. He waited until Peri's breathing was soft and rhythmic. Closing the door behind him he had to wonder how it was that his wife could shoot and score without even saying another word.

The truth was he and Gia *were* similarly wired. The last of a brood of five boys, Jake had been at one time the object of Papa P's concern. He wasn't like his older brothers—thick, meaty boys, who among them boasted a medical history of twelve broken bones, a hundred and seventeen stitches, multiple strains and sprains, and more black eyes than one could count. Papa P used to pretend to be angry about "eating up my profits" when one of his sons would come into the back room requesting a cold beefsteak to put against a shiner. Jake, who had only one black eye in his entire life (sustained from one of Peri's mighty tennis serves), preferred a bag of ice to a hunk of meat.

"You tenderloin," his older brother, Mikey, had called him.

"Sponge-cake," David said.

"Quiche Lorraine," somebody else mumbled.

Papa P clears his throat and Jake is brought back to present time. He looks at Gia and is not surprised to find her still cemented to the same spot in the doorway. He is worried about her. Kindergarten was difficult. There were tears when Peri left her and tears when Peri picked her up. The notes the teacher handed to Peri and then Peri handed to Jake the second he walked in the door after work were painful to read. Written in the teacher's hand, but supposedly authored by Gia, the words ripped through Jake's heart as he read them silently: "Today I didn't participate in 'Sharing' because Marjorie Task brought in her cocker spaniel and I was so scared I had an accident in my pants." "Today, I was distracted and couldn't complete my math lesson because of Joey Sunday's bloody nose." "Today, I…"

And then finally, the letter they'd received in June, right before school was out. The note was written on a small sheet of pink stationery in the teacher's lovely slanted script. Jake started to read it in Gia's voice, only to find

101

that the teacher herself authored this note. She didn't mince words: "Your child needs a psychological evaluation."

Jake lay awake that entire night. The teacher was inept he decided. After all, she was only twenty-four years old. Not at all experienced in these things. Maybe they'd been wrong in choosing a private school. "It's the teacher's fault," Peri said. She shoots, she scores, even in the dark.

Sometimes, possibly even right now, Gia retreats inside herself to what must be a less frightening world. Jake watches as she unconsciously plugs and unplugs her nose using first her forefingers, then the middle fingers, on down to the pinkies. Then she pulls a bundle of her soft, honey hair across her cheek and under her nose, creating her own air filter. Finally she reverts back to short, shallow breaths through the mouth.

Jake can't watch her anymore. He knows he should put her out of her misery, let her go sit in Papa P's office. Let her spin around on the chair and fiddle with the old adding machine. Peri says it borders on child abuse, these Saturday morning missions of his. Today it was the market to help Gia conquer her fear of blood and knives and raw meat. Last Saturday it was the pet shop to get Gia acquainted (she wouldn't even touch one) with some new cocker spaniel puppies to help her overcome the animal phobias. The Saturday before that it was a day at an amusement park to face her fear of rides. And the Saturday before that...well, Jake would do anything rather than resort to medicating a five-year-old. He himself rarely swallowed an aspirin.

Peri had agreed, reluctantly, to give him the summer for his little project— "Project G" she called it. But if Gia didn't improve, they had no choice but to start her on the medication. It was that or Gia would have to repeat kindergarten. Jake asked his wife what was so bad about repeating kindergarten. Peri shot him daggers through the air, then said, "Do you want your own flesh and blood repeating kindergarten? How humiliating! For her, of course."

Jake thought of comebacks later that night while lying in bed and staring at what must be the ceiling. Of course it was too late now, but he could have brought up the fact that he himself had repeated kindergarten. He could have brought up the fact that if Gia was her mother's flesh and her father's blood, then shouldn't she be allowed to work through things the way he had—by facing the fears head on, over time, over and over again?

It's what he'd had to do as a boy. With four brute brothers Jake was constantly looking over his shoulders. He'd been forced to carry a house key at all times, he slept with the light on, he learned to shake out each shoe before inserting a foot, and he never took for granted that his dresser drawers were filled only with inanimate objects. They all teased him but two of his brothers tormented him, the two who felt their parents had run out of testosterone hormones by the time the youngest, tallest but slightest, brother came along.

Mikey and David were the bad ones, the ones who locked him out of the house and locked him in the walk-in freezer. The ones who opened bottles of ammonia and told him to "take a deep whiff or else," the ones that made him eat chunks of raw meat and once even cow tongue, which he quickly regurgitated. Unequivocally, the worst thing they ever did was to re-enact the scene from the Godfather in Jake's bed...except it wasn't a horse head, it was a pig head.

Looking at Gia's face, Jake can no longer stand it and he says, "Sweetheart, you want to go sit in Papa P's office?"

"Okay, Daddy."

Papa P says, "She want a *pop-seek*?"

Jake wishes Papa P would ask her himself but he knows that his father is hurt by Gia's unfounded fear of him and so lately he hardly interacts with her at all.

Jake translates: "You want a Popsicle, honey?"

"No, thank you," she whispers and turns to make her escape.

"She'll be okay, Pa, you watch," Jake says when she's gone.

Papa P nods.

"She takes after me, that's all. Spitting image of her mother, but her liver is made of chicken, just like mine was."

Papa P twitches a quick smile. He offers this: "It's that Swedish blood from her mother. They're both *delicato*."

"You're telling me, Pa. I married a piece of porcelain who gave birth to fine china."

It's the right thing to say and Papa P even chuckles. The world according to Papa P is one where meaty men with strong, bloodstained hands care for beautiful, fragile women. The wrong thing to say would be that Peri thinks it's his blood that's weak.

"Hey, tenderloin, think fast!" a voice shouts from the doorway.

Jake's arms shoot up fast enough to catch a soccer ball with his bloody hands.

"Hey, now look what you did! You got Gary's tournament ball all bloody," Jake's brother, David, says, as he stands where Gia stood a moment ago.

Jake shakes his head at his older brother, who, having just lost twenty-five pounds has rediscovered his neck and his cocky side. Jake throws the ball to its owner, Gary, an oversized ten-year-old, who comes clomping into the room in his cleats leaving behind trails of grassy dirt clods. "So what, Dad, I don't care," Gary says as he examines the ball. "It already has some of my own blood on it. See?" He lifts the ball and a bloody knee up high so Jake and his dad and Papa P can have a look. Jake grimaces, thankful that Gia is not in the room.

"You'll want to get that cleaned and bandaged," Jake says.

"It's nothing," David says, as if the wound were his own. "You're just used to girls. My boys are USDA Standard—the toughest cuts, Jakey. Hell, this kid never cries. My boys love blood. They're like friggin' vampires."

Gary pushes out his front teeth. He looks like a vampire. Jake says nothing.

Papa P pinches Gary on the cheek and calls him a "wise guy." He gives him that millisecond smile before heading out front with a tray of packaged T-bones. "No rough-housing in the store," he says as the door swings closed behind him. Jake knows his father's admonition could be directed at either Gary or David—developmentally they're the same age.

"Hey, Mr. Scored-Four-Goals-Today, go play with Gia, will ya? I gotta talk to your Uncle Jake for a minute."

Gary protests. Stomps his feet a couple times.

Jake would like to protest. The bloody knee might set Gia off. It's what finally convinced Jake and Peri to seek out a child psychologist. Gia had once banged heads with one of her cousins and the resulting bloody nose almost made her faint. The poor thing thought she was going to die. "I'm losing a lot of blood," she had whispered in all seriousness to Jake.

"Come on," David tells his son. "Take her up front and get her a Popsicle."

Gary grunts but then turns, side steps his own clods of dirt, and heads out of the room. "Gee-Gee," he calls in a high, nasal voice. "Wanna play?"

"He won't do anything to her," David says when he sees the look on Jake's face. But Jake knows Gary is full of rotten tricks. Two weeks ago he had Gia in a panic, almost hyperventilating, when he chased her around the store waving a freshly cut-off chicken foot, screaming, "Come on, shake hands."

"Hey, string bean, listen to me," David says. "I know it's none of my business but since your wife called my wife I guess it's become kind of my business."

"They talk too much," Jake says, grabbing the butcher saw from the magnetic bar. He doesn't need the butcher saw—he's still trimming fat—but he just feels like holding it.

"Rachel says that Peri says they want to start Gia on some medicine for her problems, but that you don't want to do it."

"Yeah. So?"

"Jakey, Rachel's a psych nurse," David says, picking up the butcher cleaver and banging the flat side against the inside of his hand. "She thinks you guys should try it. And she knows what she's talking about, Jake, she handles wackos."

Jake delivers a killer stare. "My little girl is not a wacko for God's sake."

"Geez!" David says, raising up his hand, the one holding the knife. "I didn't mean *she* was a wacko. I just meant Rachel really knows her stuff."

Jake doesn't speak, doesn't lift his eyes from the meat. David tosses the knife on the table and leans back against the counter. "That's all I meant, Jake. Honest. I just think—"

Papa P pushes through the swinging door and David stops abruptly.

Papa P says, "What's going on?"

"Nothing, Pa," David says.

"How long you staying? I could use some chops. You always did a nice job with the chops. Thin cut, how about?"

"Okay, okay. I just came in for a couple of lousy steaks. I guess I still gotta work for my food, huh?" He grins at his father, grabs a white apron from a hook, washes his hands at the sink, then accepts the bulk of pork Papa P pushes at him.

"No rough housin'!" Papa P says and heads out front again.

David faces his brother at the long table, and cuts while he talks. "Rachel said that Peri said that you're in denial. That you're trying your own system. Spending every Saturday this summer trying to scare Gia's fears out of her."

"Oh, that makes sense—scare the fears out of her."

"Well, you take the kid to a pet shop, the zoo, a dog show, the Field Museum. You even take her fishing. Does it cure her fear of animals? No. Then the blood thing. You take her to the blood bank, and you bring her here to watch you cut meat. Has her fear of blood disappeared? No. Then there are the rides. You take her to Great America, you take her to Mall of America, Santa's Village. Jakey, she won't even get on a friggin' merry-go-round."

Jake can feel the blood pooling in his forehead right between his thick, dark eyebrows. "You know, she's just a little kid. Kids grow out of their fears. Look at me. I was scared of my own liver. Scared of lightning, scared of tests, scared of ghosts, scared of those damned monkeys from the Wizard of Oz. Scared of opening my sock drawer for fear a lizard might crawl out. And I got over it, didn't I? I worked through all of my fears. I can pull back my covers and not worry about finding animal heads in my bed or anything."

David's face lights up. "God, that was great. The look on your face…"

They're both silent for a while, cutting and trimming. One thing they have in common: they both hate butchering. David served his time in the market just like all the Mattino boys had. He was skilled with a knife, but was too antsy to stand in one place for any length of time. When he was nineteen his Uncle Angelo got him a job delivering beer. Now he's a district manager.

Jake did his time, too. But it never came natural. When it was his turn to help out in the back room he wore the same look of disgust that Gia had worn on her face this morning. And he, too, had tried the very same alternative breathing methods that she'd employed. Jake knew early on that he was no butcher. He was overly cautious with a knife, never trusting the grip of his thin piano fingers. But he'd talked himself into staying. He pretended that the decision was about tradition and family loyalty and ethnic pride, but he knew damn well that the only reason he had stayed was because his brothers had left.

In June of his senior year when Mattino's Meat Market was crazy with orders for high school graduation parties, Jake sliced off a good chunk of his left index finger. He'd fainted and Papa P had to pick him up, sling him over his shoulder, throw him in the back seat of his car and drive him to the ER. There they sewed the fingertip (which Papa P had tucked into his shirt pocket with an ice cube) back on.

"You tenderloin," his older brother, Mikey, had called him.

"Sponge-cake," David said.

"Quiche Lorraine," somebody else mumbled.

The next day, Jake applied to Northwestern University. There he chose Marketing for his major upon his mother's suggestion. She'd always contended that her youngest had the gift of gab, a nice way with the customers, and a "salesman's smile."

"College boy," his oldest brother, Mikey, had called him.

"Freddie the Freshman," David said.

"How's finishing school?" somebody else asked.

Now, forgetting that David is standing across from him, Jake laughs out loud as he thinks about the irony of it all—that even with the Marketing degree, he'd ended up back in the cutting business. He sells medical supplies. Microsurgical instruments to be exact: blades, scalpels, clamps, forceps and other sundries for intricate procedures like eye and ear surgeries. Part of his job is to scrub up and walk the doctors through the use of the implements in the operating room. The money's good, but in Jake's mind he'd merely traded one butcher shop for another. ("What's the difference between God and a surgeon?" Jake had asked Dr. Hanz just the other day. "God doesn't think he's a surgeon.")

It was Rachel, David's wife, who'd introduced Jake and Peri. Back then Peri was with Eli Lilly selling Prozac to psychiatrists. On Peri's third visit to the office, Rachel pronounced her perfect for her husband's baby brother, who was also in medical sales, and talked her into a double date.

At the bar in some downtown Japanese restaurant Jake drank the beer his brother bought him and waited for his petite freckle-faced sister-in-law to show up with his date. He kept his eyes glued to the door as he repeatedly wiped his sweaty palms on the sides of his slacks.

When Peri Anderson glided through the door Jake had no idea she was his date until Rachel scampered up behind her. Then he experienced a brief but jolting lapse in executive function, as if someone had pulled the plug. He couldn't blink, swallow, or get up from the bar stool to endure the introductions. The absurd thought that came to his mind when he shook Peri's cool, slender hand was that she looked like a long, golden, and perfect banana. He almost felt sorrow for Rachel, who, next to Peri, looked like a plum tomato. He did feel sorry for David, who took one look at Peri and fell off his bar stool.

On sleepless nights, Jake lies in bed staring at what must be the ceiling and thinks about the day David fell off that bar stool and about the way he and all of his brothers looked at him differently after Peri. Post-Peri, Jake somehow had been exalted. A simple association with a beautiful banana was all it took. He thinks about his brothers, with their short or freckle-faced or round wives, slapping him on the back and calling him "Slick" and only then do Peri's faults and peccadilloes disappear from where Jake has listed them on his side of the ceiling. He can almost see Peri's slender hand erasing each vice as he comes to terms with it—the vanity, the complacency, the smugness, the hypochondria. At times he rolls over in bed and accidentally touches her and he is startled by how cold her skin feels. When this happens he has to force himself to see David falling off that bar stool all over again.

"What's so funny?" David asks.

"What?" Jake shakes the scene from his head. "Nothing. Nothing really."

"Jake, I'm only trying to help."

Jake puts down his knife and looks at his brother. He's four years older than Jake, forty-one, but it occurs to Jake that the new, thinner David looks much younger than he does. His skin doesn't look tight, the way Jake's feels. Suddenly Jake wishes David would punch him, or pinch him, or just mess up his hair. He's tempted to reach out and touch his brother's hairy forearm, just to feel if his skin is warmer than his, warmer than Peri's, warmer than Gia's. A chill shoots through Jake as he digests the idea that maybe that's the price you pay for a gorgeous, limp-wristed, trophy wife— your skin loses its warmth and you age quicker.

"David, do I look old to you?" Jake blurts out.

"What?"

"Tell me, is Rachel's skin cool to the touch, even in the summer?"

"Jake! What are you talking about? You're talking crazy."

"You think she's so perfect just because of how she looks."

"Who?"

"Peri. She's not perfect, you know. She's not always right, either. This once, I'm trying it my way. Of course Peri wants to medicate. The woman's a walking medicine cabinet who subscribes religiously to pharmacologic intervention. Hell, she pops pills for a hangnail. We're talking about fooling around with a five-year-old brain here! These drugs manipulate your emotion molecules and there are no long-term safety studies. Don't you see how that scares the hell out of me?"

David puts down his knife and walks around to the other side of the table. He wipes his hand on his apron before he lifts it up to squeeze Jake's shoulder. His hand is damp and cold from handling the meat, but just the touch of it shoots through Jake like hot lightning. David says, "You know what? That would scare the hell out of me, too. But your way isn't working. Rachel says you could just try the medicine for a month. See if it helps."

"We are not trying the medicine!"

"I can't believe you of all people would let pride get in the way."

Jake raises his eyebrows. "Pride? You think this is about pride?" Now he raises the knife in his hand—maniacally. "I'll tell you what this is about. This is about a woman, so systemically vain that she won't stop using pharmaceuticals and cosmeceuticals even when she's pregnant, even when her doctors tell her it could be dangerous to her unborn baby. I don't think medicine can fix the problem medicine caused in the first place. She's not going to win this one."

A shrill scream pierces the air and then Gia appears in the doorway, face contorted, tears spilling. For a second, as Jake runs to her, he thinks there's blood on her face, but when he's closer he sees it's just smears of cherry Popsicle.

After some idle threats, Gary confesses to telling Gia that cherry Popsicles were made from cow's blood. "It was a joke," Gary says over and over. David sends Gary out to the car while he tries to fix things with Gia. A stick of Juicy Fruit helps a little. But not until Papa P retrieves the Popsicle box and Jake reads off the list of ingredients is she fully convinced that she has not just consumed blood. She settles down and even lets Papa P take her hand and lead her to the bathroom to wash her face.

Before he leaves, David says, "Sorry, I know that didn't help matters any."

Jake shrugs, pretending to make light even though deep down he'd like to get his hands on his nephew. "I guess it's human nature, the way boys love to torment girls."

"Until they get married, right? Then the girls torment the boys. For the rest of our sorry lives. I didn't know that about Peri, man. I wouldn't even let Rachel have a swig of my beer when she was pregnant." He smacks Jake on the shoulder and says, "We all love her, you know."

Jake nods. "I know, I know. Hell, you fell off your chair the first time you laid eyes on her."

"I was talking about Gia, you asshole."

"Oh," Jake says. Then, "Oh!"

Once David leaves, Jake washes the knives and scrubs down the butcher table. His cold hands tingle as he holds them under hot water, watching as the water runs pink. As he massages in the soap, he touches the scar on his re-attached fingertip and wonders what the hell he is doing to his daughter's emotion molecules by subjecting her to "Project G."

He hears Gia screaming again.

As Jake tears out of the room, he imagines puddles of blood, ripped flesh, fainting, and a trip to the ER. But what he finds is a grinning Gia sitting on Papa P's lap and swiveling in Papa P's chair. The screams were of delight. Jake's confused. Gia hates rides and she's afraid of Papa P.

"Hey," Jake says.

Gia swirls to face him and gives a soft smile. "We're playing market. Papa P wrote out my list and now we're driving to the store."

Papa P approximates a smile and hands Gia the small notepad he's holding. "Show your Daddy your list, and then we can get a cart and pick out everything, okay?" Papa P's voice sounds funny to Jake—higher and more nasal. He nods to Jake as Gia hands the list to him. "Take a look at the list, son," he says.

It's a first. Papa P never plays with the grandchildren. *A loaf of bread,* Jake reads. That's not entirely true. *Apple Juice.* Papa P will throw a ball every once in a while when the kids come to visit. *Maple syrup.* But he never plays at the store. *A thing of milk.* At the store, Papa P is all business. *Cinnamon rolls. The cereal with the marshmallow moons.* But now, Gia has slid off of Papa P's lap and is spinning him in the chair. *Fritos. Oranges. Chocolate Milk. Macaroni and Cheese. Yogurt. And the mint medicine.*

"What mint medicine, lamb chop?" Jake asks as he watches his father go round and round.

"That new medicine, Daddy."

"What new medicine, lamb chop?"

"I don't remember the name of it, but Mommy does. She used to sell it."

She shoots, she scores, Jake says in his head. To Gia he asks, "What kind of medicine is it? What's it for?"

It takes all her muscles to twirl her grandfather and there's no question that the look she gives her father is meant to signify annoyance, but she answers, "It's to dry up tears. When a person has too many tears it dries 'em right up." She stops spinning for a second to snap (well, almost) her finger. "Just like that."

"Just like that, huh? Who has too many tears, G?"

Gia gives Papa P one last big spin then she looks up at her father and says, "Me. I do."

Jake can't look at her. He looks at his father instead who sits slumped in the chair. Jake's only seen Papa P cry two times in his life. The other time was when Papa P's mother died.

"Didn't you know that, Daddy?" Gia ask.

It takes a minute to answer. "Yes, lamp chop, I guess I did." Jake scoops his little girl up into his arms. He swallows whatever is stuck in his throat and kisses Gia's soft hair. *We all love her, you know*, he hears David's voice say again. She shoots, she scores. She shoots, she scores. She shoots again and again. She scores again and again. How come she always wins?

Papa P nods to Jake. Jake wonders what's going through his head. Maybe he thinks it's a good idea, this tear-busting medicine. Maybe it will help strengthen that delicate Swedish blood that Gia has coursing through her veins. A small epiphany pops like a bubble in Jake's brain: *Maybe I'm not losing. Maybe Peri's not winning. Maybe Gia is winning.*

Suddenly the little girl in his arms starts gagging.

"Gia? What is it?"

"Daddy," she says covering her nose and her mouth, "you forgot to take off your apron."

Jake looks down at the gory apron. "What do you know, I guess I did. Looks sort of gross, doesn't it?"

"Looks sort of like finger-paints to me," Papa P. says, holding out a hand so that his son can help him up from the chair.

Gia claps her hands once. "You're right, Papa P. Just like red finger-paints."

Something Like That

"The best part of beauty
is that which no picture can express."
—Frances Bacon (1561-1626)

THE VERY FIRST thing I said to Chad Buckingham when he showed up at our apartment was, "Show me your money." Before I even let him in I said this.

He squinted at me and sort of froze in the doorway.

"You *are* Chad Buckingham, aren't you?" I asked.

Without a word he dug his hand into the back pocket of his jeans, retrieved a worn brown wallet, opened it up, and pulled out a stack of bills. When he fanned out the bills—dramatically and about an inch from my face—I spotted a couple of fifties among the tens and twenties.

"Come on in," I said. Then, "Liz, he's here!" I left him standing in the hall and went back to the living room where I plopped myself down on our old red and black Spanish-style sofa (a hand-me-down that seated six comfortably) and waited for my roommate to emerge from the bedroom. This was all her doing—she could deal with it.

"Have a seat," I called to Chad Buckingham as I curled my legs up under me. I pretended to go back to my Red Delicious and my *People* magazine but stole peeks at him between crunches and page turns. He stood there in the doorway, not having moved an inch. He looked nothing like I had pictured him, although I can't quite describe what I had in mind. Liz said he was British and all the Brits I ever knew were slightly built and small in stature. This guy was towering. Of course one could argue that almost anyone towered over all five-feet-nothing of me, but you'll just have to take my word for it, Chad Buckingham was one big Brit. He also wasn't bad looking. He had the scruffy appeal of a stray dog: shaggy, dark brown hair, a sweet face, rosy cheeks even. Still, you just never knew. Ax-murderers sometimes had sweet faces. I was dead against the idea from the start.

"You might as well have a seat," I called out again. "Liz is doing her hair which is a money-back guarantee that she'll be a while."

Still, he didn't move. I read some juicy tidbit of celebrity gossip about Brad Pitt then looked back up again at Chad. He'd taken only a couple of steps toward the living room. When I saw his eyes scanning the scenery I realized the problem. The problem was our living room. I guess you could say we had a "pad." Get a load of it: the centerpiece of the room was the red and black beast upon which I was sitting. You couldn't miss it. It was like ten feet long, I kid you not. Marty, our other roommate and the proud owner of the beast, had described it to Liz and me as "Mediterranean chic" when he (yes, *he*) first told us he had a couch. Having access to living room furniture was one of the main reasons I agreed to letting Marty share this apartment with us (that, and the fact that Lori Sutton had backed out at the last minute).

It was Liz's idea (it was always Liz's idea). We were just poor college kids, after all. We needed a warm body to cover a third of the rent and Marty was a decent guy, so we did what we had to do: we told our parents that Marty Blackman was a *she* and then we watched in horror as *he* and his brothers hauled in the most flamboyant furniture we had ever seen. In addition to the sofa, there were other intricately carved pieces—a coffee table that was longer than me, matching end tables that screamed "funeral parlor." There were ceramic-based lamps with deep red shades dotted with black specs and his and hers matching swivel chairs ("crushed velvet," Marty had said on the phone), one in burnt orange and the other in olive green. "I believe Marty and his brothers robbed the home of a bull-fighter," Liz had said, but she ended up loving the room, calling it "Early Latin-American." And she loved the sofa, where she spent about eighty percent of her junior year, sketching her sketches and painting her paintings.

"*Toro, toro*," Chad Buckingham said suddenly. Somewhere between my crunching and page turning he had walked to the center of the room, peeled off his black jacket and began wagging it at me. "*Toro, toro*," he said again, rolling the R's.

"Oh, please!" I said. "No furniture jokes. This is *not* my furniture."

"Certainly it's not," he said, in his real voice, which was nasal but melodious with that distinct Liverpudlian accent the Beatles made famous. I had to admit I could listen to that dialect, with its sing-song cadence and high pitch all day long.

"No, really. And it isn't Liz's furniture either. It's Marty's."

"Marty the matador?"

"Funny. Marty Blackman, our other roommate. He's a he."

"Most matadors are."

"LIZ!" I screamed, popping up from the sofa. "He's heeeeeeere! Are you coming?" I explained to Chad that Liz had a date tonight. "Well, every night really. By the way, have you met Liz? In person?"

"Actually, no. I've only spoken with 'er on the phone. It's 'er brother I know, from Philosophy class," he said as he dropped himself into the orange swivel chair.

I nodded and smiled and prepared myself for the inevitable: instant and absolute invisibility. See, Liz was gorgeous, and even though I didn't scare dogs away, once Liz entered a room, I was totally eclipsed by her lithe and willowy beauty. We'd been friends for three years and roommates for two, so I was pretty much used to it. You forgave her her beauty because she was so needy. She was also funnier than hell.

"So it was James who told you that Liz and I were driving to Daytona Beach for spring break?"

"James?" Chad said, as he started to swivel, using his feet to propel himself. "James, who?"

I caught my breath. I knew there was something fishy about this arrangement. "James, Liz's brother."

"I thought 'is name was Stewart," he said and stopped swiveling. "Stewart Peters."

"Oh, right, I forgot. He goes by his middle name now. Anyway, I understand you're willing to pay for half of the gas and not just a third?" I wanted to be straight on the details.

He started swiveling again. "Yes, yes, that's right."

"You're not a drug dealer, are you?"

"Good God, no!" He straightened his legs, raised his feet up in the air and leaned back in the chair, enjoying his ride. "Why would you think that?"

"No reason. Other than all those bills in your wallet."

He shrugged. "I work."

"And you're not a rapist or anything, are you?"

"I'm an *Or-Anythin'* actually."

I ignored this and asked if he was willing to take his shift behind the wheel.

"Of course. I'll drive all the bloody way, straight without sleep, if you want me to."

"That won't be necessary, but it will be just the two of us because Liz doesn't drive."

He stopped swiveling to cock an eyebrow. "Why not?"

"Uhhhmm. Take your pick—asthma attacks, migraines, spoiled by limos, prone to road rage. Anyway, you have a valid license to drive in the United States, right?"

"I'm an authentic US citizen, missy. Yee-ha!"

"*Yee-ha*? Please don't tell me you're a country music fan. You won't be begging for Garth Brooks or Willie Nelson or the Judds on the radio, will you?"

"No need to worry about that."

"Any recent speeding tickets?"

"And 'ow would you define *recent*?" he said, grinning. "No, no, none."

"Do you smoke?"

"Only after sex."

I shot him a disgusted look.

"That was intended as a joke, but obviously, it wasn't received as a joke, so, for the record, no, I do not smoke cigarettes. Joints, cigars, pipes...nothin'. I don't smoke. My, but we worry, don't we?"

"I'm just a very careful person. What's your business in Daytona Beach, anyway? If I may ask."

"You may. I'm meeting my baby sister there." (Still swiveling.) "She goes to Georgia State. Studying to be a bloody doctor. Gonna put 'er 'ands all over sick people.

121

Gonna specialize in infectious diseases. Gonna find a cure for AIDS, she is. Bloody unfair, don't you think, 'ow some get all the brains and the rest of us 'ave to settle for just good looks?"

He threw me another grin and I couldn't help but think how he reminded me of my dog, Sparky. Sparky could look me right in the eye and lie his tail off. The incriminating evidence—one of my shoes—could be hanging from his mouth and still his face would deny it. Shoe? What shoe? Baby sister? Medical student? Oh, sure. It was all too perfect, too produced. And his voice was just too charming. Maybe it was better that Liz was taking hours with her hair and that I was doing the interviewing. Liz wasn't careful, like me. If she drove, Liz would pick up hitchhikers.

Chad Buckingham stopped swiveling and said, "I'm just pulling your leg actually. My sister *is* a medical student at Georgia State but she can't get away. Something about a crash course in autopsies." He paused for my reaction, but I was pre-med myself so I knew there was no such thing. Finally he said, "You see, there's this girl."

"Well of course there is," I said, crossing my arms and sounding remarkably like my mother.

"Pathetic, isn't it?"

"I guess it depends."

"I assure you, it's pathetic."

"I'll take your word for it."

Chad Buckingham smiled and shook his head from side to side. Then he looked me up and down, quite possibly for the first time. My hand went to my face, to stroke the small raised scar that lined the left side of my jawbone.

"I'm sorry," he said. "I never got your name."

"Tally. I'm Tally Davidson."

"Well, Tally. Did I pass?"

"Pass?"

"The test? Will you 'ave me along or won't you?"

"Don't you think we should wait for Liz's opinion?"

"I have a feeling that it wouldn't matter a bloody lick to Liz if I were a rapist or a pot'ead or a country western fan or an accumulator of speeding tickets, just so I paid for 'alf the gas and did 'alf the drivin'."

I smiled, but I wasn't about to tell him he was right on the money.

Finally, Liz appeared, decked out in a silvery-gray sweater and gray leather pants that made her look shiny and long and thin, like a butter knife. I watched Chad Buckingham closely for the anticipated reaction, the "Liz effect" was what I called it. They never knew where to look—at her sparkling blue eyes, at her silky platinum hair that spilled onto her shoulders, or at her boobs that spilled out of whatever she was wearing. Something happened to their hands—they twisted in nervousness. And to their voices—they stuttered and stammered.

"Hi there," said Liz, in the same friendly tone she used with everyone. "I'm Liz. Sorry for the wait but my hair just wouldn't cooperate."

"Well, 'ello, Stewart's sister!" Chad Buckingham said, springing from the swivel chair. "Who doesn't, praise God, look a thin' at all like 'er brother!"

"Damn right, I don't look like my brother. Pa-lease! James takes after my father's side. My mother almost gave him back when he was born. Said he looked like Jaba the Hut from Star Wars."

"Liz!" I said.

"Well, he did. Still does. He's got those chipmunk-ish cheeks. I used to tell him he was adopted, that his real parents were circus people." She threw her head back and laughed her throaty, fiendish laugh.

"Lovely!" said Chad Buckingham, jamming his hands into his front pockets, then pulling them out and hooking them together behind his back. "You're beautiful *and* wicked."

"I am not wicked, am I, Tally?"

"She's terribly wicked," I told him.

"I just love your accent," Liz said to Chad. "Well, are you coming with us or aren't you?" she demanded. "We leave Friday at three-ish."

"Three-on-the-dot," I corrected.

"I'm coming!" Chad Buckingham said with bounteous enthusiasm.

"Chad's meeting his girlfriend in Daytona," I told Liz, just so she knew.

"Well," said Chad with a shitty grin, "she's not technically me girlfriend…"

Chad Buckingham sat in front with me, his big legs sprawled out in front of him. His bare skin showed through the holes in the knees of his jeans. I believe he wore the same white, wrinkled dress shirt he wore the day before for his bull-fighting performance. And I was sure that no comb had been run through his shaggy head of hair.

Two blocks into our eleven hundred forty-three mile road trip—we hadn't even left the University of Chicago campus yet—he rolled down his window and said, "Mind if I smoke?"

"Go right ahead," Liz said from the back seat.

I almost hit the brakes. "You told me you didn't—"

"I don't. I'm just pulling your leg." That grin again.

I let out an exaggerated sigh.

"Be careful with her, Chadwick," Liz said. (She'd started calling him Chadwick when he'd arrived at two-thirty that afternoon with a small duffel bag—which meant more room for her *three* suitcases—and a box of scones. I was the one who opened the door, but he'd waited to present the scones to Liz.) "She's not what you'd call the most 'tease-able' person in the world. Tally's serious. Serious as a malignant tumor."

"Why, thank you very much," I said to the windshield. "I've never been compared to a terminal illness before."

"Tally's a genius," Liz offered.

"Here we go," I said.

"She could join Mensa if she wanted to," she continued. She had an endearing way of trying to balance out her beauty with my brains. She tried to share the spotlight, honest she did.

"Ahhhh," said Chadwick, taking this opportunity to turn sideways in his seat to better see Liz.

"No, really, she's pre-med."

"Like my sister," Chad said to my profile.

"Got one B+ in her entire life. Had to take a Valium."

"That's a lie!" I shout.

"Oh, right," Liz said, with a laugh, "it was me who had to take the Valium. And she has this photogenic memory."

"Photo*graphic*," I corrected.

"And modest, too, I see," Chadwick said.

"I'm just correcting the vocabulary, that's all."

"We do that, see," explained Liz. "Correct each other. Improve each other. Bail each other out when necessary. Tally holds me back when I cross the line and I give her a good shove when she needs to assert herself. That's why we make great roommates. We are so completely and utterly opposite."

"I'll say," Chad threw in.

Had I known him better I would have punched him in the arm.

"No, really, by being so different, we harmonize," Liz went on. "Tally's smart, serious, careful and organized. And she's so precise. I'm comfortable with coming close, rounding off to the nearest whatever—dollar, number, rule, commandment. I'm what-the-hell, come-what-may, or something like that. Anyway, I'm the essential dumb blonde."

"*Quint*essential," I corrected.

"Basically, I provide the entertainment."

"I'll say," Chadwick said again.

Three hours into our twenty-hour trip and the "entertainer" in the back seat had not stopped talking, had not even come up for air. Her cell phone had rung a dozen times; each time she informed the caller—her boyfriend Jeremy—that she was in the middle of a great story and would have to call him back. The "great stories" were of course all about her, how her mother died when she was eleven, how her father adored her, and had her "limo-ed" to school everyday. Then she made Chad endure the story of us—Liz, Marty and me—and how we all met and wound up sharing our apartment. How she discovered me admiring one of her watercolors in the student art show sophomore year and pretended it was someone else's and started grilling me about how I "felt" about the piece. How she "saved" Marty's life last year when he fell off the bleachers at the homecoming game and broke his leg (she dialed 911 on her cell phone). As usual, she provided too much information: "You should have seen Tally when I first met her—so plain and bookish—I did a total makeover on her." And she blatantly exaggerated: "Marty's leg bone was sticking out this far!"

As usual, her listener sucked it all up. I did catch Chad rubbing his neck a couple of times and then his forehead, but in the end, Liz gave herself a migraine. After giving a blow-by-blow description of her symptoms she popped a couple of her "friends" and at last nodded off.

"Wow!" Chad lipped to me when he turned around to face the front.

"Mmmm. Hmmm," I said.

"My neck is so stiff," he whispered, massaging it. "What about you? Do you want me to take over for you?"

"No, I'm fine. Your shift doesn't start for another hour. Everything's all planned out. You might want to take a look at the trip summary."

"Trip summary?"

"Yes, I got it off the computer. Rand McNally puts it out. Take a look." I pointed to the sun visor above him. He grabbed it and I said, "See, it's just over eleven hundred miles. With four rest-slash-food stops I figure it'll take about twenty hours. If we divide it into four-hour shifts, that would mean two four-hour shifts for you, two four-hour shifts for me, plus an extra two-hour shift at the end for me. We'll eat dinner tonight at seven and breakfast tomorrow at eight. Is that agreeable to you?"

"Yes, sir!" he said and saluted. "But may I ask, is it allowable to deviate from the plan, for emergency bathroom breaks, possibly?"

I shot him a look. "Of course, I've worked in several of those for Liz. I've also worked in a possible ER visit or drug store run. See, here are the various hospitals along our route—in Indiana, Kentucky, Tennessee, Georgia, Florida. She gets bad asthma attacks. And driving gives her migraines."

"Talking seems to give her migraines as well," Chad said, folding up the trip summary and storing it back under the visor.

Mmmm. Hmmm, I thought, as I increased speed to pass a semi. Chad was already going through stage two of the Liz Effect: straining his brain to decide whether Liz's relentless chirping was nauseating or engaging, and, either way, whether or not a bloke could take it. Actually, he didn't know how lucky he was—he had an entire cross-country road trip to figure it out. I could almost hear the conundrum as he tossed it around in his head: "*'Ow can*

the very thing that pleases the eye so, displease the ear so?"
I popped my gum and wondered as I overcame the truck:
didn't guys know that beauty almost never came in a nice
quiet package? Even a Ferrari is loud.

Suddenly my thoughts turned into spoken words:
"You're wishing she came in a quieter model, aren't you?"

Chad turned to face me. "Amazing! A photographic
memory *and* a gift for clairvoyance."

I scrunched my nose. "I like to think of it more as sort
of a second sight."

"Ahhhhh," was all he said but then he grew quiet and
pensive and I wished I hadn't opened my mouth. The block
of silence was thick, covering some twenty or thirty miles.

Liz experienced a miraculous cure when we stopped
for dinner just outside of Indianapolis. Putting her lips into
motion for chewing just revved them up for talking. I was
used to listening to Liz while I ate. It was what we did. It
was why she was shaped like a butter knife and I like an
inverted tablespoon.

"My boyfriend Jeremy? He's threatening to follow us
to Daytona. So if either of you guys spots a brownish Jeep,
do whatever you have to do to lose him."

"Why would he follow you now?" I asked. "He passed
up the opportunity to come with us. Didn't want to 'Do
Daytona' with a couple of females."

"Yeah, but then he found out about Chadwick."

"Yes, but Chadwick—Chad, has a girlfriend. He's
meeting her. Didn't you tell Jeremy that?"

You could tell Chad didn't like us talking about him as
if he weren't there. At the same time you could tell he was
pleased to be the source of Jeremy's jealousy.

"You know, she's not officially me girlfriend."

After dinner Chad took his shift behind the wheel. Liz called Jeremy and lectured him about trusting her and giving her some space. Then she fell asleep. I was so tired I thought I would sleep, too, but I couldn't. It wasn't that Chad was a bad driver, it was just that I didn't easily deliver my life into the hands of a stranger. There was something about Chad—he didn't seem to take things as seriously as he should. Take his major, for example. Drama. *Drama.* He sang and danced. Tapped even. He played the piano and the saxophone. He'd done Shakespeare and Second City.

He read my face. "You're turning up your nose at me."

"I am not."

"Because medicine is such a serious, noble profession. Well, my experience 'as been that doctors sometimes make people sicker. Botch things up, they do. Sometimes they even kill people. I intend to spend my life making people laugh. Or at least smile."

I wasn't turning up my nose at him, not really. Well, maybe just a little. But he'd yet to make me laugh. That much was true.

"Mind if I put in one of me tapes?" he asked as I eyed the speedometer.

"Go ahead. Just as long as it's not country."

"Do you consider 'Johnny' country?"

"Johnny Cash?"

"Johnny Lennon," he said, pulling a Beatles cassette out of his jacket pocket.

"Hey!" a wide-awake Liz suddenly shouted from the back seat. "Is that a brownish Jeep? Oh, God! I think it is!"

"He wouldn't!" I said.

"He would," she said.

I slowed down to let it pass and we all stared at the poor grandmother in the *tan van*. It wasn't Jeremy. It wasn't even a brown Jeep.

"Told ya," I said.

"Told me nothing, Tally. Mark my words, that boy will follow me to Daytona. I was so stupid to give him the name of our hotel. Why did I do it?"

I shake my head and turn the music louder. I hadn't heard the Beatles in a long time and it made me a little homesick for my mom, the biggest Beatles fan that ever lived. Before I knew it my eyelids grew heavy and I stopped fighting. I slept.

When I woke up it was half past midnight. Chad's shift was over a half an hour ago. I rubbed my eyes and looked over at him. He seemed fine. He really had a nice profile. My eyes traveled from his long, full eyelashes, to his strong nose, to his boyish rosy cheeks, to his huge hands gripping the wheel, to the speedometer. Yipes! He was going ninety!

"CHADWICK!" I screamed.

You would have thought the boy was a toad the way he jumped.

"What?! Tally, are you mad? I almost veered off the road!"

"You're going ninety!"

"'Ow can I be going ninety when I set the cruise control for seventy?"

"That's a question without a good answer." I waited for him to adjust it. "Anyway, your shift is over. Pull over and I'll take it from here."

He didn't say anything. Just saluted me again. It was beginning to bug me.

He slept for the next couple of hours, snoring occasionally, which I found funny. There, I realized, he did make me laugh. He happened to be asleep, but still.

Out of nowhere, Chad said, "'Ow old were you when you decided to become a doctor?"

He startled me, as I thought he was still asleep. I looked over at him. His eyes were still closed. "Oh, I don't know. Let's see. I think I was seven. My grandpa got real sick. He had perforated diverticulits. They had to chop off about a foot of his colon. They got him up and walking just hours after his surgery. Anyway, he had internal bleeding and they missed it and he died. My grandma sued and ended up rich but sad and lonely. My mother told me that doctors were human and made mistakes. I didn't think they should make mistakes."

"If you ask me, laughter's the best medicine ever created."

"When did you decide you wanted to be an actor?"

He laughed. "Oh, Lord. I didn't set out for acting actually. I've taken a side road to be sure. It was comedy I wanted to do. I grew up in Liverpool. Me mum was a teacher, elementary, and me dad owned a pub. Mum died three days before my eighth birthday. I was the oldest of five. We were eight, seven, five, four and one. The only way I could 'andle it was to focus on me brothers and sister. I made it my goal to make 'em laugh so 'at 'ey could forget about being sad. I would teach 'em skits and songs and later when we were older we'd walk up to Dad's pub and perform. I never knew if we actually earned the laughs and the applause or if they were merely the result of being the owner's children. The fact that my father always bought a round may have 'elped."

"I'm sorry about your mom."

"I'm sorry about your grandpa."

"OH! MY! GOD! This time it *is* a brownish Jeep. It really is!" Liz yelled from the backseat.

And it was, but it wasn't Jeremy's brown Jeep.

"Settle down, Liz!" Chad said, turning around to face her. (I liked how he said 'settle' without pronouncing the t's.) "What's the worst that can happen? If 'e follows you, break it off with 'im. Tell 'im to get lost. Tell 'im you're with me."

"Chadwick, you're sweet."

The sweetest, I thought. Now that Liz was awake, she sucked all of our attention to her, like a beautiful blond vacuum cleaner.

"Wouldn't that just be the most rotten thing a guy could do?" Liz asked. "Follow his girlfriend across the continent—"

"*Country*," I corrected.

"Country. Just because he doesn't trust her. Tell him, Tally. Tell Chadwick how loyal I am to my boyfriends."

"It's the truth. She has been loyal to all five hundred and thirty-nine of them."

"Tally!"

"Okay, two hundred and forty-seven of them."

"Tal."

"It's not the most rotten thing anyway," Chad said. "I've done much rottener."

"Like what?" Liz and I both said at once.

"Oh, Lord, I really shouldn't tell you, should I? You don't really know me and you might get the wrong impression."

"No, you really should tell us. What? What did you do?" Liz begged, reaching over and pounding Chad on the shoulder with her fist.

"I was quite young actually, so please take 'at into consideration."

"How young is young?" I liked details.

"Fifteen. Sixteen at the most. I 'ad this girlfriend, Rachel, and, well, she was me first. She was me entire school's first actually, but I didn't know 'at then. Anyway, I became obsessed with Rachel. She was quite lovely really and I never imagined in all my days 'at she'd tumble with me. 'At's what we called it, *tumbling*. Well, one night she breaks a date. Tells me 'er aunty and cousin are in town and she 'as to entertain them. I was put out, but I knew 'ow her mother could be. I 'ad nothing else to do so I dropped by the McDonald's where I worked."

"You had McDonald's in England?" Liz asked.

"This was 'ere in America, Lizabeth. We moved to Chicago when I was twelve. But yes, they do 'ave McDonald's in England."

"Let him finish his story," I told her. (I liked how he said "*Mac*-Donald's" with the accent on the *Mac*.)

"Well, as long as I was there hanging around, my manager said I might as well run the drive-up since they were short-'anded. So, I'm at the drive-through window and this car pulls up. This shiny, black Corvette. Lord, I love those cars. And this kid orders, I don't know, shakes or something, and when I lean over to 'and them out the window, there's Rachel in the passenger seat! Well, I want to strangle this guy, so I dive through the window, through those little flip doors, through the car window, and I land on top of 'im! The horn goes wild and Rachel's screaming, "Chad, he's my cousin. Honest!"

"Was he?" I wanted to know.

"What do you think?" he asked me.

"I don't know. How would I know?"

"What do you think, Lizabeth?"

"I think your ass must be a lot smaller than mine to fit through that window."

The next few hours were spent sharing our bests and worsts. The best thing we ever did in school. The worst thing we ever did in school. Our best job, worst job. Best friend, worst friend. Best vacation, worst vacation. This was the stuff Liz thrived on. She was telling Chad the truth when she said that basically she was the entertainment.

"Okay, okay," she said, leaning over the seat, her face right there between Chad and me. "The best meal I ever ate was at this place called the Polo Club somewhere in New York City. My father's friend took us there for my sweet sixteen. He and his wife and my dad and I had four waiters for our table. All to ourselves. They practically wiped your mouth for you. The food was for angels."

"And your worst meal?" Chad asked her.

"Every damn one I've ever cooked!" she said, laughing.

We were starting to run out of best and worsts. There was about two seconds of silence, then Liz said, "What's the meanest thing you've ever done? Tally, you first. Actually, I know what it is, but I want you to tell it."

"What? What are you talking about?" I asked.

"You know."

"I don't know. Meanness is your department. Meanness and wickedness."

"Come on, spit it out, Tally," Chad said.

"I honestly don't know what she's talking about. I'm not denying it; I just don't know what she's referring to."

"Well, while it comes to you, I'll tell you mine," Liz said. "In high school, my best friend was Casey Deans. Her boyfriend died in a motorcycle accident a week before our senior prom. I begged her to come with me and my boyfriend but she said no. So I promised her that after the dance I'd have Bobby drop me off and I'd sleep over. But I got bombed and slept instead in Bobby's car. Not only did I not show up at her house I made her lie to my dad the next day and tell him that I spent the night at her house. We weren't really friends after that. I've always felt bad about it."

"You better not ditch me like that in Daytona," I warned.

"Oh, come on. Give me a little more credit. I was fifteen," she said.

"You said you were a senior. You were seventeen or eighteen," I corrected.

"Okay, something like that. Did you remember your meanest thing?"

"No."

"*Meow. Meow.* Does that ring a bell?"

"Oh, that. That wasn't mean. That was practical and I had every right."

"Let's 'ear it, girls," Chad said.

"It's nothing," I said. "The girls in the apartment upstairs from us had a cat. The darn thing was psycho, running around all the time. It kept me up at night. And pets aren't allowed in our building anyway. So I reported them and they had to get rid of the cat."

"There! Isn't that the meanest thing?" Liz asked Chad.

"Actually, I say 'Bravo, Tally' since I despise cats."

I smiled and then asked him what was the meanest thing he ever did.

"Me? There's not a mean bone in me body. Some lean, mean muscles," he said, flexing a bicep, "but no mean bones. I'm just a softy...well, there was that time at Disney World three years ago. I imagine 'at would qualify as mean by some standards."

"What, what did you do? Tell me, tell me," Liz begged.

"You might blame it on the temperature. It was almost one 'undred degrees everyday we were there. Me mates and me were melting, tired of waiting in the long lines.

135

Then just as we were passing by the men's room I spotted a wheelchair parked near the door. I was struck with an ingenious idea. I swiped the wheelchair, 'ad me mates push me around all day, and we were first on all the rides!"

"That's just terrible!" I said. "Just think about that poor handicapped man without his wheelchair!"

"It wasn't 'is *personal* wheelchair. It said 'Property of Disney World' or something like that."

"I think it was pure genius," Liz told him.

"After all, I was quite young. Thirteen or fourteen," Chad said.

"You said it was three years ago. You were eighteen or nineteen," I corrected.

"Oh, something like that. Why is it you are so bloody obsessed with insignificant details?" he asked me. "Maybe it's a doctor thing. My sister is exactly the same way."

"AAAAHHHHHHHH!" Liz screeched. "It's a brownish Jeep. Oh, no wait, it's purple-ish. No, it's— No, it's not. Okay, okay, another false alarm. Go back to your bickering."

"I need to take a whiz," Chad said to me. "Can we pull over at the next rest stop?"

"Only if you promise not to steal any wheelchairs parked at the men's room door."

"Maybe I will and maybe I won't."

I almost smarted off back to him but he'd pushed the Beatle's tape back in and was singing along with Paul McCartney to that little tune "When I'm Sixty-Four." *Indicate precisely what you mean to say. You're sincerely wasting away.* He sounded just like Paul McCartney. Okay, I'll admit…that did make me smile.

Walking back to the car after our bathroom break, Liz said, "Tally you look absolutely awful. There are bags, no, suitcases, no, satchels under your eyes. You go ahead and sprawl out in the back for a while. I can manage the front seat for a little bit."

I was tired and so even though I knew Liz had an ulterior motive, I hopped in the back and fell asleep listening to Liz tell Chad all about Jeremy. The last thing I heard her say was this: "Jeremy would be the perfect boyfriend—he's fantastic looking, smart, and rich—if only he had a different personality. Nicer. And better manners. A conscience wouldn't hurt either."

I woke up to the sound of her throaty laugh. It was morning. I looked at my watch. It was almost ten o'clock. We were only an hour away from Daytona Beach. When I inquired as to why no one bothered to wake me up to take my shift, Chad said, "You were sleeping so soundly. You never stirred. And this one, well, she never stopped talking so she kept me awake."

Liz said, "Let me see your eyes, Tally. See, no more bags. Good. You needed the sleep."

Sure, I did, I thought. *And you needed the time to move in on Chad Buckingham.*

I rubbed the sleep from my eyes and looked out the window. Palm trees! I had never seen them before and I wanted to shout, but I knew Liz, who had vacationed every spring in Florida, would just laugh. They were so exotic! Tall and graceful, they reminded me of Liz.

When we arrived, Chad insisted on helping Liz and I get settled in our room since there were no bellboys to be found. After he tried out both of our beds, informing us that either one would suit him fine, he offered to buy us lunch and so we followed him down to the poolside café. After lunch we walked Chad to the hotel lobby where his "unofficial" girlfriend was supposed to pick him up. Liz hugged him. I just rubbed the scar at the base of my jawbone and told him to meet us back here in the lobby on Saturday morning at eight.

"Eight*ish* or on the dot?" he asked me, smiling.

"Let's just say if you're not here by eight, we leave without you." Before I could say I was just kidding, a hot red convertible pulled up out front and honked. Two blondes in baseball caps and sunglasses waved excitedly to Chad.

"Thanks for the lift, girls," he said and trotted to the car. Then, "See you Saturday!" as he threw his duffel bag in the back seat and then hopped, literally hopped, in himself. I walked to the elevator wondering which one was technically *not* his girlfriend.

Liz and I did nothing but lie on the beach all day and hang out in the bars all night. Liz kept a constant lookout for Jeremy, who called several times each day to say he would be arriving shortly. I knew he was bluffing, but Liz thought she spotted either him or his brown Jeep a thousand and one times a day. It was tiring to say the least. But by Wednesday she stopped looking and relaxed.

We met so many people from all around the country. We danced with lots of guys, always giving fake names. I was Lottie and Liz was Sloane. We ate and ate and ate, then forced ourselves up each morning for an exhilarating run on the beach. I hadn't been so free from stress and strain in a long time. It felt wonderful not to have to worry about studying and papers and exams. I found myself wishing the trip wouldn't end.

Friday, the day before we were to leave, Liz announced that she was sick of sand so we spent the day sunning out by the pool. Liz lay lifeless, nursing a gargantuan hangover while I turned the last few pages of a medical mystery I had brought along. I had just reached the part where you find out the x-ray technician did it, when Liz let out a heart-stopping gasp.

I looked up to see Jeremy walking toward us. He had two tall drinks in his hand. Fancy drinks with paper umbrellas. It wasn't until he was standing almost right above me did I realize that it wasn't Jeremy at all, but someone who looked incredibly, unbelievably, exactly like him.

"Hello," he said to me. To *me*. "Would you care for a Fuzzy Navel? I somehow ended up with two of them."

I turned to look at Liz. Surely, he must be addressing her and not me. After all, he was wearing sunglasses and so I was unable to see exactly where his eyes were directed.

"Yes, you," he said and laughed.

I sat up a little straighter. My hand found its way to the scar on my jawbone, but just in time I smiled and said, "Why thank you very much, but I don't drink—"

"I do! I do!" Liz said, bobbing up and down. "I drink like a fish. Like a shark actually."

"Ahhhhh!" Jeremy's double said and walked over to Liz. *Poof!* I was a drawing sketched in invisible ink.

His name was Ryan. He was from Sacramento and he was just what Liz had been wishing for: Jeremy with personality. And good manners—he did buy me a lemonade and asked me some polite questions about nothing.

Later, Liz roped me into joining Ryan and some of his friends at a pizza place a few blocks from our hotel. The night was bearable, even kind of fun, until the owner announced their tenth annual spring break wet tee shirt contest.

"I'm outta here," I told Liz. "Come on, let's go."

"No! I'm staying. I might even enter!"

"You wouldn't!"

"Depends on the prize. Go ahead and go. I'll be fine. I'll be home by midnight. Or something like that."

I caught a cab and then a late night movie in the hotel room. Jimmy Stewart and that one actress with the wavy blond hair and dimples. You know who I mean. Then, even though it was ninety outside I took a hot bath and called my mom to say hi. When I turned out the lights at one a.m., Liz wasn't back. At one-thirty I wondered how long it had taken Casey Deans, her best friend in high school, to figure it out—Liz wasn't going to show. I got up and secured the dead bolt.

A little after two I heard someone knocking on the door. Even though I wasn't asleep I considered pretending I was. Where would she go? What would she do? I shuffled over to the door, unbolted it and opened it up. There was Chad Buckingham standing there with the worst black eye I had ever seen.

"Chad?! What's going on? Have you seen Liz?"

"Liz? Tally, I can barely see you. May I please come in?"

I waved him in, duffel bag and all. I stood there staring at him. Finally I shook my head and sighed. Then I grabbed the ice bucket from the credenza and said, "Make up a good one while I get you some ice. Maybe I can muster up some sympathy."

"Well, I warned you from the start it was pathetic."

I gently touched the swollen skin at his temple. "I'll say."

It really was pathetic. And typical, for a guy. Turned out the blonde who was not technically his girlfriend was officially someone else's fiancée. She'd led Chad on, even let him stay at her family's summerhouse. Chad was in the pool when the fiancé showed up. "He followed her from Chicago. In a Jeep, no less."

"I wonder if he's related to Jeremy," I said.

"Did 'e ever show up?"

"No, and good thing, because I think he's been replaced."

"Is that so," Chad said and winced as he repositioned the ice pack I'd made for him.

"So I suppose now you have no place to stay," I said, trying to keep the hope out of my voice.

"Pathetic, isn't it?"

"I'll say."

"Actually, that's not why I'm 'ere. Not at all. I just didn't want to oversleep and miss our eight-o-clock-on-the-dot departure in the morning. This way, you can't leave without me."

"Well, I should anyway. You can't drive with that eye. You're of no use to me now," I said, smiling.

"The swelling will be down by morning. I'll be fine by my shift."

"I guess you can have Liz's bed. If she shows up though, you're on the floor."

"She won't, Tally," he said with a gentleness that touched me.

"I know," I said.

He kicked off his sandals and plopped down on Liz's bed, careful to hold the ice-filled towel in place. I climbed back into my bed and pulled the covers up around me. I was nervous so I turned out the light.

"They should have a class, you know," he said in the dark.

"For what?"

"Blondes 101. Or something like that. I'm partial to them and it's been me ruination. I may give 'em up for Lent."

"Lent is almost over."

"Still."

In the morning I was beside myself. Liz had never even bothered to call and now I was worried that something terrible had happened to her. I wanted to quickly shower and dress before Chad woke up, and as luck would have it, Liz called while I was showering. When I came out of the bathroom Chad was dressed—maybe they were traveling clothes—in that same white dress shirt and the hole-in-the-knees jeans that he'd worn the first day I'd met him. "She's fine," he said. "She's with what's-'is-name and she wants to know if you'll hate her forever if she drives back to Chicago with 'im."

"What? She can't— She always— Why do I even— The nerve of some people!"

"I'll say. 'Ere's 'er number."

After speaking to my unremorseful roommate, I told Chad I didn't know if I could forgive her for this one. "It's Casey Deans all over again. Well, if you ask me, she just topped her own record for taking advantage of people. If that's possible."

We sat on the beds facing each other. Chad listened to my tirade. He seemed genuinely concerned. When I was finished he said, "I have a confession to make. I think I may have topped my own record of taking advantage of someone."

"Worse than stealing a poor man's wheelchair? How? When?"

"Last night. I kissed a girl without her permission. While she was asleep. It wasn't right, but I couldn't help myself."

I touched my lips with my fingers. I could hope, couldn't I?

"You looked so lovely with the moonlight shining in your hair."

"*Me*?"

"Yes, you. What's so surprising about 'at?"

"Well, first of all, I don't have the right hair color."

"Never mind about 'at. I'm a reformed man. I'm boycotting everything yellow: blondes, bananas, lemons, sunshine, lightning bugs, dandelions…"

I was at a loss for words, so I said, "We'd better get going. It's already after eight."

I drove. His big old legs seemed to take up the whole front seat. He was fidgety. The car was terribly quiet without Liz. Five blocks into our eleven-hundred-mile trip back home, Chad said, "My mother was blond. Maybe that's why I'm partial to blondes. *Was* partial to blondes."

"Hmmmm," I said.

We decided on fast food for lunch. When the kid at the drive-through window handed me our sandwiches I couldn't help but think of Chad flying through those tiny flip doors.

Chad wanted to know what was so funny.

"Nothing," I said.

Five hours into our twenty-hour trip home he said, "I'll do double shift if you tell me what you're thinking."

"I was just thinking about how I would look if I dyed my hair blond."

Chad Buckingham smiled and said, "Don't do it!" and put his hand on my shoulder. Where it stayed for the rest of my shift.

◼

Rescuing Grace

"It is sweet to feel by what fine spun threads
our affections are drawn together."
—Lawrence Sterne (1713-1768)

ON SOFT BLACK nights when Matt has eaten too many rich foods and his entire body is protesting the assault, Peter pushes his way into his older brother's dreams. *Peter, Peter, Pumpkin Beater.*

Earlier that evening when he sat at his mother's kitchen table and she placed the enormous slice of her famous Emma's Spice Cake with Cream Cheese Frosting in front of him, Matt should have politely declined. "Eat," his mother had told him, hands on her aproned hips. For the good of his stomach, he should have declined.

There was something about Emma's Spice Cake with Cream Cheese Frosting. Oh, it looked innocent enough, but it was more than just cake. It was part celebration—Matt's father, Royce, had just turned fifty. It was part condolence—

Matt's wife, Grace, had left him three weeks ago. And it was part victory—Dwight Eisenhower, his father's man, had just been elected thirty-fourth president.

Matt ate the cake, every crumb, with ice cream even, two scoops, and real cream in his coffee.

There wasn't much to say. Emma stirred the cream in her coffee long after it was blended. Matt picked cake crumbs from the tablecloth. Royce cleared his throat a few times. Finally Royce broke the silence. "How are things at the bakery?" he asked Matt.

"Fine, fine."

"How's Willard?"

"Willard's peachy." Matt didn't intend to say *peachy*, it just slipped out. Peachy was not the best way to describe Willard Lindsor, Matt's boss and his father's close friend. He awaited his father's rebuke. *One should refer to one's boss with respect.* But Royce didn't look up from his cake; he just cleared his throat again.

It was true though, things were peachy with Willard. He and Matt got along well. Last year Willard had told Royce that the boy showed promise. Six months ago he promoted Matt to bread salesman. Matt loved his new job—delivering fresh bread, rolls and doughnuts to cafés, grocers and diners in small towns along Route 2.

"You're keeping an eye out for deer?" Royce asked his son.

"Yes, sir."

Lately Matt's been partial to two-word replies. That's about all you could get out of him these days. In fact, Grace had listed Matt's clipped conversations as one of the top reasons for leaving him.

Emma warmed up Matt's coffee. The room had grown quiet again. Even the small sounds, those usually absorbed by laughter and conversation, were amplified: Royce chewing cake, Emma setting her coffee cup on its saucer, the hot-water radiator hissing. A train, whistling as it passed on the other side of Royce's cornfields, sounded as if it were right on top of them.

"What about that colorful fella in Byron?" Emma asked with strained cheerfulness. "What's his name? You know, the cook."

"Lux. From Lux's diner."

"Right. Lux. Any interesting stories?" she asked, arching an eyebrow.

"No, not really."

Actually, there was a story about Lux, the ex-navy man turned cook, but it was raunchy and Matt didn't want to share it with his mother. He wasn't much good at kitchen table talk. That was Peter's department. Matt stared at Peter's chair and wondered how could he not be sitting in that chair.

Royce cleared his throat one last time. "Mind if I turn on the radio?"

Matt jumped up to do it for him, welcoming the static and the din of voices from the election returns.

Home in bed, Matt approaches sleep with greediness. It eludes him. He doesn't toss and turn, but lies lifelessly on his back while his stomach, which has declared war on the dairy products he's consumed, performs death-defying acrobatics. He thinks back to when he was a boy and sleep was easy. You never gave it a second thought. You lay your head on your pillow and you just hopped on sleep like a bum catching a train on the fly. Now, Matt couldn't hop on sleep if it were perfectly still, parked in the train yard.

Anxiousness inhabits his body and he finds himself lining up his worries on a tic-tac-toe-like grid on the ceiling. *Will I ever get to sleep? Will I dream about Peter again? Will Grace come home?*

He thinks about Grace while massaging his belly. She's only downstairs, after all. "Going home to mother" meant walking down one flight of stairs, for they'd lived in the apartment above Grace's parents for the first year of their marriage. Even so, he's only seen her three times in the three weeks since she left him. On Saturday mornings he would lift the front window shade to watch her catch the bus to Rockford Memorial Hospital where she worked as a nurse. His heart ached to see her dark wavy hair tucked up under her nurse's cap and her shapely legs in those white stockings.

She'd threatened to go to Chicago, to live with her cousin, Theresa. There were nursing jobs to be had in Chicago. She'd hop on a train and just go. But she hadn't left yet. At night Matt could feel her presence through the floors when he walked around the apartment in his bare feet, opening and closing the doors to all the rooms in the apartment except for the nursery. (He hadn't stepped foot into that room since he hung the rocking horse wallpaper back in May.)

The rumbling and gurgling in his stomach leads him to obsess about ulcers, hernias, intestinal obstructions, and stomach cancer. With a groan, he heaves himself out of bed and points his body in the direction of the medicine cabinet.

Finally, with his stomach calmed down a bit, he free falls into sleep, hoping to dream of Grace. Sleep feels like swimming. He dives deep down, remaining under as long as his breath holds out. When another abdominal cramp pinches his insides, he swims to the top for air. When the pain subsides, he dives down again. Ripe for nightmares, this restless state of sleep.

Peter comes to him, happy. He's not the least bit angry with Matt. In fact, he's smiling—that crooked smile of his, which had always reminded Matt of a happy jack-'olantern. He is still sixteen and handsome. He waits for Matt to take a final puff on his cigarette. When he flicks it to the ground Peter yells, "Go!"

Matt floats along side his kid brother. Peter is sixteen, Matt is nineteen. Usually in his dreams, Matt can't see himself, for as in real life he occupies his own body, but there he is—running as fast as his legs will take him. This is puzzling and Matt wonders if in fact he is dreaming, or maybe, he's actually reliving that night, a year ago this Friday. He looks around his dream: same cloudy October night, same hammock of a moon hanging in the charcoal sky, same soft-moaning wind pressing in. He can smell the organic aroma of autumn, feel the dampness on his cheek, and see a spray of his own breath in the air. It can't be a dream.

At top speed, the boys skate across their gravel driveway, arms flailing to keep upright, race around the barn passed the rusty John Deere, and trample through their father's stripped corn fields. Peter, with his second-child determination, maintains an arm's length lead throughout the race. They reach the creek, winded and breathless, Matt more than Peter due to his pack-a-day habit. Matt bends over, hands on his knees, and pants.

Peter shakes his head. "When you gonna quit smoking?"

"When you start up."

"Which is never."

"Exactly," Matt tells him, straightening.

They hear leaves crunching. In the thin evening light, Grace and her cousin Sally materialize from behind a stand of pine trees. Matt and Peter smile as they watch the girls cross the narrow creek, carefully stepping on the large stones that Matt set in place years ago, back when he and Grace pretended they hated each other.

Grace is wearing blue jeans and that red and black flannel jacket Matt likes so much. Pretty, round-faced Grace, with full lips, wavy brown hair, and flawlessly smooth skin that is cool as marble in the summer and warm as fresh baked bread in the winter.

Sally's a pretty girl, too, with pearly-gray eyes the color of rain clouds, offset by sunny, blond ringlets that bounce when she talks. Peter and Sally, newly acquainted, greet each other shyly.

Matt pretends that he doesn't see Grace's tears when he pecks her on the cheek. He takes her hand. This is the night of the Pumpkin-Bashing Party. In an effort to deter pumpkin smashing on Halloween night, Grace's grandpa hosts his annual party the day before Halloween.

As Grace's grandma serves up hot cider, Peter stealthily visits the mugs of certain friends, adding a splash of vodka from a bottle he's hidden inside his jacket. The pumpkin smashing commences with Matt and Peter going at it with competitive zeal. They hurl pumpkins, jump on pumpkins, kick pumpkins, whack them with baseball bats and wooden mallets. When they've expended their share of testosterone and are sickly satisfied to see pumpkin guts spilling from their victims, they join Grace and Sally who are sipping unadulterated cider by the fire.

The firelight holds Grace in a warm glow and suddenly Matt finds himself filled with desire. He slings his arm around her and pulls her to him. She holds out her mug, pretending cider has spilled out, and gives him a "not here!" look. Embarrassed, he lets go and directs his attention to his brother who is being crowned king. Matt smiles and claps along as the kids chant *Peter, Peter, Pumpkin Beater.* But then he grows sad, wondering what everyone would think if they knew Grace was pregnant.

Peter wears the crown Grace's grandma carved from— you guessed it, a pumpkin—with verve and panache, holding it on his head with one hand as he chases Sally around the fire. Peter and the vodka are making spectacles of themselves. Matt thinks Peter must have it bad for Sally. He can usually gage the level of his brother's infatuations by the extent to which he makes a fool of himself.

The sky turns licorice-colored and a light fog settles upon them. The sliver of the moon looks as if it were draped with soft, white mesh. The fire dies out and the kids scatter. Some are heading over to the viaduct to hop freight trains, some are trekking over to Zander's farm to do some cow-tipping, and a small but brave contingent are formulating a plan to scare Beulah the witch out of her house near Muller's Dairy. Grace whispers to Matt in no uncertain terms that train hopping is insane, cow tipping is barbarian, and Beulah Thermon is just a poor old crippled woman. They decide to head over to Bing's Drive-In on South Main Street for a root beer. Tromping through muddy fields, they cut over to walk along the train tracks.

"Don't you just hate *walking* to a drive-in?" Sally whines as her curls bob.

"Hop on!" Peter says, offering his back. He's still wearing the pumpkin crown and Matt wonders how it is that he doesn't look ridiculous. He knows *he* would look ridiculous. Sally jumps up on Peter's back, piggyback style, and they zigzag walk on the railroad ties. Matt watches them. Suddenly, he feels so much older than Peter. Years older. He fights a fatherly urge to tell him to quit walking on the railroad ties, but he knows Peter would only laugh and say, "You worry too much."

To Peter, the sun shone each and everyday…somewhere in the world. And nothing could stop him from dancing in that sunshine. If Matt wanted to worry about good grades, good manners, good graces, that was fine. Meanwhile, Peter tap-danced. And Matt watched, wondering how choosing carefree over careful came so easy.

Matt sees Peter gently drop Sally to the ground. Peter runs off the tracks with Sally chasing behind, giggling. He flings his pumpkin crown into a ditch and then hurls the empty vodka bottle high into the air. On its return the bottle shatters on the steel tracks. Peter laughs devilishly as he and Sally disappear around a bend. So young, so free. A baby will age you, Matt thinks. *I'll be a hundred when I'm thirty.*

He turns to Grace. "You smell like campfire," he teases, hugging her closer.

"Well, you smell like cigarette smoke. When you gonna quit?"

"In nine months," he says, trying to smile.

"Make that eight."

Rounding the bend, they see Peter and Sally up ahead, sitting on the tracks, locked in a passionate first kiss.

"Maybe we should tell them," Grace says, surprising Matt. She'd made him promise over and over again that he wouldn't utter a word about her condition until after they'd eloped. She'd made him cross his heart and hope to die. Matt knows she's scared. She's certain her father will disown her when he finds out about the baby. He's about to ask her if she's sure, but suddenly she drops his hand and says, "Wait." They both freeze and listen... The muffled but familiar *CHUG-chug-chug-chug-CHUG-chug-chug-chug* approaching from the west brings terror to Matt's stomach.

"Train! Train!" he and Grace shout in unison. "Get the hell off the tracks!" Matt screams and takes off running with Grace close behind. He runs on legs that feel wobbly and unconnected from the rest of him. All the while he hears his father's voice yelling warnings in his ear: *Never walk on the wood. Never jump a train on the fly. Never cross in between cars. It can take a mile for a train to make a complete stop.*

For God's sakes, never sit on the tracks. But there they are, Peter and Sally, not just sitting on the tracks, but oblivious to everything but each other.

As Matt gets within a hundred feet or so of them, the steam whistle blows, nasal and diluted, but lusty enough to blow the stardust out of the lovers' eyes. Since Peter's arms are already wrapped around Sally, it takes nothing for him to bring her along with him as he dives off the tracks. They roll and roll, dropping into a ravine, and by the time Matt and Grace reach them, they're laughing so hard they can't stop.

Puffs of angry steam escape from Matt's nostrils as he watches the two of them. But when he opens his mouth to speak, instead of harsh words, he releases a loud and monstrous belch.

The burp startles him awake. In the dark he fumbles for the alarm clock, thinking it's his alarm ringing. But the clock just ticks and Matt realizes it's his own body sounding off. He clutches at the pain in his stomach, giving up on sleep, which is over-rated, and dreams, which are terrifying. He knows how it all ends anyway. Hell, it's two a.m. He might as well get up. He washes and dresses. In the small, cold kitchen he brews dark coffee, enough to fill a 2-quart thermos.

At three a.m., he starts up his turquoise blue '50 Chevy and drives the short distance to The Colonial Bread Company on Cedar Street. In the garage, Matt finds his bread truck, washed, gassed up, and loaded with the order he'd placed the night before—hundreds of loaves of sandwich bread, hot-dog and hamburger buns, rolls, and doughnuts. When Matt first started delivering, the yeasty aroma of the fresh baked goods drove him wild. Now, he can't even smell the bread. Now, it's just bread. His product, what he sells, what he stocks. A commodity. It's not bread so much anymore as it is what puts bread on the table.

He jams the stubborn gear into drive and sets out on his 125-mile run. Heading south on Main Street, he passes deserted storefronts, empty gas stations, and dark, sleeping houses. Route 2, which runs along the Rock River, is all curves and bends, but Matt could drive it with his eyes closed.

He's a careful, defensive driver, obeying the speed limit and the no-passing zones, always with an eye out for deer. His boss had warned him about his predecessors, one who was fired after his third speeding ticket, and another who swerved to miss a deer and instead hit a semi. With his eyes focused on the road, he takes no notice of the glorious autumn scenery as morning emerges—clear skies the color of a newborn's eyes, trees with leaves that are buttered and jammed with varying shades of goldenrod, ochre, plum, and whose branches form a soft canopy overhead. Once his favorite season, now Matt tolerates autumn. He's found he can't breathe around campfires. He grows queasy when he smells pumpkin. Gets jumpy when he hears a train whistle.

His route takes him through tiny, blink-your-eye-and-you'll-miss-it towns—Byron, Stillman Valley, Oregon, Forreston, Davis Junction, Rochelle—towns he'd never had reason to visit. He'd discovered early on that no matter where you went people were just people. It was the diners that had surprised him; they were a world unto themselves, spilling over with a cast of characters.

His first stop is Lux's All-Nite Diner, sandwiched between the post office and a beauty parlor that Lux says is run by "queers." Every other day Lux dares Matt to drive into town on a Saturday for a cut and a shave to see for himself. Matt loads Lux's order onto a dolly then backs his way through the front door. It's not quite four in the morning. The usual two customers are perched at the counter, coffee cups glued to their hands.

"Kid!" Lux greets him. "Look, Sandy, Peanut, it's the kid. Damn, I like that kid. He's a shit load better than the last ass-hole that delivered my bread. I swear that ass-hole sat on my hamburger buns. Probably farted on them, too."

"Morning, Lux. Guys," Matt says and heads to the kitchen to unload the order.

Lux pops his head in. "Got time for some hot cakes, kid? I can tell you ain't eaten nothin' yet."

Matt smiles. It's hard to resist Lux's hot cakes. He would never admit it, even under torture, but they were better than Grace's, better than his mother's. He heads out front and hands Lux the invoice. Lux pays him from the register. "So, you want cakes or don't you?"

"If you make it quick," Matt says, smiling. He sits at the counter and shovels in pads of hot, spongy pancakes coated with maple syrup. Lux throws in some scrambled eggs for the hell of it and Matt finds the food soothing to his sensitive stomach.

"Well?" Lux says, leaning over the counter, talking into Matt's face. Matt can smell the alcohol.

"Well, what?"

"Well, I don't know. How's the cakes, or you get laid lately, or when you gonna let the queers next store cut your hair, or you think they'll close down that dirty hole-in-the-wall they call a diner up on Kilmer Street?"

"Delicious, not recently, never, and hell-if-I-know."

Lux and Sandy and Peanut laugh at Matt. He smiles. He likes this place. He's different here. He's not Peter's brother or Grace's husband or his father's son. Grace would be appalled if she heard Matt talking like this. His mother would cover her mouth with her small hand. His father would wonder what kind of boy he'd raised. Still, they are entertained by the "cleaner" stories Matt brings home about Lux. Stories about his card tricks, and his skill with a griddle and a spatula. His way around words, like instead of saying *I wasn't born yesterday*, Lux says, *I was born at night, but I wasn't born* last *night*. And the way he sings. Lux has a voice smooth as his maple syrup. Smoother. In all honesty, Matt has misrepresented Lux to his parents, who must imagine him as a sort of vaudeville performer. If they ever met the real Lux, they would think there'd been some kind of mistake. This man, with the yellow crew cut, ruddy complexion, wrinkled white tee shirt with a pack of cigarettes folded under the sleeve could not possibly be the man about which their son had been speaking. Matt doesn't tell his parents about what Sandy and Peanut have told him—about Lux's drinking problem, or the way he cusses, about his indecent tattoos, that he slaps his girlfriend around, that he used to hop freight trains for the thrill of it, or that he did some jail time in the forties for assaulting some guy. Peanut, drunk himself one morning, told Matt that once, Lux had tried to kill himself, tried to hang himself in the kitchen.

And Matt will never tell them about the morning, a few weeks back, when he found Lux passed out on the floor behind the counter. It had scared the hell out of him. After he found a pulse, he ran back to his truck for his thermos of coffee, and forced cupfuls down Lux, until he sobered up some. Luckily, Sandy came along and took over so that Matt could continue on his route.

Matt finishes up the breakfast, wipes his mouth with a napkin, throws a quarter tip on the counter, and blasts out the door. He's got a schedule after all. Next stop is Kilmer Street Cafe and then on to greasy spoons and mom-and-pops and corner grocers and tiny taverns. If he veers off his schedule, even by a couple of minutes, the City of Seattle Flyer'll hold him up in Davis Junction. Its rattling cars—a half mile of them—would only put him off schedule by five or ten minutes, but early on it had become a game of Matt's to beat that slick, silver passenger train.

At the end of the day, Matt pulls the truck into the bakery garage. He's spent. His eyes burn, his head aches and his driver's foot cramps up on him. Before, home and Grace and a hot meal would be waiting for him, making it all worthwhile. Now, there's nothing to go home to. And he can't even look forward to a good night's sleep.

He eats standing up at the kitchen sink: a hot dog, stabbed with a fork and roasted to blister black over the gas burner, and creamed corn, cold, right out of the can. He walks through the apartment opening and closing doors. At the nursery door, he pauses, but then walks away.

Even without dairy products, Matt's stomach turns somersaults and he sleeps only sporadically, dipping in and out of consciousness.

Once again, Peter comes to him, happy, hysterical even. Matt doesn't recall last night's dream ending with the caption: *To Be Continued*, but here it is, right where he left off. And there Peter is, rolling around in the ravine with Sally, laughing like a sloppy drunk. Behind them the Union Pacific rolls past and it would be a toss up as to who or which is emitting more steam—Matt or the train.

This time his voice works: "Get up, you idiot. Don't you know you scared the shit out of us?"

"What?" Peter says, sobering at the tone of his brother's voice. "Oh, the train?"

"Didn't you hear us screaming?" Grace asks.

Sally blushes and says "Sorry" as she stands and brushes off her clothes.

"We better get these girls home," Matt says, extending a hand.

"You worry too much," Peter says as he accepts Matt's hand and allows him to heave him up. Peter hangs on to his brother's hand longer than he needs to, gripping it harder than necessary. He says something else but his words are drowned out by the rattle and clank of the jostling freight cars.

The four of them climb out of the ravine, silent with their own thoughts as the train continues to chug along. Then, without warning, Peter grabs Sally's hand and pulls her away from the group. They run alongside the train while Matt wonders what kind of vodka it was that has stolen his brother's sanity.

"Peter!" Matt calls out sharply, before breaking into a gallop of his own. "Don't be stupid!" It frightens Matt to think about how far his brother might go just to impress this girl.

Once again, Matt finds Grace running a few steps behind him. "Are you guys crazy?" he hears her scream. They catch up to Peter and Sally, begging them to stop running. Peter ignores them, running toward a freight car ladder. He positions himself, grabs the rung, and pulls himself up. Sally does the same.

"All aboard!" she sings, throwing her head back, letting the wind pull her fine blond curls.

"Come on, you guys, get off," Matt yells, still running alongside.

Then, something he never in his life could have predicted happens: Grace, the most careful, levelheaded person he's ever known, leaps into the air and catches a train on the fly.

"Grace?!" Matt screams as he chases the train. "What are you doing?" Then he trips on a fallen tree branch and collapses like a folding chair. Lying in the dirt, he watches Grace and Peter and Sally drift slowly away from him.

The rest of the dream plays out in slow motion: Matt pulling himself up, forcing his legs to run. Watching in horror as his show-off brother decides that holding onto the ladder isn't intoxicating enough; he has to climb to the roof. And standing triumphantly upon the roof isn't thrilling enough; he has to start jumping the cars, which are spaced about a foot and a half apart.

Matt's brain goes into circuit overload as he watches Peter move quickly down the line, falling into an easy rhythm—step, step, step, *hop*, step, step, step, *hop*.

Matt pleads with Grace to get down, but he doesn't take his eyes off Peter, who continues to step, step, step, *hop*. "Grace, think about the baby!" he shouts, still not taking his eyes off of Peter, but keeping close to Grace, ready to catch her if she decides to jump. She doesn't move, but she does begin to cry. She calls out to him.

On raw impulse, Matt jumps up and pulls her with all his might from the ladder. Not until they are safely on the ground does he realize the madness of his actions—they could have easily been pulled under the train. Grace lies sobbing in his arms. "I don't want to live, Matt," she whimpers. "I don't even want to live."

"It'll be all right, honey, I promise," he tells her. "Everything will be all right." He holds her close, even as he is torn between holding her and leaving her to chase after his crazy, intoxicated, infatuated brother. Grace clings to him, her arm tightly around his neck. He kisses her hair and wipes away her tears. How could he know that Peter has accidentally broken his rhythm, and stepped when he should have hopped. Matt hears a shrill scream. It's Sally.

The train's steel wheels shriek against the tracks. The brakes expel a desperate whoosh of air. They grind and screech. Someone sounds the bell and it doesn't stop clanging. Matt all but drops Grace to the ground. He runs, trying not to think. *Don't think. Don't think.*

When he reaches Sally she's hysterical, talking gibberish, shaking violently. Peter is nowhere in sight. The train finally comes to a complete stop and Matt sees some of the crewmembers running toward them with flashlights. It will take Matt months and months before he can again remember his brother as sixteen, fresh-faced, and so good-looking it makes your heart ache, instead of how he found him that night: in pieces.

Matt wakes in a cold sweat. With his eyes wide open he waits for morning, which for him is the middle of the night. He blames his stomach but he knows that what steals his sleep is the guilt. He knows it. Grace knows it. The guilt about saving Grace. Rescuing Grace instead of Peter, his own flesh and blood. If only Grace hadn't hopped that train. If only they'd gone cow tipping instead. If only Peter hadn't swiped that bottle of vodka. If only...Matt was haunted by "if onlys." If only he'd told Peter about Grace being pregnant maybe he would have understood why he had to save Grace first. If only.

At the bakery he wonders how he can face the day. He turns the key to his truck and drives in a daze. He drives too fast for conditions. He passes in no-passing zones. He takes turns at torturous speeds. He brakes fast. He drives too close to the cars in front of him. Maybe he'll just keep on driving—never turn back. For without Peter, without Grace, without the baby—who had come too early and died during delivery—there was nothing. It boggled his mind to think that by saving Grace he'd lost her.

He parks in front of Lux's and kills the engine. Something's wrong. The place is dead. No lights, no movement. The doorknob won't budge when Matt gives it a twist. He knocks. Looks through the window. There's no life at all. It's strange, but then, maybe Lux is just sick or sick of being open twenty-four hours a day. Matt walks around back, but everything is locked up tight. His stomach growls, wanting Lux's pancakes. Reluctantly, he starts up the truck and takes off up Kilmer Street. He'll try again on the trip back.

Since Lux's was closed, Matt is early to his other stops. He asks around about Lux, but no one has any information to offer other than "sometimes he lays one on and can't get up." Ahead of schedule, Matt stops off the road in Stillman Valley and helps himself to a couple of the doughnuts that were to go to Lux's. A train whistles in the distance—did it always sound so sad, like a plaintiff wail? Or did it only start to sound that way after Peter's accident? Matt glances at his watch. Time to go. Got a train to beat.

He has all but forgotten about Lux when he pulls up to the crossing grade in Davis Junction. Is he mistaken, or is there a car stalled on the tracks? He drives closer and sure enough, it's a car all right, a rusty gray Ford that looks like Lux's. The whistle blows and Matt doesn't even have to look to the right to know the train is there. Without thinking, Matt screams, "Peter! Look out! Look out!" He floors it, connects bumper to bumper with the car and pushes it forward until both cars clear the tracks. Matt feels the whoosh of air and hears the train's horn as it whizzes past him. He releases the breath he's been holding, slams the bakery truck into park, and runs to the car. At first, he doesn't see anyone and he begins to feel foolish for rescuing an empty car. But then he sees a man slumped over the wheel, and as he approaches, he sees that it is Lux. He knocks on the window, then tries the door handle. It's locked. He bangs on the window, confused. He doesn't even realize that he's shouting Peter's name instead of Lux's. Doesn't realize it until a policeman is standing next to him, saying, "This man is Lux Pearlman, buddy, not Peter. Can you tell me what the hell happened here?"

In the end, the policeman told Matt more than Matt could tell him. Mainly, Lux had done this before, a couple of times. "If he wants to do away with himself, he should just blow off his head instead of putting innocent people in danger," the cop says, banging on the car window.

On the way home, Matt gets lost. Somehow he misses a turn and ends up in Freeport, adding forty-five minutes to his drive home. He blames the trees and the sky. The leaves are on fire with color, and the sky is the color of Peter's eyes. Matt's own eyes are watery as he wonders when autumn arrived. He hadn't noticed.

He pulls up in front of his house, well, Grace's parents' house. He shifts to park but leaves the engine running. Why bother expending the energy needed to walk up those stairs? There's nothing there. Unexpectedly, Matt is seized by fatigue. He leans back in the seat and closes his eyes, surprised and relieved to find the sleep train waiting for him. He climbs on. All aboard! He sleeps a thick, cocooned, dreamless sleep. There are no images, no sounds. Just soft, sweet sleep.

Matt is startled awake by fingers tapping on his window. For a moment he believes he's in heaven, because never has Grace's round face looked more like an angel's. Still groggy with sleep, he rolls down the window.

"God, you're okay," Grace says, swallowing. "You looked dead, Matt. God."

He opens the truck door and gets out, letting the door slam shut. "I- I guess I fell asleep. I haven't been sleeping so well. I- I saved this guy today, Grace. From a train. I saved him."

Grace stares at him. "From a train?" she asks.

"It was Lux. Remember Lux, the cook? I thought it was Peter, but it was Lux. But I really thought it was Peter."

Grace looks at him funny. "Matt, your truck is still running."

"I'm tired of running, Gracey. All we've been doing is running."

Grace opens the door, reaches in the truck, turns the key and removes it from the ignition. She hands Matt his keys.

"Thanks," he says right before he feels his legs go weak. He can feel himself falling and he hopes Grace can catch him. He saved her once. He couldn't save everybody, but he saved her.

Matt feels like he's falling in slow motion. Grace is strong enough to break his fall but not strong enough to hold him up. They both collapse to the ground. "Oh, Matt," Grace says. Matt feels her arms around him. They sit in the street among the fallen leaves.

Maybe it's not too late, Matt thinks, reaching for a perfectly shaped and colored oak leaf. "For you," he says to Grace as he hands it to her. "It looks like an oak leaf but it's really an olive branch." Grace smiles, smoothing the leaf against her cheek.

Matt gets up first and pulls Grace up. She leans on her husband and together they climb the stairs to their apartment. Maybe Grace will make hotcakes for dinner.

◖

Arlene Speaking

"No one knows like a woman
how to say things which are at once gentle and deep."
—Victor Hugo (1802-1885)

WHAT WOULD IT be like, you may wonder, to be voiceless in a world that never stopped talking? Perhaps you already know…perhaps you are shy or reticent or maybe someone has led you to believe your opinion counts for nothing. Or, possibly, you are one of those people who, when you open your mouth, find either stupid words flying out or your own foot forcing its way in. Perchance you have emigrated here from another country and you aren't confident of your English or you are embarrassed by your accent. Maybe you stutter or speak through your nose. Maybe your teeth have gone bad or your breath has turned malodorous or your dentures are ill fitting. Maybe you found along the way that no one ever listened to what you had to say anyway. Maybe you just have nothing more to say.

Even then, you're not *really* voiceless, are you? At least not in the way that Arlene Allerton is voiceless. A traumatic neck injury is what robbed Arlene of her voice, paralyzing her vocal cords and rendering her once velvety-smooth speaking voice rough and raspy, sometimes barely audible. Her own great grandbaby recoils from the sandpaper sound of it, making her feel freakish, like a mute monster.

When Arlene lost her voice she lost more than her voice. She lost her job, too. For thirty-four years she had worked as a switchboard operator at the busiest hospital in New Orleans. After the vocal cord damage, she'd had to give up her position and take a spot as a housekeeping aid on the night shift. Her daughter Lucy had tried to talk her out of it, saying the work was beneath her, but Arlene accepted it for what it was—a safety net. You had to have insurance until Medicare kicked in, didn't you? Since Harvey was out of the picture she'd had to look out for herself. (He took their nest egg right along with him back before the state of Louisiana repealed the "head and master" law which gave control of marital property exclusively to husbands.) Plus, she took comfort in knowing that here was a job that wouldn't require much talking.

There's not much to Arlene anymore. If you saw her you might think she looked more like a little girl with wrinkles than a senior citizen. Always tiny, she now barely measured five feet. Skin covering bones. As a youth, she had been athletic and plucky, wiry like a boy. Her body was solidly snug and she learned early on how to throw a good punch, having trailed a clutch of brothers. A powerhouse in a petite package, she'd had no problem asserting herself both physically and vocally. Two husbands changed all that, each contributing to her voice loss long before she truly lost it. But somehow she'd managed to maintain her physical stamina. Some people are strong simply because they have no other choice.

From the very start the night shift suited her. She was surprised by this, always being a morning person. It was odd to sleep during daylight, but after Harvey left, she slept with the light on anyway, so it wasn't difficult to adjust. She didn't pop out of bed like she used to, and she did need a two-cup caffeine jump-start, but by the time she parked her old car in the hospital lot, she was ready for her day, or, in this case, night.

For the first two weeks on nights her daughter wouldn't talk to her. Mad about the whole thing, Lucy was. Didn't think a sixty-one year old woman should be doing "manual labor" and at night no less. Lucy wanted Arlene to come live with her and her daughters—one, an unwed mother of one, and the other, an unwed-high-school-drop-out-mother-to-be. No thank you was Arlene's answer; she'd raised her own four daughters, spoiled them so that even as adults they expected their mother to solve all their problems, to dole out money she didn't have, to baby-sit on a moment's notice, to wait on them hand and foot. Lucy was the worst. Arlene had practically raised Lucy's daughters and now was being recruited for the great grandchildren.

Arlene's family tree ran long on unwed mothers: Arlene, her mother before her, two of Arlene's daughters, and two of her granddaughters. As a young mother, Arlene had vowed that her daughters wouldn't fall into the same trap she had. What went wrong? Driven by loyalty and guilt Arlene had spent years helping out with the grandchildren, letting her daughters stay out all night, carrying on as if they were without a care in the world. After grand abuses—like the time Lucy asked Arlene to watch her baby while she took in a movie with a friend and then didn't come home for two days—Arlene would protest, threatening to put an end to her grandma services. But she was soft inside, and she loved the babies.

Arlene would have married Jerry Conner, Lucy's father, but he high-tailed it out of town the second Arlene informed him of her condition. With little help from her own mother or family, she raised Lucy. The job at the hospital was her saving grace. When she met Lloyd, one of the hospital's carpenters, Arlene felt kissed by the angels. They married and soon Arlene was pregnant with her second child, Sheila. All went well with the pregnancy and delivery, and Arlene settled easily into her maternity leave to care for her two daughters. But the baby was a fussy one, and one night, after several sleepless nights, Lloyd grabbed Arlene's arm just as she was about to rise from bed to nurse the child. He told her she was spoiling the baby, to let her cry for god's sake. Reluctantly, Arlene lay back down. But if there was ever a sound she could not stand it was a crying baby. After nearly twenty minutes of listening to the baby wail, Arlene rose to get her. Instead she got a fist in the eye. The first of many.

Not having to speak was just one of the advantages working nights had to offer; the bigger benefit was that she would no longer be so easily accessible to her daughters who were all guilty of tying up the switchboard with their petty complaints and faux melodrama. Working the night shift, Arlene felt free from the buttons and the buzzes of the switchboard but mostly she felt free from her daughters.

The best part was the quiet. If it weren't for the nurses and their obstreperous merriment, or the medical machinery with the interminable blips and bleeps, if it weren't for that, you could float on the quiet, or, not quiet, for a hospital is never truly quiet, but the forced hushedness of it all, the whooshes and the snoring and the drone of forgotten television sets. At night, there were no noisy floor buffers, vacuum cleaners, or water pick-up machines. There were no food service carts with rickety wheels. There were no visitors blocking doorways and breathing up all the oxygen. No one was paged over the loud speaker. Yes, Arlene blended in well at night, damp mopping, dusting, emptying waste cans, cleansing the bathrooms, the water fountains, and the pay phones, washing glass door panels, changing bed linen and towels, performing all her duties with an obsequious smile, rarely making eye contact with anyone other than the housekeeping officer.

It was wonderfully calming to be able perform one's job without words. And when she needed words, she simply whispered, which, on the night shift, was a perfectly acceptable way to speak. None of this, "Speak up, will you?" or "What's wrong, hoarse voice?" "Cat got your tongue?" "Laryngitis?" Usually, when Arlene spoke, people would swallow hard and clear their own throats, as if somehow this would be of help.

Well, speaking softly led to walking softly, which led to tiptoeing, creeping, sidling. Sometimes, Arlene startled people. One nurse—the one whose make-up appeared to have been applied with a paint-by-numbers technique— actually accused her of *lurking*. She didn't lurk, but she did have a distinct knack for blending in with the scenery: her gray hair, sallow skin, and taupe-colored uniform dress provided no contrast to the muddy walls of the hospital corridors. Not to mention her diminutive size. She enjoyed the obscurity, likened herself to a milk stain on a white linen tablecloth. To baby powder spilled on a clean white sheet. To a pair of white silk gloves dropped on snow-covered ground. To a ghost in the clouds. Oh, how she wished she had possessed this talent for fading into the woodwork back when she was married. Invisibility would have come in handy when Harvey or Lloyd got all juiced up.

Her favorite was the third floor, D wing: Maternity. *Knock, knock. Housekeeping.* She'd go about her duties, delivering clean linens, a box fan, an extra pillow, or some other sundry a new mother might request, and then sneak a peek at those pink- or chocolate- or caramel-colored babies as they nursed at their mother's breast or slept in the wheeled bassinets. The babies were her delight. She cooed silently at them, careful not to let the mothers catch her. Her housekeeping officer didn't allow much interaction with patients; neither did the nurse with the paint-by-numbers face. But Arlene had a heart for the young ones, and the ones who bore them—teenage mothers like her granddaughters, like her daughters, like herself, who had not an inkling of what lie ahead. She'd been sixteen, but now they were even younger—yesterday a fourteen-year-old, a fourteen-year-old! gave birth to a chubby, feisty boy. That's where Arlene was headed now, to the fourteen-year-old's room, 308, to deliver a vaporizer. Apparently, the poor thing was suffering from a bad cold and was having difficulty sleeping.

When Arlene arrived she found both mother and child in a state. The mother was pacing the room, cradling her unhappy baby. Who was shrieking louder was hard to tell. Arlene tried to be inconspicuous, tried to go about her business as quickly as possible, but just as she plugged in the vaporizer and adjusted the directional piece, the girl pleaded, "Take this baby!" and pushed the screeching child into Arlene's arms.

"They said he's waking up all the other babies in the nursery," the girl blubbered. "Like I'm supposed to do something about it. Like he'll listen to me or something. He's fixing to blow out his lungs, that's what he's doing."

Arlene cradled the baby and instinctively began bouncing him in her arms.

"I tried to nurse him, but he doesn't want me," the girl said, twisting her dingy white tee shirt around her body. She looked more like ten than fourteen. "I don't think I got a drop of milk in me. And besides, it really hurts. No one told me it would hurt," she cried, and then flung herself onto the bed.

Arlene stood there bouncing the bundle—which felt remarkably like a nice solid Easter ham—until memories of her own colicky baby came to mind and she began patting and pacing in addition to bouncing. If she'd had a voice of any kind she would have hummed. She did whisper a soft, "There, there," in her hoarse, husky voice, but who could hear it over the din? Arlene moved the blanket away from the baby's face to get a better look at him. He was red as nail polish and madder than her second-ex Harvey, when the Saints lost a game. The way his wee face was scrinched up also reminded Arlene of newborn Lucy. Lucy had been the kind of baby that made a woman consider permanent options, like tubal ligation. Colicky, demanding, inconsolable. Something that did work to soothe a wailing Lucy was to blow lightly on her face. Arlene looked up at the mother who had now buried her head under the pillow, which undulated to the rhythm of her whimpers. What the hey, Arlene thought, and blew lightly on the baby's face. Immediately the baby's crying subsided, replaced by hiccuppy gulps. Arlene blew again, circling his small face with her cool breath. He sighed and quieted, going limp in her arms as he finally gave in to sleep.

Arlene blinked with surprise, just as she always had when the trick worked with Lucy. She looked around the room, wishing there was someone to whom she could brag. See! No matter that her hands were coarse from cleaning, or that her voice was rough as a whiskery kiss, she knew how to hold a baby securely to her, and to blow sweet angel breezes his way. In Arlene's arms, the baby almost purred.

"It's a miracle!" whispered the girl, sitting up now and throwing the pillow aside. "I'm not kidding," she said a little louder, "it's a miracle! What'd you do anyway?"

Arlene just shrugged and walked and patted, feeling more powerful than she ever had in her life, demonstrating her soft blowing technique. Catching her reflection in the window she was surprised to see herself against the dark sky looking so tall, so visible, so indispensable. She felt mighty. She felt magic. Then she came to her senses and felt in danger of losing her job. But as soon as Arlene gently deposited the baby back into his mother's arms he started howling all over again, and the girl thrust him back to Arlene. "Please don't leave me," she pleaded. "Do it again. Make him stop. Make him stop!"

Arlene cleared her throat and whispered to the girl that she couldn't stay, that it was against the rules. She was sorry but she'd get fired. But when she tried to return the baby again, the mother refused to take him, holding her arms stiffly at her side. "No, no, I can't," she cried, turning away. "I'm just so tired," she said, flinging herself once again onto the bed. "I'm just so tired."

And so Arlene stayed. She planted herself in the rocking chair near the window and blew on that little red-faced boy as if he were hot soup needing to be cooled, and rocked as if there were no tomorrow. Or no housekeeping officer. Or no set-in-stone hospital policies. Arlene Allerton rocked and blew as if she didn't need the damn job. Or the health insurance.

After a while—she didn't know how long—when the baby's breathing was soft and steady, Arlene rose and gingerly laid the child in the bassinet, rolled the bassinet over next to his sleeping mother, and tip-toed out of the room. She nearly collided with the nurse with the paint-by-numbers face, who gave her a suspicious look before heading into the room to do what nurses did best—bother a patient just when she had finally fallen asleep.

Arlene breathed a sigh of relief as she pushed her cleaning cart down to the women's restrooms. What could she have been thinking? If anyone had seen her she would have certainly been fired! She swallowed hard and wondered how she could have been so stupid. If she lost her job and her insurance, the expensive phonosurgery her doctors were encouraging her to undergo would be entirely out of the question. Not only that, without a job, she'd end up living with Lucy and her daughters, the baby, and the baby on the way.

Oh, why did so many young women end up this way? Arlene could predict that young mother's life. She thought about it as she cleaned the toilets. It would be not unlike her own—sporadic support from family members, sub-adequate housing, food stamps and WIC, sleepless nights, aching loneliness, and the misguided conviction that a man was the answer to all of the above. And then maybe another man. Or like Lucy, who was on her fourth man, having just thrown out the third after he'd punched Arlene in the neck three months ago when she'd inadvertently powdered her great-granddaughter's behind with his cocaine. (A plastic sandwich bag filled with a white powdery substance stuffed into the pocket of the diaper bag next to the baby wipes? Who wouldn't have thought *powder*?)

There should be a home, Arlene thought. And if she were a better person, she would have created a place for young women and their babies. Oh, sure, New Orleans had crisis pregnancy centers, but what Arlene had in mind was one of those big old Victorian homes, a nice clean place with sun-filled bedrooms, nice hot baths, and a community kitchen. A place with rules but also love and support and help with crying babies. If only there had been a place like that for her, maybe she would have finished high school, not rushed into marrying Lloyd, maybe she could have done things differently for her daughters. Arlene remembered a time when she was so sleep-deprived and hopeless she felt like throwing crybaby Lucy out the window. That had scared her more than anything, that the crying wouldn't stop and that she might one day do it.

She finished with the bathroom and pushed her cart back down the hall. She heard a baby crying and recognized it immediately. She continued down the hall, but hesitated at the nurse's station. Should she tell someone that the mother in 308 was in trouble? That if someone didn't help her she might not be able to overcome a desperate urge to throw her baby out a window? Did anyone realize the mother was just a baby herself? But nurse-paint-by-number-face wouldn't even look up from her paperwork so Arlene shuffled herself along. She stopped at the drinking fountain, right across from room 308. The baby's crying sounded almost sheep like now: *baa-baa-baa.* Arlene bent at the fountain for a drink of water. A hundred thoughts flashed through her head, too many to process. She shut them out. Some things are meant to be thought out, others needed to be talked out, and then there were those that simply needed to be acted upon without thought or discussion. With a throaty laugh, Arlene gave her housekeeping cart a little push with her foot and watched it roll slowly down the hall. "There, there," she whispered even before she was through the door.

◖

Dangling

"The heart has often been compared to the needle of a compass for its constancy; has it ever been so for its variations? —Yet were any man to keep minutes of his feelings from youth to age, what a table of variations would they present—how numerous, how diverse, how strange!"
—*August W. Hare (1792-1834)*

A HOT STEAMING plate of creamy Fettucine Alfredo sits before her on a beautifully set table. Her husband Oliver is the chef; she, his only customer. Even though it's a Wednesday night, an ordinary Wednesday night—not even "National Men Make Dinner Night"—there is wine, there is candlelight, and there are silver serving dishes. Samantha knows her husband's intentions are good and loving, but everything about this meal gives her a pain in various parts of her compact and muscular body, especially the fact that if she doesn't properly adore this meal and if she doesn't properly praise the chef, she will later pay with more than mere indigestion.

Sam tastes the pasta and it's good, as is the salad with the homemade balsamic vinaigrette. "Wonderful," she says with her mouth full.

"Really?" Oliver says. "You're not just saying that?"

"Really. It's so good," she tells him. "And I'm so hungry." She sucks in a couple of noodles that don't quite make it all the way into her mouth. She has discovered that if she talks with her mouth full, Oliver thinks his food is so delicious that she just can't stop eating for even one second.

"And the salad?"

"Mmmmm. The salad is superb."

"That's a new dressing. I substituted garlic olive oil for regular olive oil. It's not too garlicky now is it?"

"No, no, it's perfect. Delicious."

"But do you like the other dressing better?"

"Which?"

"With the regular olive oil."

"I like them both, Oliver. They're both good."

"Good. Now chew your salad well. My grandmother nearly choked to death once on a radish slice."

They have been married for three hundred and forty-three days. Sam knows the exact number because Oliver keeps track and each morning writes the number of days along with a happy face on the wall calendar in the kitchen. Oliver sometimes can't remember his own phone number ("I never call myself") but he knows to the day how long he and Sam have been blissfully wed. For the first forty-three days of their marriage, Sam considered this to be one of the best things that could ever happen to a thirty-eight-year-old woman on her third marriage. Imagine, someone actually celebrating a life with her! It was no secret that her first two husbands were more likely to keep track of how many blissful days they'd spent apart from her. But yesterday was day three hundred forty-two and something about that number made Sam sick to her ears of this tallying thing. Last night after Oliver had gone to bed and she had downed a half bottle of white wine by herself, she changed one of the happy faces to a sad face, went right over that little smirker with a Sharpie permanent black marker. This morning at breakfast, when Oliver went to the calendar to write in a three, a four, a three, and a smiley, he saw the sad face and got all shaken up. "I was just teasing," Sam said. "I just wanted to see if you'd notice," she said.

That Oliver is in touch with his sensitive side is what attracted Sam to him in the first place. The first two husbands had been counterfeits that put themselves first and last in all situations and Sam had vowed that if she ever married again number three would be tender, compassionate, a true gentleman. What she got was a grandmother—someone who fears she's dead in the street if she's fifteen minutes late getting home at night, someone who harps on her to dress properly for winter weather, someone who appears out of nowhere with salt water if she so much as mentions a scratchy throat. After almost a year of marriage she has found that the very things she loves about Oliver are the very things she hates about him.

She's known it for a while now—she can only tolerate her husband in small amounts. Two hours a day would probably do it. The other night Sam dreamed that she asked Oliver—in a nice way, mind you—if he would consider getting his own place for a while, that she needed some space. Her dream version of Oliver was fine with this. He even went apartment hunting with her. The real Oliver would go to pieces if she proposed such an idea. Itty-bitty pieces.

After dinner, Sam helps Oliver with the dishes. She washes by hand in hot, hot water. They have a dishwasher but rarely use it because it takes an entire week for them to fill it. "Besides," Oliver says, "it gives us time to talk." Oliver usually talks about people Sam doesn't know, some real, some fictional. Sometimes Sam listens and sometimes she only pretends to listen. "Be careful," Oliver says, "that water is scalding hot."

When Sam was little she drove everyone around her crazy. She changed her first name from Suzanne to Samantha when she was six. "I am not a Suzanne," she told her mother. "Never was, never will be."

In rare moments of self-examination, Sam wonders if she is responsible for her mother's drinking problem. Growing up, her mother's favorite line had been: "Just wait, *Suzantha*, someday you'll have a child just like you." The thought still sends shivers up Sam's spine and is the foremost reason why, in spite of the fact that she actually likes children and harbors a secret desire to have a baby herself, she remains childless at thirty-eight. Even *she* doesn't want to raise herself.

With the dishes done, Oliver heads upstairs to take his shower. Pinched by guilt, Sam picks up the Sharpie permanent black marker and writes in the number three hundred forty-four on the calendar. Biting the cap of the marker, she stares at the number, tempted to put a "one" in front of it for surely tomorrow will make it *one thousand* three hundred forty-four days of marriage. At least it feels like it. Instead she follows the number up with four exclamation points and the happiest smiley face you have ever seen. There. Exonerated.

Oliver and Sam go to bed right after dinner. Or, they get *into* bed right after dinner. Sam works for the mayor of Chicago and each night she lies in a blanket of paperwork. Even with all the work done on her laptop, there's still paperwork: questionnaires, computer printouts, fan mail, hate mail. Sam tells people she loves her job because it used to be the truth. When she was little and people asked her what she wanted to be when she grew up she would tell them "the boss." And now, she is, sort of. What she didn't know then was that even the boss has a boss, and even that boss has a boss, and that one, and that one... In any case, she's good at what she does, which is energizing people to do things that she, or the mayor, wants them to do. She does this by using strong language, using flattery to her advantage, and by leveraging favors— "you wipe mine, I'll wipe yours."

"I got Jeremy to shut his mouth about the neighborhood playground thing," she tells Oliver, who lies propped up beside her, taking in his classical music intravenously. He lifts one earphone of the headset so that his wife may repeat her statement. "That neighborhood playground thing that Jeremy wanted. I got him to dump it."

"I am woman, hear me roar," says Oliver, letting the earphone snap back into place. Sam can read him easily. He's feigning hurt about the sad face she drew on the calendar, but that's not what's really bothering him. What's really bothering him is what they'd argued about last night: that Oliver is ready for a baby and Sam is not. Not after only three hundred forty-three days of marriage. She's not ready and she's not even sure she's qualified for the job. "How does one prepare oneself to screw up a kid the way my mother screwed me up?" she had asked him. "Are there classes? Dysfunctional Family 101?" Oliver hadn't found anything funny about that kind of thinking.

She finishes her last e-mail with a "thank you in advance for your cooperation" which is the politically correct way of saying "get this done, or it's your ass." She snaps closed the lid of her laptop and glances at the clock. It's after eleven but she's not tired. Outside the bedroom window a buttery light from the apartment building next door filters through the sheer curtains and she wonders if there might be a place opening up there. The best of all worlds—to have her husband right next door.

She feels Oliver staring at her. "Sammy, you have bags under your eyes. You've got to get more sleep." Oliver's been on a campaign to increase their sleep intake after reading an article recently about billionaires crediting much of their success to a solid eight hours of sleep each night. Sam's been existing (subsisting) on five hours a night for years now. Oliver says that she's not only sleep-deprived but dream-deprived as well. "Dream deprivation can bring about severe disorientation," he had told her in a serious psychoanalyst voice, "because the dreams that are deprived during sleep find a way to take place during the waking state."

"Thank you, Dr. Freud," Sam had said, but she had to admit to severe irritability and lately a disorientation manifested by uncharacteristic forgetfulness. She forgot the name of the mayor's personal secretary the other day—a woman she knows better than her own mother. It was a frightening experience, one that someone of her power and rank could not afford. No, she wasn't sleeping well and it was starting to affect her thinking.

"Ready?" Oliver says.

She flicks the light off as an answer. His lips find her cheek in the dark. Even when he's mad he still kisses her, a diehard subscriber to the philosophy of never going to bed angry with your spouse. Within twenty seconds Oliver is asleep, inhaling and exhaling in a serene, steady pattern. This makes Sam crazy. All three of her husbands could out-sleep her: Kent because he was lazy, Travis because he lacked a conscience, and now Oliver because he needs the dream time to fuel his muse. This is not a good thing in a marriage because it leaves the insomniac awake and resentful of the slumbering spouse. It leaves time for the insomniac to wonder how she can love and hate her slumbering spouse so extremely and simultaneously. In five minutes and five fingers Sam can go from loving Oliver to hating him, pick up her other hand, and in the other five fingers go from hating back to loving him.

She wonders how this measures on the normal scale. Are other people given to bouts of erratic and even perverse changeableness, or is it just her? Does she love Oliver? Yes. Does she hate him? Yes. Can she (and this is the biggie) live with him? She's not sure. Ever since the first week of their marriage she's had to stifle powerful urges to throw him out. Sam admits to being a slob, but she explains it away as an attribute of the very creative. Day number six of their marriage, Sam came home after a horrible day at work to find that her stay-at-home-writer-husband had organized her desk and all of her piles. Her piles! Oliver had put her perfectly arranged piles of disorder into some kind of order! There was hell, yes there was. There was also a moratorium on touching any of Sam's piles in the future.

"What will I do when I have writer's block?" Oliver had whined. "Organizing things helps me organize my thoughts."

"Go alphabetize the pantry," Sam had said. She's always wondered how Oliver can stand working at home, all alone in quiet rooms that smother you like quicksand. She couldn't do it, she needed the commotion of people and things. She's one of those who is happiest in the throes of chaos.

As for Oliver...two things make him happy: grand-mothering Sam to death and writing his damn mystery novels. Yes, Oliver writes mystery novels. You may have heard of him—Oliver St. Luke—or maybe not. He's working on the seventh novel in his Jack Reddy series and has enjoyed a comfortable level of success in the mystery genre. Sam thought it would be fascinating to be married to a novelist but she has found it to be quite maddening. First of all, novelists are a misunderstood bunch. People think they lounge around the house drinking cups and cups of coffee, wearing roomy clothing, and waiting for the ideas to come. Oliver's reality is being stuck in the spare bedroom wearing Dockers and Polo shirts, drinking bottled water, and rejoicing if he ends the day with one or two polished pages. Sam hears him sometimes in "that room" as she refers to the second bedroom, clicking on the keyboard, talking to himself, humming to himself, whistling to himself. And then there's the issue of material—writers are always fishing for material and Sam soon realized that her whole life was up for grabs. He talks about his characters as one would talk about relatives and friends. Plus, writers are a moody bunch.

Once he got over the shock, Oliver, she was certain, would enjoy having his own place to write. He'd been complaining recently about the noisy couple that lived above them. Wouldn't he appreciate a change of venue? Of course he would. And he wouldn't have to stay there every night. No, mostly they'd be here together, but, say, for the duration of her menstrual cycle or while the mayor's re-election campaign was underway or when she wanted to watch a chick flick while eating M & M's in her bathrobe, or just when she had a really crummy day. They would have this understanding, a code even. Sam would pinch her nose or pull her ear and that would mean, "Oliver, please go home." And he would.

When she's in an honest mood, say, like when she's out drinking with her pals from work, Angela and Felisha, she confesses things—he's not who she thought he was, he's so predictable, he's fastidious, he creates worry out of nothing. His arm around her sometimes feels like a leash, he speaks so slowly that she finds herself finishing his sentences, and he's so damn nice—nice to telemarketers and Jehovah's Witnesses and airport solicitors and even ticket-issuing police officers. Sometimes it's the wine talking, but sometimes it's the truth talking.

Sleep is stubborn and tomorrow is a huge day, the mayor meets with the governor on the school referendum. She's just got to get some sleep, some good quality sleep, with good dreams and no more nightmares. She made the mistake of telling Oliver the other morning about her nightmare—she'd dreamed she was drowning. He told her that meant something in her life was out of control. Sam had laughed. One book on dream interpretation and Oliver was an authority. She told him he was full of horse dung; she had everything under control.

On the morning of her three hundred forty-forth day of marriage, Sam Mitchell (she'd kept her maiden name even though it had hurt Oliver deeply) wakes, showers, dresses, kisses her husband good-bye, and falls down a flight of stairs.

Sam has a very low threshold for pain and absolutely no patience for what comes with the fall—a trip to the emergency room, a broken leg, a cast, crutches, patronizing pity, lost work-time, the whole shebang.

For days she camps out on the couch and watches the news channel, the shopping channel, the weather channel, and the cooking channel. She peruses the real estate section of the Tribune for a nice cheap apartment for her husband. Oliver, clueless, rents movies that she has been too busy to see and stacks books, which she has been too busy to read, next to the couch. Most, she notices, are his novels. "I'm not into mysteries," she had told Oliver when they first met and he asked if she'd read any of his books. "I've had enough mystery in my own life, enough to fill a book," she teased. Once they were married she promised to read them, of course she would read her own husband's books. But she's yet to whittle out some time for leisurely reading, laying blame on the mayor for monopolizing her free time.

Now Oliver loiters above her with a pitcher of ice water and a glass. "I read somewhere that drinking a lot of water aids in mending broken bones." He sets the pitcher and glass on the end table and bends to straighten the tower of books he's stacked. "Turn on that lamp if you decide to read," he instructs. "You don't want to strain your eyes." Sam smiles a yeah-sure, but then strains her neck to see the TV. Oliver shrugs and goes back to his room to work on his book. Sam watches him as he walks down the hall. Sometimes she likes him better from the back. His shoulders look broader from the back; he looks less like a maven from the back.

Throughout the first week, to aid in her convalescence, Oliver serves Sam her meals on the couch. And he periodically offers snacks—homemade fudge brownies ("watch out for the nuts"), herbal tea ("blow on that now, it's hot"), and Godiva chocolates ("a little pick-me-up"). At night he massages her feet, helps her undress, asks permission (he always asks permission) to make love to her, cast and all. Sam says yes, but it proves awkward and makes her feel old and sad. She has never been this immobilized in her life. It frightens her and shortens the length of her temper. It's hard to imagine that Sam Mitchell could possibly be any more impossible to live with, but it's true. Since her fall, she hates everyone and everything.

Six days on the sofa, boob-tubed, muscles starting to atrophy, she is bored beyond the yawns. Oliver emerges less and less from his room to play nurse-maid, explaining that he's reached a critical point in the novel, where Veronica Booth finds her brother bludgeoned to death. (It crosses Sam's mind that a "regular" writer would say "beaten to death" but a mystery writer has to say "bludgeoned to death.")

The visitors, those who couldn't stay away the first week—her mother, Angela, and Felisha—have dwindled down to absolutely nobody today. She has one more week of vacation to use up—the mayor insisted. One more week with Oliver. Now she will go mad.

Out of sheer boredom, she has taken to calling her husband from his room fifteen million times a day for any little old thing.

"Ah-lee-ver!" she sings like a child. And again, even louder, "AH-LEE-VER!!" when he doesn't appear in the expected number of seconds.

"Yes, my sweet," he calls. "Coming, my darling," he shouts. But then he doesn't come. At least not right away. He's been getting progressively slower in responding to Sam's pleas. Sam cocks her ear, listening for his light footsteps on the wood floors—her cue to put on her pathetic face.

"What do you need, hon?" Oliver asks, the remains of a concentrated frown still on his face.

"Quick, look," Sam says, pointing to the TV. "What's his name, that actor?"

"Sam!"

"There. Him. Is that Robert DuVall?"

"I don't know."

"I think it's Robert DuVall, or else it's that other guy, you know, that other guy who was in that western you like. Bushy eyebrows. Thick mustache."

"Hon, I don't know who it is and I don't want to be rude but I'm in the middle of a good roll right now. Veronica just walked into Paul Serell's office. She doesn't even know yet about the bomb and—"

"Veronica, Ba-bomb-i-ca. I'm sick of Veronica. I sometimes think you love her more than you love me."

"You're jealous of a fictional heroine? Now, that's rich, Sam. You know what? I think you need to get out of here.

You're going batty. Come on, I'll take you for a ride. And buy you a Starbucks if you're good. Come on." He holds out his hand. "Be careful with those crutches, now."

It was Carl Reed, from the newspaper, who had introduced them. At his New Year's Eve party. Sam had been divorced from Travis for two years then, happy to be free, totally comfortable with showing up all over town by herself. Look how "two thousands" she was! But there was something about New Year's Eve—it had gotten her in trouble before—that made her want to have someone's arm casually and territorially slung around her. Angela assures her that it's an actual phenomenon, this need to be attached to an earthly being as one year changes over to the next. She read about it somewhere.

Oliver didn't look like an author, not then, not now. Sam thought Carl was joking when he pointed Oliver out at the party. "Oliver St. Luke, my favorite author," Carl said later, introducing them, "meet Samantha Mitchell, my favorite pain-in-the-ass." Author, this guy? He wasn't wearing tweed, or smoking a pipe, or brooding in a corner. His looks were a smidgen above average—slender build, sandy brown hair, kind green eyes. But he was given to nervous mannerisms and he didn't look interestingly tormented like some authors Sam had met. He didn't even look interesting. But what intrigued her about him from the start—and this will sound as ice-cold shallow as it is—was Oliver's immediate interest in her. He was smitten and she'd never had smitten before. She'd had drop-dead handsome and irresistibly unapproachable, even slightly abusive, but never smitten. Right then Sam experienced an epiphany, one that illuminated exactly what she wanted from a man: to be loved like a car, totally and unconditionally, regardless of age or mileage.

"Sammy, this guy is crazy about you," Angela told her after she and Oliver had been together a few weeks.

"I know," Sam had said. She was crazy about someone being crazy about her. In three months they were married.

"This guy is head-over-heels for you," Felisha said after Sam and Oliver had been married a few months.

"I know," Sam said. And that night she went home and tried to start a fight. She sat down to yet another beautifully prepared meal, took two bites of the Mediterranean veggie wraps (selected, certainly, with her elevated lipid levels in mind) and told Oliver that the wraps tasted "funny." The worse thing was that Oliver had agreed. And apologized! He had thought so himself, but had attributed it to his taste buds being off due to a slight head cold. Then he scraped the perfectly fine wraps from the plates and shoved them down the disposal.

"You do not deserve a man like Oliver," has been her mother's mantra for the last year. "He's a good man, a sweet man, and a real gentleman."

"You don't understand," Sam tells her. "The man grandmothers me to death: 'fasten your seat belt, chew your food well, remember your vitamins, watch your step.' It's unnerving to say the least."

"It's unnerving that you finally found someone who loves you?"

"I know it sounds crazy, but yes."

"And it's unnerving that this wonderful man wants to have a baby with you?"

"Mother. I'm not wired that way and you know it."

"It might be just the thing to mellow you out. Remember that dog we had? She was meaner than you are, but after her first litter she softened considerably. She never bit anyone after she had those puppies."

"I take offense to being compared to a dog."

"I'm hanging up *Suzantha*."

Sam hates her when she calls her that.

The ride turns out to be a not-so-good idea. It starts with, "Buckle up, now," and ends with Sam feeling jealous of every *walking* individual in the city of Chicago. She yearns to be a pedestrian once again, chasing a cab, surviving a near-miss with a city bus, walking in spiky, impractical high-heeled shoes.

"Take me back," she says.

She's had enough of the couch so she goes to bed. If he serves her dinner in bed she swears she'll scream. He does serve her dinner in bed but she manages to stifle her scream. But if he fishes for compliments on his lamb chops she will scream. He does, asking if she likes this marinade or the one he used a few weeks ago. Again, Sam maintains self-control while she properly adores the meal and the chef. But if after taking away the tray he comes back and plumps her pillows, she really will scream. He does come back and he does plump and Sam does scream: "WILL YOU JUST STOP? Can't you see you're grand-mothering me to death?"

"I'm just trying to be helpful," Oliver says, taking a step backward, "that's all."

"Well, stop it."

"Okay. Fine. Whatever you say."

"You know I need space, Oliver. Air to breathe. You're smothering me."

"I am not."

"You are too."

"I am not."

"Can't you just go somewhere? For a few days maybe? I need some space. I'm not kidding."

"Space? What are you talking about, space? What you need is more sleep. Sleep on it, why don't you."

"All I've been doing is sleeping."

"It's the book, isn't it? I know I'm preoccupied. Listen, tomorrow if you wake up and still think you need space, I'll go to my brother's for a while and finish the book there. Okay?" He wiggles her big toe. "Just sleep on it, okay?"

"Sleep on this!" she screams and throws a pillow at him.

So, tonight, it's microwave popcorn and a can of diet Mug root beer for dinner. Sam munches and sips and thinks about how nice it is not to have to answer questions about the quality, temperature, or saltiness of the popcorn. Yesterday she ate cold condensed vegetable soup straight from the can. It was so freeing. Yes, this was exactly what she needed, this space.

Oliver was great about going. He said it couldn't be easy to live with a writer. He's been staying at his brother's for a week now. He's been wonderful, really, so respectful of Sam's needs. He's only called once in five days. Yesterday. And that was only to return her call. She couldn't find the paprika.

"What do you need paprika for? You're not cooking, are you? Not in my kitchen."

"Don't be silly. I needed it for...my popcorn. I like a sprinkle of paprika on my popcorn."

"Since when?"

While Oliver is gone Sam smokes in bed. She stands on a rickety chair, cast and all, to change a light bulb. She doesn't call the gas company when she thinks she smells gas in the kitchen. She uses her hands instead of a wooden spoon to shove leftovers down the garbage disposal, she hangs a huge, heavy framed oil painting over their bed, she doesn't change the batteries to the smoke detector, she drinks water straight from the tap, she doesn't bother locking the two extra dead bolts, she talks on the phone to her mother during an electrical storm, she leaves candles burning unattended, she eats nutritionless meals that upset her stomach, she doesn't bother with the multi-vitamins, she doesn't turn on the air-purifier, she tells telemarketers that she's home alone, she drinks entire bottles of expensive wine by herself, and she goes outside to get the paper with soaking wet hair. If she could drive, and if she owned a convertible, and if she lived in the mountains, she would floor it to ninety on some winding road with the top down.

She calls Felisha. "I kicked Oliver out."

"You're the biggest idiot."

"I know."

"You don't know, girl, or you wouldn't have done it."

"My marriage is going south."

"Your brain is going south."

"He grandmothers me to death."

"A normal person would call it 'treating you like a queen' but you're not normal."

"I mean it, we're dangling by a thread."

"Oh, please."

"I'm hanging up and calling someone who will sympathize with me."

"Angela's not home. She's got a date with that guy who hits her. And you say your marriage is going south. I'm hanging up now, *Suzantha*."

After an itching attack that results in Sam straightening out a hanger and shoving it deep down into her cast (the doctor had warned her against doing this) for relief, she prepares to watch yet another movie when she realizes she is fresh out of videos. The usual prime time garbage is unpalatable so she picks up one of Oliver's books. She starts to read and in the sharp quiet that the four walls put forth, Oliver's characters come alive: she can see their faces, hear their voices, smell their fragrances and odors.

She stays up all night reading and by dinnertime two nights later she is on book six.

And who would have thought it, but Oliver's books are good, really good, and this takes Sam by surprise. The intrigue, the criminal mind, the gratuitous sex! She realizes she's been unfair. She had assumed Oliver had written mystery books in the old detective style with predictable plots, seedy motel rooms, bosomy women, and macho men, but his books are different. They're layered and complex and the writing is as good as some of the literary fiction she'd read.

The main character, cool and likable Jack Reddy (hence the titles: *Camera Reddy, Reddy or Not, Reddy for Bed, Get Reddy, Reddy and Willing, Ever Reddy*), is not your stereotypical detective. He's not even a detective. He's a staff photographer for the Washington Post who accidentally solves crimes via his photographs. Jack is deceivingly innocuous, a Columbo-type, but a lot hipper and a lot better looking. His love interest is the infamous Veronica Booth, the fictional character of whom Sam is supposed to be jealous. And well she should be. Sam had never formed a clear picture of Veronica in her head; she was just a vague, faceless person connected to a shapeless body. In reality—in fictional reality—Veronica Booth is bigger than life. She's redheaded, big chested, and despite being almost six-feet tall, favors high heels. She's emotionally naive, but quick-witted, and possesses a surprisingly childlike infectious giggle. A beat reporter for the Washington Post, she tries so hard to make a name for herself that she misses the really good stories, the low profile, non-political but pivotal stories, the ones Jack Reddy covers. At first Veronica isn't interested in Jack—he's not classy enough, he's not rich enough; they are only friends in the first book. In the second, third, fourth, fifth and sixth books, they go from being lovers to enemies to partners to spouses to ex-spouses, and then to lovers again.

By the time Sam turns the last page of the last book, she is dumbfounded. And not only because the books are such good reads but because she has learned some things about her husband through his alter ego, Jack Reddy. Like Oliver, Jack Reddy is a kind and decent man, a man who cares a little too passionately about the people in his life. A man who was raised without a father by an indifferent mother who never bothered to worry about her only son's welfare or whereabouts. Oliver had never shared much with Sam about his childhood, saying only that his mother had raised him to be independent. Sam had only met Oliver's mother once, at their wedding, and had immediately sized the woman up as a cold fish. Could there be parallels? Just how much of himself does a writer put into his main character? Could this explain Oliver's bent toward grandmothering?

And then there was Veronica Booth, gorgeous, spoiled, terrifyingly ambitious, and yet she loves children (in *Get Reddy* she throws herself out into traffic to save a three-year-old boy). Sam wonders about art imitating life and life imitating art and art imitating the opposite of life. That night she sleeps and dreams that she visits Oliver one night for sex at his new apartment and he smothers her with a bed pillow.

"So I've got to know, what happens in book seven?" Sam says into the phone the next morning. "Do they get remarried? Do they have a baby? Give 'em a baby, why don't you? Veronica would be a great mother."

"Sam?"

"Give 'em twins."

"Am I to understand that you read one of the books?"

"I read all of the books. The books are great. Come home, why don't you."

Tonight Sam cooked for Oliver. Okay, some frozen cuisine thing, but she made the effort. Then they went to bed and re-enacted a wild sex scene from *Reddy and Willing* right down to falling off the bed and knocking over a ceramic-based lamp. It was the most fun Sam had had in a long, long time, cast and all. But now Oliver's lying next to her, acting funny.

"What?" she asks. "Are you mad about the painting above our heads? I assure you I used the strongest brackets I could find. It won't fall on us, Oliver."

"It's not that. It's—"

"What?"

"I don't know."

"What?"

"I just want to make sure you know that I am not Jack Reddy."

"What do you mean?"

"I just hope all this…tonight…isn't because you read my books and now you think that deep down I'm this cool, hip guy, because you're wrong."

"Hello? Excuse me but I think I know the difference between fiction and real life."

"Well, he's not me, okay?"

"And I'm not Veronica Booth, either."

"I know *that*," he says, a little too quickly, a tad too emphatically.

"And what's that supposed to mean, I would like to know."

"Nothing except that you and Veronica are nothing alike. To answer your earlier question, Jack and Veronica do get back together and they do have a baby. Not twins, but a baby. And Veronica gives up her stellar career to raise their son."

"You're right, I'm not like her at all," Sam says and turns her back to Oliver.

"But could you ever be?"

She turns around. "Oliver, I'm five-four, flat-chested and I never wear high-heels. I have a pint-sized sense of humor, I don't giggle, I swear like a trucker, and my hair is only red because I have my girl put henna into it every six weeks."

"You know I'm talking about a baby."

Of course she knows he's talking about a baby. For months now, since day two hundred thirty-nine, when he drew two big smiley faces and a tiny one on the calendar next to the number, Oliver has been talking about a baby.

"You would just grandma it to death," Sam says, turning around to face her husband.

"No, I wouldn't."

"You'd be so overprotective, so overbearing. You would worry about every little thing. You wouldn't let him go sledding or ride his bike in the street, or let him have a B-B gun or a bow and arrow set."

"Yes, I would. Well, maybe not the B-B gun. He could put an eye out with that."

"Oliver!"

"What?" he says, and then he does what he always does when he doesn't know what else to say to Sam but he wants to be close to her: he tickles her. She doesn't giggle, only squirms. "And don't tell me you need more space. Next time, you can go. My brother would be happy to put you up. I'm staying. You can be the one to go."

Write it down: Sam Mitchell is having a speechless moment. But when she finds the words, she says, "Do you want me to go?"

"No, I don't want you to go! Do you want me to go?"

"Yes, sometimes."

"I'm not going. Not anymore."

"Oh. *Oh.* Well, okay then."

"Okay then," Oliver says with a tone of finality she has never heard before.

Sam, again at a loss for words, rolls over so as not to look Oliver in the eye. Why does marriage always have to be so complicated, so mysterious? And why does she keep marrying chameleons? Men who start out someone and end up someone else. People should stay the same, constant, steady. She hasn't changed one iota. She's the same person Kent, Travis and Oliver married.

Without turning around, Sam says: "And you know you wouldn't let him have ponies at his birthday party because someone might fall off, or let him play pin-the-tail-on-the-donkey because someone might get maimed with the straight pin, God forbid."

"Why are you so sure we'd have boy?"

"We couldn't have a girl, I'd screw her up royally."

"You would not," he says, trying to turn her around to face him.

"I would," she says, pushing him away, "I know it. Let me be, will you? Just let me sleep on it, okay?" She punches her pillow then buries her head in it, profoundly aware of her powers to confuse, confound, and bewilder.

Oliver leans over to kiss his wife. He kisses her right on the soft spot of her neck, right in back of her left ear, her one and only tickle spot. She lets go with what for her is a giggle.

"Sleep on this," Oliver whispers and continues with the kissing.

Pulling the Air

"Who loves the rain and loves his home,
and looks on life with quiet eyes,
him will I follow through the storm
and at his hearth-fire keep me warm."
—Frances W. Shaw (1872-19??)

I SIT ON my porch steps in the gathering twilight, in the beam of a moon that's just about full. It's just about June, just about eight, and just about the most perfect almost-summer night we've had, after a cold and soggy spring. Fireflies blink their soft intermittent light and my boys, four and two, tailgate them, eager to bottle up as many as they can before I announce their bath time.

Porter, my older one, particular about what he touches, pretends to grab at the lightning bugs, but really, he only pulls at the air. It's my fearless two-year-old who has actually caught the five, six, no, seven bugs that are imprisoned in the mason jar that sits at my feet. There would be even more bugs in the bottle, but Cole, not knowing his own strength, has accidentally squished a few between his thumb and forefinger on his journeys to the jar. See, he just did it again. He approaches with his victim: this one has died with his light still on.

"Sorry, Mom," Cole says, then kisses the air twice. This is his usual apology— "Sorry, Mom. Kiss. Kiss."—whether he's spilled milk, punched his brother or eaten chocolate before breakfast. Sometimes I think the world would be a better place if everyone apologized in just this way. My husband, for one.

We've made a deal, the boys and I. Since Daddy is off flying jets to other continents and it's an unseasonably warm night, I've agreed to sleep on the screened porch with them if they promise to let me sleep until seven. It never fails, Saturday comes and the two of them wake up two hours earlier than usual, wanting pancakes and terrible morning cartoons. I find it hard to believe that I gave birth to early risers, but here they are.

I blame it on my husband, Dennis. He's an early riser, cheerful and go-get-'em in the morning, ready to fly around the world before the sun even rises. Dennis is a pilot for American Airlines. Right about now he should be on his way back to Chicago from Lisbon, Portugal.

"Hi Daddy!" Cole screams to the sky. He does this whenever he spots a plane in the air. In Cole's two-year-old world, his father flies *all* the planes. Sometimes I feel as if this might be true, for once Dennis started flying international, he's been gone more than he's been home. And, even though that's an overstatement, I've earned the right to interject it into casual conversation because I'm the one who is here, day in and day out. Even when he's home he's not really home. If he's not in the air, he's on the greens. And if he's not golfing, he's water-skiing with his brother, Glen. If they're not water-skiing they're snow

skiing. Throw in racquetball and basketball and my boys
have a father they see on the fly.

Porter runs to me, his arms pin wheeling, his face almost
lucent with happy pride. "I got one, Mama! I got one!" he
cries holding out a fist that is clenched so tight I fear we'll
have another fatality on our hands. But as I remove the lid
to the jar, Porter giggles and says, "It tickles!" so I take this
as a good sign. It is. His hand opens to reveal a perfectly
intact lightning bug. He shakes his hand over the lip of the
bottle and the bug is his. I slap the lid on tight and wonder
if this is what God intended when he gave us dominion
over the earth. Porter must like the feel of sovereignty
for he runs off to claim more prisoners. If he only knew
that lightning bugs were really (entomologically-speaking)
winged nocturnal beetles, he might in fact barf. He loathes
beetles, especially the June bugs that fly in late spring and
for some reason seem to be found in abundance in our
backyard.

I sip the glass of iced-tea that Porter made for me
earlier (heavy on the sugar) and hear myself sigh. The
commencement of summer always makes me blue. Of
course, so does the arrival of spring, fall, and winter.
Thanksgiving, Christmas, and Easter. The first day of pre-
school, spring break, the last day of pre-school. I never
used to be this way—transitionally challenged. The mood
swings started two years ago, right before Cole was born
and I started to suspect Dennis's infidelity. There was this
flight attendant. Imagine Dennis's shock when my sister,
who had accompanied her husband on a business trip to
Germany, found my husband nuzzled up in a little cellar
café with someone other than his wife. What were the
chances? Talk about a small world, my sister said.

At first I was angry with her—my natural reflex to want
to kill the messenger. But then I checked Dennis's flight
schedule and yes, he was in Germany. I was seven months

pregnant with Cole and I wanted to end it all. But I couldn't end *me* without ending *Cole*, so instead I sought the counsel of our pastor and my mother. You'll love this part: it was my mother who told me to stay and stick it out. Father Donovan advised me to leave Dennis. I lie awake nights wondering why a Catholic priest would encourage a woman to leave her husband, to break a covenant, to sabotage a sacrament. Then I realized why. Father Donovan had listened to my husband's confession for years. Did he know something I didn't?

Of course I stayed. What else could I do? I was bigger than an apartment complex and I hadn't worked a day since graduating from college. What could I do with a zoology degree anyway? I was five years into a marriage that had been deemed "iffy" by more than a few friends and family members. Dennis, confident and cocky, was the kind of guy who created his own parking spaces. I was diffident and shy, the kind of girl most comfortable on the second floor of a big, quiet library. He was flashy, like a lightning bug. I was an ant, a lowly little worker ant, minding my own business until I found myself blinded by his light. Of course I stayed. But I stayed for my kids.

"Bath time!" I say in a voice that would lead one to believe I have dominion over my children when quite the opposite is true.

"One more lightning bug, Mama, please. Just one more!" Porter pleads, infusing his voice with drama.

"Okay, okay, but just one more." I give in only because he has the sweet face of a cherub.

"How do they light up, Mama?" he asks me, trailing an exceptionally bright blinker into the bushes.

"Light bulbs," Cole says with a straight face. Cole was born clever, with a serious "old soul" kind of face. A face only a mother could love, my mother once said, propelling me to tears. I lie awake nights hoping that the blue period

I underwent during the last months of gestation didn't predispose my baby to melancholy. Sorry, Cole. Kiss. Kiss.

I access my cerebral zoology file, stored way in the back of my brain since college. "Well, fireflies produce their light by oxidating luciferin," I inform my eldest, who remains dumbfounded that his mother, a girl, actually liked bugs enough to study them.

"Lu-ci-fer-in," Porter repeats. "That sounds like the devil, like Lucifer."

"Luciferin is a pigment that's found in luminescent organisms like fireflies. It furnishes practically heatless light when it undergoes oxidation."

"Mamaaaaaaaaaaa!" Porter hates "college talk," but I insist in never talking down to my children.

"Well, you asked," I remind him. I'm about to tell him that lighting up is the bug's way of courting, but this fun fact will give rise to questions of a different nature, questions I'm simply too tired to entertain. "Go on," I say, giving a couple of claps, "get your one last bug."

Porter runs from me, stopping near the hedges where he stands still as a tree and waits for a flicker of yellow light. This time he traps one quickly, cupping it inside his hands, which he holds far away from his body as he runs to me. Cole catches another as well, but as he approaches I see that, although this bug is not squished to death like many of his cousins before him, it certainly is maimed. I give Cole a *not-again!* look. He says, "Sorry, Mom. Kiss. Kiss." He and his brother drop the bugs into the jar, then Cole adds another fistful of grass. I reattach the lid with a pang of guilt. I've always felt it was wrong to keep flying creatures from flying. As for me, I hate flying. I never fly.

While the boys are in the tub together, I pull three sleeping bags down from the cedar closet. I also grab an air mattress, but only one, because the boys have been brainwashed by their father into thinking that air mattresses are for sissies. This from a man who has taken his sons camping a total of one time.

Her name was Angela, the flight attendant. (Plug your nose with your thumb and forefinger and then say it: *Angela*. That's exactly how she said it, all nasally and Brooklyn-sounding, the one and only time I heard her voice when she called here for Dennis.) Dennis explained the affair as a "one-time major slip-up in a weak moment of alcoholic-induced stupidity when you were seven months pregnant and holding out on me." (Just for the record and not because it has anything to do with anything, I will say that I had a large cyst on my right ovary during my entire pregnancy that caused me quite a bit of discomfort.)

The boys and I lay out our sleeping bags and eat popcorn while we tell knock-knock jokes. Then we review our agreement: "I'm sleeping until seven. Seven o'clock, when this clock says seven-double-dot-zero-zero. Understand?"

"Yes, Mama."

"Yes, Mama."

Somehow I know I'll be up at five.

The night has grown cooler so I close all but two of the porch windows. We pray—for Grandma's "gold-bladder," for Grandpa's "diet-bead-eez," and for "Daddy in the sky." I sing their two favorite songs: The Beatles' "When I'm Sixty-four" for Cole and "Mr. Sun, Sun, Mr. Golden Sun" for Porter. Before turning out the light I have to pry the jar of lightning bugs out of Porter's hands.

"Please don't let them go, Mama, I wanna keep 'em."

I explain that lightning bugs will die if they can't fly. Surprisingly, he accepts this and asks me to release them after he is asleep. "All that hard work!" he exclaims, falling back on his pillow.

"Yeah," agrees Cole.

"They'll be around all summer," I say, setting the jar on the table. "Now sleep."

I sit in the wicker rocker and hum softly as they drift off. Sleep comes quickly to Porter, but Cole needs to tire his mind first, so he whispers to himself and pantomimes with his hands, until finally, they drop to his side. Porter goes out like a light but Cole fades like a sunset.

I get up to pour myself a glass of wine, but then I remember the jar of bugs. I grab it, slowly open the creaky screen door and step out into the night. I open the lid and shake the bugs out into the grass. They are weak; they don't even light up. *They'll die if they can't fly*, I told Porter. Funny, Dennis told me the same thing, when, after the Angela incident, I'd begged him to give up flying. I was having a hard time forgiving and forgetting. What it boiled down to was this: when Dennis was home and I could keep my eye on him, I trusted him. When he was flying all over the world...well, that was a different story. When he was away I was tormented by thoughts of my husband with women of every race, color, and ethnicity. Upon his return home, I could barely look at him. I had myself talked into believing that an office job could be the savior of our marriage. But Dennis said he would die if he couldn't fly. And, I, being a person who thought it wrong to prevent flying creatures from flying, let him fly.

Heading toward the kitchen for my glass of wine, I pass my grandfather's grandfather clock. It chimes out the eleventh hour. I stop in my tracks and slap my heart with my hand. The tears fall without warning. Lately, this happens often and when I least expect it—while pumping gas, in the confessional, while driving Porter to school, in the shower. This time there is an identifiable stressor: the clock striking eleven. It's silly really and I've never told anyone before, but when Dennis and I were first married, we played this little game. It was so hard for us to be apart, even when he flew intercontinental and we were separated for just a day or two. It was Dennis's idea—that at eleven o'clock p.m. Central time, we would take a moment and just think about each other for a few minutes. Then when Dennis returned home, he would tell me exactly where he was, his exact location above the earth, when he was thinking of me. "I was right over the Rocky Mountains." "I just touched down at JFK." "I was one minute from the Grand Canyon." We continued this later when he started flying international, and still later when Porter came along. Porter loved to hear his Daddy tell him that he was thinking about him just as he flew over Sydney or London or Tibet. It didn't matter that Porter knew none of these places, just that his Daddy was loving him from high up in the sky. But after the Angela incident...well, one time I heard Porter ask Dennis where he was at eleven o'clock last night on his flight to Madrid, and I heard Dennis tell him that he didn't remember. "Sorry, Bub, I forgot to look," was what he said.

Before the Angela incident, I used to lose sleep worrying about plane crashes and near misses. I would pray for angels to surround Dennis's plane and keep the crew and the passengers safe. Dennis always found my fear of flying hilarious. "It's safer than riding in a car." But like all fears, the fear of flying has nothing to do with logic.

After the Angela incident, I stopped worrying about Dennis's plane going down and started worrying about our marriage going down. How do you mend trust? I don't care what it is, anything that breaks, even if repaired, is left with residual scars. Sometimes the scars are superficial, sometimes they reach deep down to the tissue of your heart. He said the affair meant nothing, that it was stupid. He said it was an isolated incident, that he was committed to our marriage and to our children, and that it would never happen again. But what he didn't say, never did say, was "Sorry, Danielle. Kiss. Kiss."

Still, I forgave him (or did I?) if only because he was the father of my boys. I'd been down the broken family road myself and I wanted to spare my boys. I would make this work for them. I could do it for them.

But putting the incident out of my mind proved more difficult that putting hot fudge sundaes out of your mind when you're nine months pregnant. I'd never met Angela, never even saw her face, although my sister described her to me in full and painful detail upon her return from Germany. All that really mattered was that she was blond and skinny and I was sort of blond and fat with pregnancy.

I say I never saw her, but possibly I did. Once, before I even knew about Angela, I accidentally opened a piece of mail that was addressed to Dennis, thinking that it was addressed to me. Enclosed with a short note that said, "To my favorite party pilot," were three Polaroid snapshots of my husband dirty-dancing with a young, and I mean young, blonde. Dennis sloughed it off as a practical joke, the work of Marty O'Donnel, a pilot friend of Dennis's, who, in my opinion, had the face and the demeanor of a leaping orthopteran insect.

I pour some wine into a glass and sip it standing near the window. I hear a faint rumble of thunder in the distance. Somewhere there's a storm, but again, I don't worry about weather and planes crashing anymore. I worry about my own crash landing. The wine isn't that good. I pour what's left down the drain, head back out to the porch, and curl up in my sleeping bag. I fall asleep wondering if Portuguese women are beautiful.

I wake up to what I think is the sound of my alarm clock but then I realize it's the phone ringing. From the kitchen it peals violently, each ring amplified in the stillness of the night. I run to it.

"Danielle!"

"Dennis?"

"Honey, I know it's three a.m. and I don't want to scare you but—"

"Dennis! What is it? What's going on?" I'm half-expecting a late-night confession of some kind. Part two of the "one-time major slip-up in a weak moment of alcoholic-induced stupidity."

"Oh, God, there's been a terrible accident. The plane and terrible weather and—"

He's sobbing now and I can't make out what he's saying. My heart races. "Dennis, are you all right? Tell me what happened!"

There's fumbling with the phone. Someone clears her throat. I hear a nasal voice say: "Mrs. Pouriman? This is Angela Downing. I'm a flight attendant with American."

"Yes?"

"Denny's pretty shaken up. We all are. We crashed while attempting to land at O'Hare. We lost two crewmembers and sixteen passengers. We—"

"Dear God! Let me speak to my husband!"

"Danielle." His voice is calmer now. "Danielle, it's horrific. Eighteen people are dead. *Eighteen* people."

"Oh, my Lord. I'm so sorry. Are you hurt?"

"Just some bruises. I'll be okay. I'm at the hospital."

"Are you sure you're all right?

"Yes, yes."

"Tell me what happened."

"Oh, God. It all happened so fast. We'd had a smooth flight. Then just as we approached Chicago a thunderstorm bore down on us. Every time the lightning flashed, you could see a wall of black surrounding us. We circled a couple of times but they gave us clearance to land. We made a hot approach; the touch down was very hard. Marty applied the reverse thrusters, but the plane didn't slow down. Then we started to fishtail violently and— Honey, I can't. I'll tell you later. Angela's going to drive me home."

"NO! I'll pick you up. I'll get Jennifer next door to come over. I'll be there in half an hour."

I find him in the emergency room wearing a hospital gown, sitting in a wheel chair, and smelling like jet fuel. The Angela person is nowhere in sight. *Just some bruises* turns out to be three fractured ribs, deep lacerations, and abrasions on Dennis's back and chest. They'd stitched up his lip and a gash that extended from the middle of his right cheek to his ear. Since his clothes were ruined, they tell me he can wear the gown home. "You don't have to return it," the nurse said. I sign some papers and we leave.

In the car Dennis continues to cry, holding his head in his hands. I try to keep my eyes on the road.

"There will be an investigation," he tells me. "They'll call it *pilot deviation* which is absolute horseshit."

A purely selfish thought runs through my head: maybe he won't fly after this.

"Dennis, I'm sure they'll know you weren't to blame. They gave you clearance."

"Danielle, it wasn't me. Marty O'Donnel and Gene Hitt were piloting. I was asleep in first class. The storm woke me. The turbulence was unbelievable. I was just about to get up and tell those guys to get it under control when we hit ground. The plane fishtails, we go off the runway and crash through the fence. We do a complete one-eighty and the plane literally breaks in two, drenching us all in jet fuel. I was able to push out a piece of loose fuselage and escape through the gap. Danielle, your life really does flash before you!"

Dennis cries softly the rest of the drive home. I'm torn between wanting to pull over and wanting to get home as soon as possible. I keep driving. When I pull into our driveway it's just starting to get light.

"We lost Marty, Danielle," Dennis says. "He was burned so badly. Gene's in critical. It was a nightmare."

"I'm so sorry. It is a nightmare. Everyone's worst nightmare." Just this moment I'm feeling very bad about comparing Marty O'Donnel to a cricket.

Suddenly Dennis is almost in my lap. With tenderness that I fear has been reserved for others as of late, he caresses first my right cheek, then my left. He looks me in the eyes, something he hasn't been able to do for quite some time.

"It's just like they say…your life…it flashes like a slide show before you: I saw myself riding a tricycle and then at Old St. Mary's school and then playing basketball at Drake and then I was dancing with Marla Fuller and skiing with Glen and changing Porter's diaper and catching lightning bugs with Cole. And the last thing I saw before I thought I was going up in flames was you. You, in that yellow dress and that straw sun hat you wore when we went sailing last summer. And in one final flash, I got it. I suddenly realized what matters. But then I was afraid it was too late. Danny, I've been a shit."

He pulls me to him, then winces in pain. But he holds me tight and buries his face in my neck, soaking me with his warm tears. "Danielle…" he says and then nothing more. But I know what he means. He means, "Sorry, Danielle. Kiss. Kiss."

Knotted Pearls

"The Grecian ladies counted their age
from their marriage, not from their birth.
—Homer (10ᵗʰ century B.C.)

CELIA STOOD AT the kitchen sink, up to her wrinkled elbows in soapsuds. The dishwasher was broken again. Harry, that is, her husband.

Never once in fifty-four years of marriage had Harry lifted a domestic finger in the house. "Woman's work," he called any and every chore that took place within the four walls of their modest bungalow. But suddenly and for no apparent reason, he'd starting helping Celia with the dishes. One night about a month ago he just walked his dinner plate right over to the sink and didn't move until he'd washed everything—the two blue tulip-bordered dinner plates, two forks, two knives, three spoons (Harry liked a clean one to stir his coffee with), two salad bowls, two water glasses, two coffee cups (but only one saucer), two sauce pots, a frying pan, the coffee pot and the creamer.

But just when Celia had gotten used to Harry helping out, he stopped, just as abruptly as he'd started. About a week ago. She hated to ask why. That wasn't the way their marriage worked. And it had worked for fifty-four years. If not worked, chugged along then.

Celia scraped the remains of her dinner down the disposal. She clucked her tongue, feeling ashamed about the waste. Harry's appetite was also waning—he'd hardly touched his plate. The meat loaf had been picked at, the lima beans simply rearranged, the rice pushed into a steeper mound. Tomorrow she would phone Dr. Lin and inform him of their poor appetites. They were already so thin. "His and Her bean-poles," was how Celia described Harry and herself to the doctor on their last visit. "G.D. walking skeletons," was how Harry put it.

With the last dish in the drainer, Celia shut off the faucet. The sound of muffled applause trickled in from the living room. Harry must be watching that game show he likes so much. Oh, what's the name of it? It's the one with that adorable Regis Philbin. Celia pursed her lips and tried to think of the name of the show. It eluded her, like so many things these days. Just the other day she couldn't remember the name of her own dog. They'd had Chickadee for eleven years, how could she forget her name? And where was that dog anyway? Celia seemed to be losing her all the time. She'd show up in the oddest places: in the bathroom lapping up water from the toilet, asleep in a laundry basket of soft towels Celia could have sworn she had folded and put away.

There were other things, too. That incident at church a couple of weeks ago. So embarrassing. The lady that sat in the pew behind her tapped her lightly on the back and whispered that the zipper on the back of her dress was undone. All the way down her back! Well, that piece of forgetfulness she blamed on Harry. He was the one who always zipped up her dresses.

But last Wednesday had been the worst day yet. She'd gone to the grocery store to do the weekly shopping and in the checkout line suddenly she forgot how to write out a check. Where did you write the dollar amount? Was the "pay to the order of" line meant for the store's name or her name? In the end, the cashier, just a baby with a heart tattoo on her cheek, had to help her write out the check. The incident was so disturbing that Celia got lost on her way home. She drove up and down a strange street countless times and finally realized she was just two blocks from home. And when she got home, Harry wasn't even there. She had plopped down in her recliner and just sat there for the longest time, knowing the ice cream would be melting in the grocery bag.

More applause from the living room, then Regis Philbin's voice saying, "Let's play Who Wants to be a Millionaire." Thank God, Celia thought, upon hearing the name of the show. She'd never thought memory lapses could be physically painful, but they were.

Now, Harry, he had a steel-trap memory. He could shoot off answers to those trivia questions quicker and with more accuracy than most of the show's contestants. Harry could have been a millionaire two or three times over if he ever wound up in that "hot seat" and she told him so.

"What would we do with a million dollars at this stage in the game?" Harry had asked her. She'd looked into his eyes to see if he was kidding. He wasn't.

Why, this stage of the game would be the absolute best time in life to win a million dollars! (But of course she didn't say this to Harry.) The best time because there wouldn't be years and years of investing it and worrying about it and protecting it from the greedy ones who always managed to come out of the woodwork when they smelled greenbacks. Here's what she'd do with the money: give the bulk of it to her niece, Carol, and her family; give some to church, of course; some to the American Cancer Society; some to the animal shelter and the rest…the rest just pee away! There, she'd said it—well, almost. Harry would say "piss" away, but Celia couldn't bring herself to say that crass word even though it better described the act of spending the money wantonly and foolishly.

First, she'd march herself down to Mitchard's Jewelry on Rutgers Street. She'd pick herself out the best diamond ring they had in the case, the one with the biggest sparkle. She'd never had an engagement ring, just the thin gold wedding band that Harry'd slipped on her finger at the Justice of the Peace in Tulsa, Oklahoma. There was no need for an engagement ring since there was no real engagement. "You'll marry me, right?" was how Harry, then a handsome cadet, proposed. She married him three days later.

Celia wiped down the sink after scouring every inch of it. Even kitchen cleanser with bleach wouldn't get the stains and scratches out. A new sink! Part of that million would go for a new sink. What the heck, a whole new kitchen. The only renovation her kitchen had ever seen was a few coats of fresh paint every eight or ten years. Harry didn't "believe" in re-decorating. In eighty-three, he had to buy her a new range but only because they no longer made parts to repair the old one. "A man's gotta eat, don't he?" he'd said to justify the purchase.

At the appliance store, Celia had cleverly led Harry to the ranges by way of the dishwasher aisle. "Look, Harry, dishwashers! Why, I bet we could save a lot on our water bill with one of these efficient models." Harry said, "We got a dishwasher—you," and pushed her out of his path.

More applause from the living room. "Did someone win a million, Harry?" she called. No answer from the living room. Celia quickly covered her mouth to stop herself. You would think a woman who had been married to the same man for fifty-four years would remember that he didn't take kindly to being shouted to from other rooms of the house.

After wiping her hands dry, Celia hung the dishtowel on the metal bar inside the cupboard under the sink. She wondered if Harry remembered his medicine with dinner. He didn't like to be reminded to take it ("I'm not a G.D. baby!") until he forgot to take it ("Why didn't you remind me?"). She unscrewed the lid to his medicine bottle and shook the tiny pink pills into her hand. She counted out eleven. Same as yesterday. She clucked her tongue. "He needs his medicine," she said out loud, returning all but one pill to the bottle. That one, she sat on the counter.

She headed out to the living room to ask Harry if he was ready for his nightly dish of ice cream. If he was, she would camouflage his pill in the ice cream, just like her sister Martha used to do with Carol's medicine when she was small. She'd gotten away with this tactic before. Although lately, Harry was taking just a few bites of his ice cream and, when Celia sifted through the melted remainder looking for his pill, often she found it.

Dr. Lin said it was common for people with cancer to lose their appetites. Harry said nothing tasted good anymore, said, "The G. D. chemo wiped out my taste buds."

"Harry, you ready for your ice cream?" she said to the back of his chair. No answer. She peeped around only to find his burgundy vinyl recliner empty. She looked down the hallway and saw that the bathroom door was closed. She shook her head. That was another topic for Dr. Lin—her husband's bathroom habits. The man was in that bathroom all the time.

Back in the kitchen, she scooped French vanilla ice cream into a small glass dish. After squirting the small mound with chocolate syrup she placed the pill in the center and then sprinkled chopped walnuts around it, making sure to cloak the pill. The things a wife must do to keep her husband healthy. Left to his own devices, the man would not have lived passed fifty.

The contestant on the millionaire show was not nearly as smart as Harry. "You're missing it!" she called down the hall to her husband, who couldn't still be in that bathroom, could he? She hoped he wasn't ill. She worried about her cooking. Lately, cooking seemed to confuse and confound her. She'd been forgetting to add ingredients thereby ending up with tuna casseroles without a flake of tuna, bread puddings without a lick of sugar, and banana muffins without a smidgen of banana. Or she'd remember the ingredients but not in their proper state, like when she remembered to add eggs to her potato salad, but added them raw. And last week, she forgot to cook the hamburger patties and didn't even realize it until she'd bitten through the bun and tasted cold mush. "Now that's what I call rare!" she'd said, trying to make a joke. But Harry didn't laugh because he'd already gotten up from the table, probably in absolute disgust. Probably took the dog, what's-her-name, out for a walk. It was a wonder Harry didn't send her flying for that one. Years ago, he would have. Nowadays, the silent treatment was his punishment of choice. And in a house that was already quiet as a graveyard, the silent treatment was pure torture.

She hadn't even heard the toilet flush. "Harry, you don't want to miss this! This young man is going to poll the audience because he doesn't know what part of an orange is called the 'zest.' Imagine that!"

Later, she woke up in Harry's recliner, with the bowl of melted ice cream in her lap, Chickadee nuzzled at her feet, and that staticky "off-the-air" fuzz blaring from the TV. For a second, Celia thought she was home, in her mother's house, that is, and she wondered where everyone was—her sister Martha and the twins Edward and Eaton. She missed them so. How terrible to be the oldest of four siblings and to outlive them all. Edward was just fifty-nine when his heart gave out. It didn't seem fair that she, the only one without children of her own, should still be standing. Her niece, Carol, misses her mother so much. Carol's been good to Celia, inviting her and Harry for holidays and checking in on them every other day or so even though she had a busy schedule as a high-school teacher. Celia tries to remember, did she come today? Was Carol here today? For the life of her she can't remember. She can remember Carol's wedding day almost thirty years ago—she was barefoot and put daisies in her hair and almost drove Martha to drinking—but she can't remember if she'd stopped by today.

Surely Harry had already turned in. It would be just like him to hand Celia his dirty dish and say, "Night, Cilly," using the nickname he'd coined for her the first day they met. How sweet and romantic it had seemed way back then—endearing even. It didn't become annoying and patronizing until years later, about the time Celia realized that they would never be able to have children. Once she'd even asked him to please stop using the nickname. "Please stop calling me 'Cilly.' I just don't like the sound of it anymore."

"Why not, Cilly?"

"Harry, please."

"You used to like it, Cilly."

"It used to sound different, like a sweet twist on Celia. Now it just sounds like you're calling me *silly* all the time. That you don't take me seriously."

"Believe me, Cilly, I take you serious. Every Cilly word you say."

Celia knew she should get up and put herself to bed. If she sleeps in this chair all night she'll be stiff all over in the morning. She heard the sound of water in the bathroom —either tinkling or lapping, she couldn't tell which. Harry'd been sleeping in the spare bedroom since he started the chemo treatments. "So I won't bother you," he'd said considerately. But she missed his botherings—the snoring, the talking in his sleep (did other husbands swear at football players in their sleep?), the flatulence, the hogging the covers. She missed having him—gruff as sandpaper—next to her. It was when she was alone in bed at age seventy-four that she realized that another person's breathing—just that simple exchange of air—made one feel safe, and a part of something. Now it took her a long time to get to sleep.

Her body decided for her. Stiff or not, she was staying put. She closed her eyes and dreamed that she and Harry were young and were gliding in a canoe on a narrow, winding river. They had a picnic of wine, cheese, and sweet green grapes. Was it a dream? Hadn't they done that with Mary and Roger Boyd? Gone canoeing on the Kickapoo River in Wisconsin? Hadn't they?

In the morning, she woke up in the chair and was not surprised by the stiffness in her neck and back. In her legs, behind the knees. But it was her own doing and so she gave herself a heave-ho and visited the bathroom before starting breakfast. Harry liked a big breakfast. Or at least he used to. Bacon, eggs over easy, fried potatoes with onion, Swedish pancakes with lingonberries. She heard rustling in the spare bedroom but didn't dare peek in. If you woke Harry before he was ready, the man was a bear. No, these days, she found it was best to let him wake up on his own. But that could mean noon or later on some days. Sleep is medicine, Dr. Lin told her. So, he sleeps. And sleeps.

In the kitchen, Celia started first on the potatoes, slicing them with a sharp knife on the cutting board. Chickadee appeared from who-knew-where and began scratching at the back door. Celia let her out and then stuck her head outside to test the day. A gorgeous June day, void of humidity. A good day for a walk. Maybe Harry would be up for a walk along the river after breakfast.

Returning to the potatoes, Celia grabbed the knife, but by the blade rather than the handle, and blood began to squirt from a wide gash on the palm of her hand. "Harry! Harry!" she screamed when she could breathe. "Harry!" When he didn't respond, she picked up the phone to call 911. But in her panic, the order of the numbers wouldn't come to her. 191? 119? Her niece Carol's phone number, which hadn't changed in twenty-five years, came to her, so that's who she called.

"I cut my hand," she found herself saying weakly into the phone when Carol answered.

"Aunt Celia, is it you?" Carol asked.

"Yes, yes, I cut my hand. There's a lot of blood."

"Tell me exactly what happened, Aunt Celia."

"I was making breakfast for Harry."

"Harry?!"

"And I know it sounds ridiculous but I think I just forgot how to use a knife. I thought you held on to the blade and cut with the handle. I'm going crazy, aren't I?"

"No, you're not going crazy. I'll be there in ten minutes. In the meantime, run your hand under cold water and then wrap it in a dishtowel. We'll have it looked at."

"All right. Should I wake Harry?"

"Aunt Celia— Oh, just let him sleep for now, huh?"

At the clinic, Celia felt like a child. The deep gash required thirteen stitches and Carol insisted that Celia go back to her house so that she could look after her for a bit.

"What about Harry? He'll be hungry and wondering where I am."

"He's probably still sleeping, Aunt Celia."

"Yes, you're probably right, dear. Sleep is medicine, you know."

When they arrive at Carol's, a man Celia doesn't recognize helps her out of the car and kisses her on the cheek. A good-looking fellow. "I always said you were dangerous with a knife, Aunt Celia," he said. He had sparkling blue eyes and a nice smile.

"And who might you be?" Celia asked him.

He shook his head and smiled. Taking hold of her uninjured hand, he shook it and said, "My name is Frank and I'm a friend of Carol's."

"Well, any friend of Carol's is a friend of mine," Celia heard herself say.

He took her arm and they climbed the stairs to Carol's house. Then it hit her. "Wait a minute! I know you!" she exclaimed happily. "You're Frank. Carol's husband. It's so good to see you! Where have you been all these years?"

"On safari, most of the time," Frank explained.

"Frank!" Carol said.

"Let him talk, young lady. I want to hear about it."

Carol, like her mother, was a good cook. One of her two sons joined them for dinner and Celia was just crazy about her great nephews. This one, his name eluded her, the handsome one with the dark eyes, had a sharp tongue, but he knew where to draw the line. She liked the way he held his fork—European style. Harry would say he was putting on airs. With a pang of guilt, she wondered what Harry had found to eat. Oh, he probably opened up a can of beans and ate them cold from the can!

"Maybe I better call Harry," Celia announced when dinner was finished.

"I'll call him for you," Carol's handsome man-friend offered. What a nice man! Carol deserved a man like that.

After dinner, Celia sat with Carol and one of the boys and they watched "Who Wants to be a Millionaire." Carol's son was quite the trivia buff and shot off answers quick as his great Uncle Harry. Celia surprised everyone by remembering the author of the poem, "A Tree." "Joyce Kilmore, Regis!" she shouted at the TV. "It's *B.* Joyce Kilmore." And then she began to recite the poem, a poem she hadn't thought of in possibly a half of a century: "I think that I shall never see a poem lovely as a tree."

She would have completed it to the end if she hadn't been interrupted by the bark of a dog.

"Why that sounds just like Chickadee!" she said to Carol. Then Chickadee ran into the room and up onto her lap. "It is you! What are you doing here?"

"Phil, Dad and I need to talk to Aunt Celia, okay?" Carol said to her son.

Phil! That was his name. Easy to remember, just think of the Phil in Philbin, Celia told herself as her great nephew kissed her cheek and said good night.

"Aunt Celia," Carol began in a serious voice, so serious that Celia had to ask her if something terrible had happened. "Well, you cut your hand today. Remember?"

Celia nodded, turning her bandaged hand this way and that. "It's fine now. It's nothing."

"Aunt Celia, it's not fine and it is something."

"What's wrong, dear?"

"Aunt Celia, Frank went and got Chickadee because we want you to stay with us for a while."

"That's sweet of you really, but I couldn't. Who'll take care of Harry?"

"Aunt Celia," Frank said, "Harry's gone. He died over a month ago. Don't you remember? He died at St. Katherine's Hospital. The cancer had spread to his brain."

Celia was confused. She looked at her niece. "But you said that Harry was still sleeping."

Carol came and sat at Celia's feet. She took hold of her left hand. "I know I did. Aunt Celia, your doctor told us that it might be easier on you if we went along with your thinking that Uncle Harry was still alive. They call it validation therapy, that's the fancy name. But now I think the truth is best. Aunt Celia, Uncle Harry died and you do have Alzheimer's, it's been confirmed. The disease has gotten worse since Uncle Harry died. We're worried about your safety and we want you to come and live with us for as long as you can. I'm home for the summer and I'm so excited that we can be together. You'll help me not to miss my Mom so much."

"Did I ever tell you that Harry originally asked your mother out on a date?" Celia asked Carol.

Carol smiled. "You're kidding. Tell me about it."

"Well, it was Martha who Harry came a courting, but Martha had it bad for your father, so she wouldn't even come out of her room. She told me to go downstairs and tell that old Harold Finnigan to go away. Well, Harold Finnigan had to show off his brand new old jalopy to someone and even though I was six years younger than him, I was at least someone. So I hopped in. The rest is history."

Carol said, "That's a great story. He did love you."

Celia looked at her dog. She hugged her and said, "Yes, he did, didn't he? Even if he never admitted it. But I know he did." She sighed, shook her head. "In his own mean ol' way. Did I tell you he started helping me with the dishes?"

"No way!"

"Yes, before he got bad. But not anymore, now he just sleeps. And spends too much time in the bathroom." She turns to Frank. "Young man, I'm sorry that I've forgotten your name, but if I give you directions to my house, would you mind just running in and checking on my husband? Just make sure he's okay for me?"

"Of course I will, Aunt Celia."

"Have we met before? You have nice eyes. And, are you serious about my niece? You could do a lot worse, you know. She's a wonderful cook. A good housekeeper. She loves children. She's a teacher, you know."

Frank got up from his chair and sat on the floor next to Carol. He gave her a little squeeze and told Aunt Celia that he was very serious. "In fact, I'm thinking about proposing. What do you think?"

"Do you do dishes?" Celia asked.

Among the Trees

Gifts that grow are best;
Hands that bless are blest;
Plant! life does the rest!
Heaven and earth help him who plants a tree,
And his work its own reward shall be.
–From "Plant A Tree" by Lucy Larcom (1826-1893)

THE BOTTOM OF his cane was encrusted with mud. With each step, his great grandfather's walking stick penetrated the damp, springy earth, denying him sure-footedness. But he continued on in the dark. Thick, dank air clung to his face like heavy aftershave as he made his way through row after row of aromatic conifers. What possessed him to leave his warm bed on this austere March evening could not be put easily into words. Howard Garland had awakened from a thin sleep and couldn't remember where he had planted his trees. The uncertainty dangled above his bed, tormenting him, until finding the trees evolved into a full-blown obsession, forcing him to throw his feet over the side of the bed and sneak out of the room.

Howard had secretly planted the row of forty-two pine saplings when he was twenty years old, with the sole intention of pleasing Sarah Ann Archor, one dairy farm over, who loved green things and wished her father raised beautiful things like trees, rather than stupid things like cows. In the end, planting the white pines did nothing to win over Sarah Ann, but it did spark a life-long passion for tree farming in Howard. That row of pines, now over sixty years old, stands a lofty eighty feet high, forming a majestic wall of lush green on the southern border of his family's three-hundred-acre farm. Or perhaps it was the northern border.

His wife would think the worst if she were to wake up and find Howard's side of the bed empty, especially now after his second heart attack. Claire would conjure up terrible pictures of Howard dead in the basement, dead in the nursery, or dead under one of the thousands of Christmas trees on their farm. He had no business wandering around in the wet fields at this time of night and in this state of dress—he'd simply pushed bare feet into boots and pajama-sleeved arms into a suede jacket—but the hiccups in his memory frightened him more than the hiccups in his heart. Small slippages, nothing to worry about, the doctor said, quite common after open heart surgery. But the other day, Howard couldn't remember all the words to the Lord's Prayer, and then the word for shaping the trees (shearing), and then it was his wife's maiden name. What kind of husband couldn't remember his wife of sixty years' maiden name? Claire Rose... Claire Rose...

Outdoors just a short time and already his fingers and toes were numbing at the tips and his nose was running. He realized too late he should have grabbed his blue cap. Howard Garland never seemed to remember that his old head was more bald than hairy. The coarse wind coiled around his body, penetrating his clothing and skin, passing through muscle (he had no fat to speak of, no insulation) and landing deep down in his bones. Still he persevered.

Of the row of forty-two trees he had planted, only four were lost. This had both surprised and pleased Howard as he had never put anything into the earth before, not a flower, not a tomato plant. He found the care and maintenance of trees to be pleasing work, far more so than the care and maintenance of his father's cows. He wanted to see that stand of trees one more time. Howard had it in his head that his time was up, that any day now, he'd die. For the last three months he'd greeted each day as his last and climbed into bed at night astonished that he was still kicking. It was exhausting. He was ready to go. Everything was in order: his sons and grandsons would take care of Claire and the farm. There was just one thing—he wanted to see those trees. He'd find them and then climb back into bed where soft, dimpled Claire would warm his feet. And then maybe he could die.

He'd started his journey with a flashlight but it was gone now. Had he dropped it? He couldn't remember. Maybe he'd left it behind when he stopped to retie a boot string. Good thing for him the moon was generous tonight. The sky, chockfull of twinkling stars, provided adequate light for walking. He stopped for a breath. Standing under the trees, head back, looking up at the vault of sky, he felt, for the millionth time, as if he were in a cathedral. How many little epiphanies had he experienced among these trees? One memory was especially fresh: the night his first son was born. A perfect Christmas Eve, nineteen forty-nine. Mother and baby were asleep in bed, one exhilarated yet exhausted, the other nursed and contented. Unable to sleep, Howard grabbed his pipe and his grandfather's walking stick and started in the direction of his father's cow pastures. Wandering longer than he had intended, he found himself unable to turn back to the house. He walked aimlessly, but then maybe not, for he came upon his pines at the edge of the adjoining farm, and wondered what had led him here. Ten years old by then, taller than he, they were picture-perfect Christmas trees. He brushed some heavy snow from their branches and vowed never to cut down even one. He hadn't known it when he had gently laid those tiny seedlings into the ground, but he knew it now—planting trees was important. Planting trees was pledging faith in the future. He had walked back home, swiping tears from his cold cheeks, thankful for his new son, the first member of the fifth generation of Garland farmers, who would grow good and tall like a tree, and wondering if there was a way in the world that he could tell his father how much he loathed all things bovine. He considered cows to be the dumbest creatures alive, dim bulbs. "Any animal you can keep in with a single strand of wire doesn't have a full load upstairs," he'd say. He'd been kicked and stepped on one too many times. He promised himself that night in the moonlight, his first night of fatherhood, that he would drum up the courage to show his father his trees and talk to him about getting out of the dairy business and into the tree business. In the meantime, he would enjoy his new son and dream of a place called the Garland Family Tree Farm.

As it happened, Howard's father learned of the trees on his own one spring day while he and his sons were inspecting the north end of the property after a tornado had blown through. When Howard's father pulled up to the row of small pines, sturdy and well-tended, he sat with the truck idling while he rubbed his stubbly chin and adjusted his cap. He smiled and addressed his sons: "Looks like that twister blew us in some trees." Howard didn't say a word. A week later, after the morning milking, and just as Howard was about to approach his father to discuss the trees, a truck pulled up and some men began unloading dozens of balled and burlapped baby evergreens. Howard's father tugged on the rim of his son's baseball cap and with a smile said, "Looks like the twister blew us in some more trees."

They planted them together. These were firs, Douglas and Fraser. In the fall, they added Colorado blue spruce and more pines. Howard confessed about planting the trees to impress Sarah Ann and shared with his father his ideas about transforming the old dairy farm into a tree farm. His father's reply: "Cows have kept this farm afloat for some ninety years, son. But you go on and keep planting them trees and maybe your kids or your kids' kids can farm Christmas trees someday."

Howard continued planting, collecting seeds from his own trees, and his neighbors' trees, and ordering them from catalogs. Acre by acre, pastures were transformed into fields of sprite trees. Howard began selling Christmas trees to friends and neighbors, until, finally, in 1960, Howard's father told him to "sell the damn cows," and they were able to devote themselves fully to the trees. With the help of his father and his three sons and one daughter, Howard added annually to his acreage until the present time, when they'd managed to fill two-hundred of their three-hundred acres with trees. Howard's sons, David, Larry, and Peter, took over the farm ten years ago, but Howard still kept his hands in the business, that is until the second heart attack. His only usefulness now: he was still the resident expert at detecting bow-legged fir aphids, silver spotted tiger moths, and other pests that threatened the trees.

Winded, Howard had to stop. He slid onto a wooden bench—one of the nice touches of the Garland Family Tree Farm—and waited for his breathing to return to normal. He looked up again at the sky, finding pleasure in the way the moon, complete and radiant, resembled the Holy Eucharist. The leaders on the trees seemed to be pointing up to the illuminated host, an image he'd witnessed countless times over the years. He thought of the time David, five or six then, tagged along with him to watch him give the trees their "beauty treatments"—the twice-a-year shearings to train the trees into the symmetrical shapes that customers have come to expect. (Often, the staff had to work round-the-clock to get to all the trees—by flashlight and moonlight.) The moon was buxom and bright that night, too, serving as a gigantic light bulb. Little David cast miniature moon shadows as he trailed his father. At one point David stopped in his tracks and gasped. Howard asked what critter had spooked him, but David was looking up, not down. "Do trees pray, Daddy?" he whispered. Howard followed his son's gaze up to the tips of the highest trees pointing to the host-like moon. It was another one of those powerful epiphanies. "Yes, son, I guess all the created praise their Creator."

Howard rose from the bench and resumed walking. Perhaps it was because he was on foot that his directional sense was off. Before his heart surgery, he would take the golf cart out to his trees, short-cutting his way through the firs. He always cited some excuse—to check for needle blight or weather damage—but the real reason was that seeing his trees grounded him somehow. They represented his family's posterity. He'd read somewhere that conifers can reach heights of 250 and 350 feet, and that many conifers can live for a century, and some species even a thousand years or more. Howard wanted his trees to live a thousand years or more. Damn his heart, even if it was eighty-two years old. And—not damn, but darn—Claire and his sons for hiding the keys to all the vehicles: the car, the truck, the golf cart, even the tractor mower. He could have been to his trees and back by now, back into bed, nuzzling with Claire one last time before flying to the moon and beyond.

A light fog was settling around him, dimming the starlight. Something made him turn left before the field of Balsam firs. He imagined turning the wheel of the golf cart to the left. Yes, it felt right. It was the northern border after all. Of course it was. How could he forget? He'd planted the trees on the border line separating Sarah Ann's farm from theirs, so the trees would be in plain view. Fortunately, the farm ran deeper than it did wide. He was very close now, just a quarter mile or so more.

The first heart attack was sneaky—Howard hadn't even known he had one. The second one came on with a vengeance, like an iron hand squeezing his heart to a pulp. He was on the tractor. His grandson, Willie, found him, freckle-faced Willie, scared of the dark, of high places, and especially of spiders. Willie had a hard time looking at his grandfather now. Like he was looking at a ghost. Howard wondered why he hadn't died then. What was there to keep him?

He did worry about the farm. Not that his boys weren't capable, but national surveys showed the percentage of U.S. households using a real Christmas tree to be declining. Artificial trees increased by seven percent the previous year, especially with baby boomers. Discouraging trends for real tree growers.

But then, they were never in it for the money. No, it wasn't about the money, but about breathing fresh, clean air every day, appreciating the land and its gifts, working with family, living a life that didn't put on airs. In the end, they made more money with the cows, but he didn't miss it for a second. Steel toe boots, constant worry about sanitation, proper cooling and storage, government regulations. And cows required such attention—eating up to eight times a day, up to eighty pounds of feed, drinking thirty to forty gallons of water a day. They needed to be milked at least two times, sometimes three times a day, early in the morning and again in the afternoon and/or evening. They smelled. And then there was the manure (which later Howard appreciated for its fertilizing effects). Anyway, he hadn't the patience for cows.

Not to say that tree farming required no patience—it took almost as long to raise a Christmas tree as it did to raise a child. A Douglas fir had a five to seven year growing season until harvest. Some trees required twelve or more years to mature. But for inexplicable reasons, Howard had always believed a Christmas tree to be a superior life form to a cow.

Howard tried to think about these things so that his mind would not register that he was lost in his own woodland. (He wasn't lost—he was no more than thirty feet from his trees.) In the dark, the rows were a tangled maze, a labyrinth that robbed him of his sense of direction. Though chilled, he began to perspire, as he turned in circles, hoping to right himself. But there was nothing to aid him for the things he'd planted dwarfed him and he never did learn how to read the night sky, couldn't tell the north star from any other, and he'd learned the hard way that sometimes moss grows on the south, east, and west sides of trees, not only the north side.

Suddenly, there they were. Looming. Present. Standing like sentries in the moonlight. Howard laughed out loud. He never in all of his dreams thought they would grow. He loved them like a painter loves his color-splashed canvas or a carpenter his table. What a great gift, to partner with God to keep the earth green and the air clean, to provide homes to birds and other small animals. Planting a tree is one thing; being outlived by that tree is something else again. It's admitting to mortality and that just maybe a tree was as useful as you were, maybe more so. It was humbling to stand in the presence of these majestic trees, their invisible muscles serving to both secure them to the earth and unleash them to the sky.

Howard shook his head. Maybe it wasn't only about the trees; it was also about Sarah Ann. He'd loved her so purely and innocently, the girl with strawberry blond hair, pulled free from braids when her mother wasn't looking, who liked to run barefooted, free and wild in her father's pastures. A dreamer, who always came up missing at chore time. A girl who wasn't afraid of telling her father how much she despised cows and how she knew that deep down she was a city girl, even though she'd never ventured more than ten miles from her Wisconsin farm. Sarah Ann's father didn't have the heart to put his only daughter over his knee and so he and all who knew her indulged her every whim.

Howard couldn't remember a time when he didn't love her—his earliest memories were tinged with a fondness for Sarah Ann. They were born a day apart, the mid-wife running from one farmhouse to the other. They'd been bathed together in old washtubs, put to nap on each other's sleeping porches, antagonized by the other's older siblings. Howard would finish her chores for her and in return she'd sing him the songs she'd written, the ones that would someday make her semi-famous and bring her to theaters around the country. She'd kissed him once in misty moonlight. Near his baby trees. They were twenty-two and the kiss was like a seal on his heart. It would take years for Howard to realize that the kiss was no more than the meeting of two pairs of caring and tender lips. He lost her to a musical in Milwaukee in which she had won the leading role. But how could he say he lost her when he never really had her?

Claire was his cousin's friend, a big-boned girl from Michigan, who'd lost her mother and father in a fire, and was unofficially adopted by his aunt and uncle when she was fifteen. Claire was warm ointment for a wounded heart. Practical, hardworking and unselfish, Claire made a good impression on Howard's mother, who told him he could do worse. He grew to love Claire for her Sunday pot roasts, her way with the children, her husky singing voice. He loved that she was quick with numbers, slow to gossip, steady in crisis, and fearless in her faith in God. He loved her, yes, but never—oh, what does it matter now? Water under the bridge. He loved Clarie and that was all that mattered. He loved her with a steady, dutiful love, the kind of love that smells like morning. The amazing kind of love that still has something to say across the dinner table after sixty years. "Did you know," Claire asked him the other day, "that when rain won't fall from the sky, but you see the dark clouds sort of leaking down, that it's called *virga*?" And Claire loved him, too. With the kind of love that sits beside a hospital bed, that presses tiny pink pills into the palm of your hand, that listens for your breathing at night and feels for the beat of your heart with a strong hand. And they loved each other with the kind of love that two people share when they know that they are the only two people in the world who remember what their babies looked like at one second old: David with his endearing swirls of dark hair on his forehead; Larry, with milk pimples on his nose; Peter, with an ice-cream-cone-shaped head; and Franny, with two delicately webbed toes. And yet, he'd never felt the way about Claire that he felt about Sarah Ann. He could admit it to no one, but loving Claire after loving Sarah Ann had felt almost…bigamous.

He sat himself down on the bench he'd positioned years ago in front of his first-planted tree. How easy it had been to grow. Easier than children, for at least trees stayed put. They didn't run off when you least expected it to Vietnam and college and God-forsaken Los Angeles. They didn't talk back or sing "druggy" songs about peace and love, or try to democratize every person at the Thanksgiving dinner table. Trees just stand, minding their own business, improving the air, shading the world, often unnoticed and unappreciated, until someone has a need for lumber or paper or maple syrup or apples, pears, or cherries—or Christmas trees for that matter. Sarah Ann said she loved trees, but did she? Did she really?

Howard longed for his pipe—given up along with fatty foods, salt, and sweets after the second heart attack. Will Heaven provide the answers to all of his questions? What had happened to their fifth baby—why had it died in the womb? Why did David have to go to Vietnam? Was that really a space ship he had seen in his father's cow pasture in the fall of 1958? Had Sarah Ann really been in love with that slimy salesman from Milwaukee?

He stopped himself. He had to keep his soul clean, no black marks at this point in the game. This close to the end. No regrets, no unclean thoughts, evil ideas, no selfish pining for earlier days and younger, sweeter love.

Here was his life, Lord: he hated cows; he loved trees; once he tap-danced at a church-sponsored talent show; he'd saved a choking boy; he'd broken the same arm twice; he never struck a man; he expected too much of his sons; he spoiled his only daughter with pretty bracelets and miniature tea sets; he cheated on his tax return once and only once; he was vain about his physique; he never cheated on Claire in action but many times in thought; he didn't understand homosexuals or body-piercing or hip-hop music. Late one Christmas Eve he accidentally got drunk while Claire was baking rum-ball cookies and he was keeping her company and sipping rum and Franny was born nine months later. He secretly liked watching European soccer on T.V. even though his sons didn't consider it a manly sport. He once read ten pages in Franny's diary, was found out and denied it to this day. He tithed to his church, he loved his neighbor, had a soft spot for the underdog. He voted in every election since he was eighteen. He never flew on an airplane, he never road a motorcycle, he never punched the keyboard of a computer. He never gambled, owned a credit card, or had his fortune told. And he never got over finding Sarah Ann's still body, bloody at both wrists, under his twelve-year-old pine trees, when that slimy salesman from Milwaukee left her and she came home that Christmas.

Printed in the United States
24482LVS00002B/61-558